CHEATIEBO, THE FOLKLORIST SERIES

1

KLANDAGI'S RESCUE

GLENDA SIMPSON

Published by Innovo Publishing, LLC
www.innovopublishing.com
1-888-546-2111

Providing Full-Service Publishing Services for Christian Authors, Artists &
Ministries: Books, eBooks, Audiobooks, Music, Screenplays, Film & Curricula

CHEATIEBO
THE FOLKLORIST SERIES

VOL I

Klandagi's Rescue

ISBN: 978-1-61314-801-3

Cover Design & Interior Layout: Innovo Publishing, LLC

Printed in the United States of America
U.S. Printing History
First Edition: 2022

Has God called you to create a Christian book, eBook, audiobook, music album,
screenplay, film, or curricula? If so, visit the ChristianPublishingPortal.com to
learn how to accomplish your calling with excellence. Learn to do everything
yourself, or hire trusted Christian Experts from our Marketplace to help.

DEDICATION & ACKNOWLEDGMENTS

The *Cheatiebo, the Folklorist* series is finished. What a thrill! The research for the historical background changed my view of the world. In addition, there were a few people who helped in various ways. The following family members and cherished friends contributed significantly to this work, and they deserve to be recognized.

First, I am dedicating the *Cheatiebo, the Folklorist* series to Pat Horn, Anne Milstead, and Warren Simpson. My heartfelt adoration and overall respect for the three of you makes this an easy decision. *Pat:* I could write 'thank you' to the moon and back and it would not be enough. You are unusually alluring. Beautiful, but much more. You are unassuming in a stealthy manner. You disarm and charm people with your low-key personality. Thanks for the myriad of hours you spent searching this manuscript for errors and consulting on content. Your efforts were a great help. I am planning some Zane Grey scenery searching from our vehicle while you are visiting. Until then, pack your bags and think of some fun ideas during your visit. *Anne:* the bantering humor we shared during our marathon editing sessions banked some special memories. Your English language knowledge was put to good use with my writing. You helped immeasurably. When you would guess where the plot was headed, I delighted in keeping you in the dark to the very last moment. You are the epitome of a godly, faithful Christian, elder's wife, church member, mother, grandmother, businesswoman, and loyal friend. *Warren,* my son: your support in this writing project has been crucial. Thanks for your patience. You are such a clear thinker, with the ability to draw sound conclusions. The Lord gave you amazing mental faculties, and I have greatly benefited from them with this endeavor and on many other occasions. Warren, you turned out to be the sort of son every mother hopes for.

Patti: you are my first-born child, so you got to welcome me to the wonderful world of motherhood. I was indescribably in love with my funny and cute little baby daughter. The admiration I feel for you continues to grow with time. The two of us have enjoyed a lot of fun times over the years. Thank you for all the help, past and future, on *Cheatiebo, the Folklorist* and for your compassionate caregiving. A million hugs and kisses.

Ruth Monroe: you, my beloved friend, are greatly beloved by me and oh so many others. Thanks for your suggestions and advice. Keep them coming. I especially treasure your wise words because they come from a heart that belongs to Christ our Savior.

Candice Pinzon and her beautiful and gifted off-spring, Naomi and Jimmy: you all helped in a number of ways with staging and being supportive of my writing project. Thanks for being so generous with your talent and photographic instruments.

Wathena: Technically I have only one sister, but you are my "custer" (cousin sister). Our mothers were sisters, and the three of us had great fun growing up in the great state of Texas. A monumental thank you for the suggested stories you dredged up from times long gone.

It breaks my heart to bid farewell to *Jackie Bond*, one of my dearest friends. She lost her battle with Covid 19 in early 2021. We first met at a little country church building tucked away in Arizona's White Mountains. The village of Lakeside caters to skiers. There is a ski resort near Mount Baldy, the second highest elevation in Arizona. Jackie's artwork often reflected the breath-taking scenery called home by the famous author, Zane Grey. Jackie was first a Christian, then a gifted artist. Her skill was intrinsic, not the result of art lessons. Examples of her stunning work can be seen throughout my home.

Finally, I would like to recognize *Deborah Tiano.* You are generous and protective to a fault, and that includes everyone and everything from biology class frogs, runaway dogs, street beggars, roving neighbor kids, old men and children at church services, and people in general. You provided honest feedback to this writing effort, and you "called it as you saw it."

AUTHOR'S NOTE

C*heatiebo, the Folklorist"* is a collection of largely fictional stories, separate but linked by family ties. Chronologically, the earliest section starts in the early 1800s, and the latest concludes shortly before the start of World War II. I believe the historical background to be accurate, based upon my general knowledge acquired over years, allowing for some writer's license. An informal bibliography is posted at the rear of the book. The names of the characters will sound familiar since they are borrowed from actual family members and are common for that period of time. The characters are composite renditions of people from my past. A steamer trunk is used as a prop and helps to transition from one section to the next. It is packed full of family memorabilia, such as family bibles, wedding, death, divorce, and baptismal certificates. There are personal diaries and many letters.

The trunk provides a treasure-trove of drama, romance, mixed in with day-to-day living to keep the narrative moving. Section 1 starts with the Willie Joe and Mattie Wainwright family. Their family roots are in the Kiamishi piney woods of south-eastern Oklahoma. The first section begins in 1917, a tumultuous period in world history. That was the year that the United States joined the war effort against the Axis forces. It was the year of the Bolshevik Revolution and the year that the swine influenza began to ravage the world over, an expanding pandemic the likes of which were not to be seen until the year 2020. It is the year that was portrayed in the movie "Lawrence of Arabia" leaving behind a hostile region that is still in turmoil to this modern age. The year of 1917 was the year that the King of England refused asylum to his first cousin, the Czar of Russia that resulted in the entire royal family being brutally executed behind their palace home by the leaders of the revolting communists. There were rumors that one family member was able to escape being murdered.

Sadly, things were not going well for Willie Joe and Mattie Wainwright either….

Chapter 1

WHEN THE GOOD LORD WAS WILLING

My given name was Cornelia, but Cheatiebo was my nick name, and later on it was shortened to Cheatie. My daughter, Glenda, decided to name this book after me, so I reckon the best place to start is with my birth.

I'm known as Cheatiebo, the twin that survived. My twin and I weighed 'bout two and a half pounds each. Back in them days odds for us surviving weren't good. It was terrible cold in that old cabin. My parents, Mattie and Willie Joe, saw the cloud bank in the north and realized the weather was about to get bad, but they had no idea how bad. The date was December 15, 1917.

The storm turned out to be what we called a "blue norther." It attacked our southeastern Oklahoma home with a vengeance. By noon snow mixed with sleet was pelting the area. Mattie was seven and a half months pregnant with me and my twin. She was suffering from a stubborn case of malaria. We'll never know for sure what caused her to go into early labor. It could have been the drastic drop in barometric pressure, or the dose of Quinine, or even the strain of splitting and hauling in a big load of firewood.

The Wainwrights rented a share-cropper's house. The old log cabin was sturdy enough but run down something terrible. Due to missing chinking, it was impossible to keep warm. Poppa wasn't much of a provider and had neglected the place. Momma tended to make excuses for him. His folks haled from France. I never heard how they ended up in Oklahoma. Daddy played the harmonica, was a hoe-down fiddler, and sang with near perfect pitch. He was the number one square dance caller in the communities where Oklahoma, Texas, Arkansas, and Louisiana came together. He had curly black hair and iridescent blue eyes. His good looks attracted the ladies of the night where he performed. Momma pretended not to know.

Momma was mostly Cherokee. She was a tall, powerfully built woman that never shied away from hard work. She was proud of her Cherokee ancestry; we all was.

My twin and I was born shortly after midnight, December 16th, 1917. Momma had a terrible time. Most folks suspected the story was exaggerated, but Mattie wasn't one to lie, not even a little white one. I can vouch for her honesty. The date was the anniversary of the first New Madrid Earthquake of 1811. The fact that my twin and I survived such a difficult birth was so unlikely, it made it hard for most folks to believe. Fact is, God answered Momma's prayers, the only possible explanation. I can still hear Momma saying, "Nothing is impossible with God" (Luke 1:37).

The sinking barometric pressure seemed to intensify Mattie's suffering. She frantically searched for the bottle of Quinine. "You girls see that bottle of Quinine? It was right up here. Never mind, I found it." Willie Joe started making a racket on the front porch, so Mattie cupped her mouth with her hands and yelled, "Willie Joe, hun, we need some farwood, it's gittin' cold in here."

Mattie wiped her sweaty face with her flour sack apron and said to the two children, "Burr, yawl git back under the covers." The fires had burned down to coals, and their breath was condensing right there in the house. Mattie helped the two children crawl under the layers of bedding.

The girls shared body heat by sitting close together as they practiced penmanship with chalk and slate. Mattie was strict and determined when it came to educatin' her girls. She knew schoolin' would be even more important for their generation.

Mattie was suffering from chills, and her feet were numb. "Here I come, hold back your feet while I slide this hot brick under the covers. Why don't yawl move over so I can slide in beside you. Keep on working, you're doin' a great job. Wow, does that ever feel good?"

Willie Joe could be heard on the porch stamping mud and snow from his feet. He had been to visit Rose and Leon. He peeked into the dimly lit cabin and shouted, "I'm back, Mat, you say something? Wind's howling out here. Sky's real black in the north. I'm gonna go nail some tin over that hole in the shed and split up some farwood. Whew, it's already blo' freezin' and spittin' snow. Mark my word, this storm is gonna be a bad one, I feel it in my bones."

About the time the feeling was coming back to Mattie's feet she was struck by belly pain. *Oh my, that feels like a labor pain.* After a few minutes she felt wetness. She decided to check herself and went behind the privacy curtain in the corner. Sure enough, a patch of bright red stained her step-ins. Mattie had spotted with her other two pregnancies. She reasoned it was most likely just false labor since the baby wasn't due 'til mid-January to early-February. The dose of Quinine seemed to help but the relief didn't last long. A few hours later Mattie was back to shivering with chills and burning up with a fever. Despite feeling terrible she rose to put supper on the table.

With a storm bearing down, Mattie didn't want to do anything that would send Willie Joe into one of his nervous spells, so she decided to keep quiet about the labor pains and hope they would go away. She wanted him to focus on bringing up the wood and repairing that shotgun hole.

A week before Willie Joe had encountered a skunk in with the hens and ran to the house for his shotgun. When he got back to the barn, the skunk had managed to climb into a nesting box and was feasting on eggs. Willie Joe took aim and blasted the nesting box before the critter had time to react. He congratulated himself on his marksmanship and hurried to the house to tell Mattie, "That skunk we got, well I just blew him to smithereens. He didn't git a chance to spray, not much." It never even occurred to Willie Joe that the loudness of the blast would cause the domineckers to quit laying. And if that wasn't bad enough the buck shot destroyed two nesting boxes and created a new fox-sized entrance to the barn. Willie Joe didn't always think things through.

After the skunk incident the family was forced to depend upon their flock of free roaming guinea fowl for eggs, and that wasn't working out well since they hardly lay in the wintertime. It takes two guinea eggs to equal a chicken's egg, but otherwise they are the same. From time to time Mattie bartered for hen's eggs, but that was costly.

Mattie wisely held her tongue on the ill-advised shotgun blast but did say, "Unless them hens start layin' right soon they's gonna be chicken and dumplings. I hear Rhode-Island-Reds are good for both eggs and meat. One thang's for sure, we'll get a few meals off that bunch of hens, just hav-ta cook-em long-enough. Mattie realized it was already mid-afternoon and decided to combine the two meals into one. Mattie knew the larder was low, but she felt confident everything would work out since the Lord oversaw food. After a short prayer she set eight guinea eggs to boil and warmed over half a skillet of cornbread and a stewer of butter beans flavored with bacon drippings. For dessert she popped the seal on a jar of wild plums.

Annie Mae, 8 and Ethyl, 5 years old were typical children, totally unaware of the starkness of their existence. In her high little voice Ethyl said, "Momma, do we get to have a Christmas tree this year? There's snow comin' down out there!" It was December, and Mattie had always done her dead level best to make Christmas fun.

"Yes sweetie, I thank we should put up a tree, and I bet I know two girls that will want to help decorate it. Just talkin' about decorating a Christmas tree gets me all excited. We'll ask your Papa to help find just the right tree."

It was December 16th, and Annie Mae counted on her fingers and said, "Only nine days till Christmas, yea!"

Mattie, speaking in a loving tone said, "Girls, get back under the cover and keep your caps on. Yawl need to stay covered up; you might catch your death. When the wind dies down, you can bundle up and build a snowman, but only if you finish up your writing lessons." The girls each placed their slate on their lap and took up a stick of chalk that clicked as they copied Matthew, Mark, Luke, John,—. Mattie took a moment to watch them working, and said, "Neatly now, very neatly, good job!" Mattie was thinking how the girls blessed her life. They were the epitome of cuteness. The older, Annie Mae had her father's blue eyes, Ethel's were a golden hazel. The children were freckled from playing out of doors, and their snaggle-toothed grins melted her heart.

Suddenly a strong gust of wind blew open the cabin's door. Ashes whipped up by the wind created a haze inside the small cabin. The smoldering coals awakened to an orange glow. Mattie slowly stood and shuffled across the bare wood floor. She was down in her back again. She groaned when she lifted on the door and slammed it hard.

"Wouldn't ju' know, now the door latch is broke." Mattie was feeling overwhelmed. The door was the latest among a growing list of repairs that plagued the Wainwright's cabin home. Little did she know that the trouble they faced would be trivial compared to what the rest of the day held in store for her.

The fact that Willie Joe was going back on his promise to fix up the place in exchange for free rent was gonna be found out any day. *We're gonna be homeless agin, sure as shootin'. That was awful hard campin' out in that old tent.* Mattie was thinking, *what's the use, worry don't ever get me nowhere.* She paused long enough to allow a full body shiver to pass and once again used her apron to dry her clammy face.

Mattie split up the last two pieces of wood, one went on the fireplace grate and the other in the cook stove. What mattered was keeping her girls fed and warm. "There girls, you can manage the rest; I got to lay down and try to git easy."

Outside, Mattie could hear the wind slamming the barn door back and forth. *What on earth is Willie Joe doing? That door will be ruint in this wind.* Just then a pitiful looking Willie Joe kicked open the door and walked into the cabin tenderly supporting his bloody left hand.

"Hit my thumb with the hammer. Help me Mat, I thank I'm gonna faint." Mattie slid off the corn shuck mattress and shuffled over to the open door. Once again, she gave it a herculean slam. Then she limped to Willie Joe's side. She motioned for him to sit on a chair while she examined his thumb.

"Oh my, looks like you knocked the thumbnail plumb off." Mattie poured warm water into a pan and added a slice of lye soap. After removing the dangling nail, she made sure the wound was clean and wrapped it with a white rag. She covered the bandage with a strip of folded blanket scrap to protect the tender part and then used a strip of cloth to make a sling. Mattie placed her hand on Willie Joe's shoulder and said, "Keep your hand up in the sling or it might start throbbin'."

Willie Joe said, "Mattie, I'm sorry about the wood. Why don't you just brang in enough wood to build up the fires, and I'll get the rest after my thumb stops hurtin', okay?"

Mattie averted her gaze to hide her disappointment, "Thangs happen, now you and the girls eat some dinner and rest a spell. I'll get what farwood I can." Then as an afterthought, Mattie said, "Annie Mae and Ethyl have something they want to talk to you about."

Both Ethel and Annie Mae spoke in unison, "Daddy, can we git a Christmas tree, please?"

Willie Joe said, "Ya know, I think I saw a little juniper bout this high over by the fence row. T'would make a right purdy little Christmas tree."

"You can talk it over while I'm gone to the barn." said Mattie. Guilt caused Willie Joe to avoid eye contact.

When word got around that Mother had transferred the title of "Storyteller" to me, my father's family handed over their records. Some of them had hoped to create a database and this effort of mine might help to speed that along. I stored the McCawl material in the same closet as the old trunk. Once I looked through the memorabilia, I recognized its potential. Much like Mother's family, the McCawls had some compelling tales that deserved to be heard by a larger audience.

I recognized that the subject matter was compelling, and that spurred me on. By this point I had a line I liked to use to introduce myself.

The idea of recording our family history in the form of a historical novel sounds like a great empty nest project, the ultimate crown jewel of my bucket list, and perhaps the perfect aging-grandmothers' Swan Song.

After considerable thought, I discussed my idea with Mother, and the sparkle in her eyes indicated her willingness to help with the project.

By then she was past eighty years old and physically worn out. I am so grateful for that final year and a half we spent together reminiscing. Truly, Cheatiebo was a unique member of humanity. Much of her distinctiveness grew out of atavism. I learned the meaning of the term while researching family history. Atavism means a person that is an evolutionary throwback and possesses traits that have reappeared after they had disappeared from the blood line generations earlier.

In common language Cheatiebo was a throw-back to Cherokee ancestors that hailed from the Appalachian Mountain region. According to family folklore, Cheatiebo was a direct descendant of Wathena, pronounced Wah-then-ah, a legendary ancestor who lived during the time of the Lewis and Clark Expedition, the 1812-1814

New Madrid Earthquakes, and the 1814 Battle of New Orleans. The mesmerizing fire-side tales she heard were the stuff found in history books. The similarities between Cheatiebo and her ancient Cherokee Grandmother Wathena defined the phenomenon of atavism.

Cheatie exhibited both physical and psychological traits attributed to Wathena. An in-depth search of the term describes a well-established branch of genetics that is still evolving. Atavistic occurrences such as Cheatiebo's continue to challenge the minds of the scientific community.

Chapter 2

A TRAIL OF BLOOD

M attie pulled on her moth-eaten tweed coat that didn't meet over her belly. She tied a black knitted scarf around her long black hair and pulled on an extra pair of woolen stockings before slipping her feet into a pair of oversized rubber boots. "I'll be back soon as I kin. Them aigs'll be done in about five minutes, don't let 'em boil dry. You and the girls go ahead and eat, I'll eat later."

Wind gusts pummeled Mattie with snow and sleet. The ground was already slippery. Every breath of cold air hurt. Once inside the barn that was actually an old shed, she fed a pitchfork of hay each to the horse and goat. She called them by name, Roanie and Banannie, names the girls had chosen. The nanny goat was a cream, almost yellow color. Mattie checked to make sure their stalls were securely latched and gave them both an affectionate pat.

The whole flock of useless dominecker hens were bunched together on the roost and had their feathers fluffed out for warmth. The old hens had sealed their fate and would be slaughtered. She didn't feel up to the effort, maybe tomorrow. Banannie would be birthing kids soon and hopefully furnish the family with a long spell of milk and cheese. The anticipated twin kids would be slaughtered for meat.

Mattie tackled repairing the shotgun hole from the outside. She picked up the hammer and spilled nails where Willie Joe had dropped them. Mattie hefted the piece of metal, a pilfered road-side sign, to cover the jagged hole. A wind gust ripped it from her hands. On her second try she held the sign in place with her hip. Mattie was trying to hurry, but her cold numbed fingers made her effort clumsy.

Mattie returned to the barn's interior and searched for the splitting wedge and sledgehammer. Finally, she found them half hidden under some pieces of kindling. She made a mental note to load up some kindling.

Mattie was in no shape to be splitting wood. Each swing of the iron hammer radiated pain throughout her body. Perspiration beaded upon Mattie's brow and trickled into her eyes. Before each strike she would hold her breath. A couple of times the pain drove her to her knees, but after a short pause she would rise and continue. Mattie refused to give in to the pain.

She was thinking, *storms like this one can be killers. Word has it that winter before last a whole family was found frozen to death in their home.* Mattie was glad they had traded the two half-grown shoats for the load of dry hardwood. She was thinking in times like these it's better to be hungry than cold.

As a married couple Mattie and Willie Joe were terribly mismatched; picture the oil and water analogy. Willie Joe had two sides to him. When he was around home and sober, he was affectionate and playful with his family, but disorganized and sadly, just plain lazy. In a public setting he relished the limelight. He was a natural entertainer, gifted at playing the fiddle, harmonica, guitar, and his singing voice had near perfect pitch. In addition to talent and stage presence, he had a certain something, some call it charisma or animal magnetism. Ladies found his black curly hair and iridescent blue eyes quite handsome. Some of them would line the stage hoping to catch his eye. During his high energy performances, he exuded a devil-may-care recklessness that never disappointed his fans. The farming communities where Texas, Oklahoma, Arkansas, and Louisiana merge were his stomping grounds. Hands down he was the area's favorite hoe-down fiddler and square dance caller.

In his later years he gained popularity among the rowdy Texans that frequented the beer joints on the Oklahoma side of the Red River. Blue laws that restricted the sale of alcoholic beverages in Texas created a large customer base for the dance halls just across the river. Quitting time on Friday saw carloads of fun-loving Texans headed north, many of them using the Red River crossing at Carpenter's Bluff, the site of a railroad bridge constructed in 1910. The crossing had been modified after-the-fact with a wooden shelf barely wide enough to accommodate single file automobile traffic. I had nightmares from crossing that bridge. The structure was not for the faint hearted. I usually kept my eyes closed. It was a long way down to the river. It became a popular place for dare devils to perform high diving stunts. Carpenter's Bluff was the gateway to small towns like Antlers, Broken Bow, Cartwright, and Idabel, all eager to welcome the influx of Texans.

Willie Joe's fans couldn't get enough of his low, lonesome hillbilly picking and singing. He could croon out a yodel with the best of the local "Jimmy Rogers" imitators. Much like the future musician Woody Guthrie, Ole Willie Joe made his mark on the area in the 1920-1940s.

Willie Joe's character was badly flawed. He fit the description 'busted, disgusted, and not to be trusted.' A clever line from Harlan Howard's country song titled "Blame It on Your Heart" fit ole Willie Joe like a glove and went like this, "—a lying, cheating, cold dead beating, two-timing, double dealing, mean and mistreating loving heart."

He gave my mother and her two older sisters Cherokee sounding nicknames when they were just little kids. That is how Cornelia became "Cheatiebo." The name meant "Sweetheart" according to Willie Joe. The silly sounding name stuck for life, and hardly anyone knew mother as Cornelia. Right away Cheatiebo was shortened to "Cheatie," but "Cheatiebo" makes a better book title.

By her thirties Cheatie had assumed the role of family historian and was put in charge of the old trunk that stored their collection of family documents and memorabilia. It was overflowing with crumbly letters, news articles, photos, diaries, and family Bibles.

Our writing project began a couple of years before Mother passed away. I could see her growing weaker, and that motivated me to ask her about her memories and the stories she had been told. Her memory had remained amazingly sharp.

Cheatie had grown up hearing fire-side folklore about her distant ancestors. The treasured stories had been repeated by a succession of Cherokee grandmothers. After Mother's passing, I agreed to take control of the trunk for safekeeping. The story-telling standard was so high it was intimidating. There wasn't really another successor, so I signed on to do my best. Once I began exploring the contents of the trunk, I became obsessed with preserving the family history. Though I am not a trained writer, I wanted to record the stories and let someone else worry about the punctuation.

I was reminded of uneducated writers that were successful without the training. I wasn't prepared for the satisfaction I derived from writing. Emotion crept into the lines that appeared on the screen as I typed them. I was writing fiction that felt real.

When word got around that Mother had taken over as a storyteller, my father's family handed over their records. They had learned of mother's talent for telling a good yarn. She was put in charge of the McCawl family archives. I stored that material in the same closet as the old trunk. Once I looked through the memorabilia, I recognized its potential. Much like Mother's family, the McCawls had some compelling tales that deserved to be heard by a larger audience.

In stark contrast, Mattie was a modest, low-key homebody, the consummate nurturer. Her favorite times were when she was surrounded by her family and close friends. She was decidedly uncomfortable with Willie Joe's circle of 'honky-tonk' friends.

For the present the Wainwrights were facing a triple threat. Considering the weather conditions, inadequate heating headed the list. Isolation from the lone doctor in Millerton County and a shortage of staples were the other two.

Willie Joe was always finding excuses for leaving chores undone. The accident with the hammer forced Mattie to take over getting in the wood. She shook her disheveled head to clear her thoughts. Her sight was suddenly blocked by a wisp of course black hair that fell from the scarf. She tucked it back under. Mattie had Cherokee hair.

There was no mistaking Mattie's Cherokee ancestry. She had inherited her mother Delia's features. Her stern and intense countenance was deceptive since she was a kind and loving person. A youthful Mattie had swept Willie Joe off his feet. She had an earthy attractiveness that Willie Joe found irresistible. She projected confidence and alertness. Thanks to her schooling she was more literate than most backwoods Okies. She was well qualified to home school her daughters, and she was bringing them along well above the kids that attended school in town. As a youngster Mattie easily mastered the book learning offered by her one room school. Once grown, she was the one that folks asked for help in ciphering, writing, or reading. Her many assets went beyond education. She was blessed with a strong back and abundant physical stamina, except for the time she hurt her back struggling to free the family buckboard from a mud hole. Mattie was loved and respected in her little part of the world.

Each strike of the splitting maul aggravated Mattie's back pain and seemed to accelerate the contractions. Mattie chose to risk her own welfare and that of her unborn baby to protect Annie Mae and Ethyl from freezing. Granny Delia had always claimed Mattie got her pain tolerance from being part Cherokee. This was the day that Mattie's ability to function under the direst circumstances would be tested as never before. The hourglass was half empty in measuring her day of travail.

Mattie was thinking about a scripture, "— to pray, nothing doubting," and if there was ever a woman that believed in prayer, it was the loving, gentle Mattie, and so she stopped to pray and then turned the situation over to Jesus with the caveat, 'Lord if you are willing.'

Mattie realized her strength was fading from sheer exhaustion and needed to stop while she could still haul the wood back to the house. She wrapped her first load of precious fuel in a big toe sack and dumped it outside the door of the cabin and then rapped upon the door, yelling to be heard over the wind, "Willie Joe, here's some wood. Hon, you 'wake? Better build up the far before it goes out; I'm going back for another load."

Mattie carried two more loads of wood from the barn. On the last haul, she added a few nails, wire, a wood chisel, some board scraps, and the hammer for fixing up the door. Before heading back to the house, Mattie stopped to drive a nail into the barn door frame next to the door's broken latch. Then she purposely bent the nail over so that it could be rotated to hold the door in place. Mattie used caution while driving the nail having just seen what a hammer did to Willie Joe's thumb. She drove a second nail beneath the first one and bent it over, thinking that two was better than one. *There, that should keep the door in one piece.* She moaned as she gathered the ends of the bundle and hefted it to her back. She carried the final load all the way into the kitchen and dumped it into a wooden box next to the cook stove.

By the final trek Mattie was spent and barely managed to stagger through the doorway. She hadn't noticed the trail of blood left in the snow. Willie Joe had let the fireplace go out. The girls were sound asleep on each side of him, and he was snoring, so Mattie thought *'oh well'* and let him sleep. She tried to hurry, but her body rebelled. She forced herself to get the fire started first and then stoked the cook stove.

Mattie was thinking about the little stash of money she had hidden away. Her plan was to buy a Ben Franklin stove like the one Rose and —. That is when she noticed the spots on the floor, red spots, blood droplets on the floor! She went behind the curtain and checked her private area. What she discovered sent her into a state of shock. An incredulous Mattie had to check a second time to confirm what she felt. Her brow wrinkled and her lips pursed. Mattie was feeling a tiny foot extending from her vagina. It moved when she touched it. Mattie suddenly felt faint and staggered to a chair. By this point her body had partly warmed, but knowing that her infant's foot was outside the birth canal washed over her like ice water and caused her to shiver. A sense of foreboding swept over her. She had never heard of anything like a baby's foot being born first!

Willie Joe and both girls were well protected from the chill by Mattie's homemade featherbed. Her time and effort had been time well spent. Temporarily changing her focus from the tiny foot, Mattie rested a spell to warm up before working on the door latch. Mattie filled a dishpan with warm water and immersed her feet. At first the water was too warm and made her feet hurt. She was forced to perch on the edge of her chair to protect the protruding foot. What was happening with the baby? For the present the question would have to remain a puzzle.

Mattie wondered if Rose had ever heard of a baby's foot being born first. She leaned over the table and rested her head on her arms and prayed, *Dear Lord, please, please help with the baby and give me wisdom on how to handle Willie Joe.* At that moment it came to her what she should do. The pains were growing sharper and more frequent and Mattie knew her labor had gone too far to stop. It was time to tell Willie Joe that the baby was coming early.

Mattie indulged in a few moments of sobbing. She visualized her Lord Jesus embracing her. She felt better and took back control of her emotions. A scripture came into her mind, but she could not recall the chapter or verse. "—casting all your anxiety upon Him, because he cares for you." Mattie decided to do just that.

"Willie Joe, wake up, you got to get up and take the girls over to Rose and Leon's. Hurry and pack the grip with a change of clothes and their nightgowns, it's going to be getting dark real soon."

Willie Joe raised his head and grunted some groggy, nonsensical words and then said, "Say again?"

"Hun, it sure looks like the baby is a comin' early. I think you should take the girls over to stay with Rose and Leon. Pack the grip with a change of clothes and their nightgowns and hurry."

Willie Joe whined, "Rat now? You want us to go in this weather?"

"I don't want to scare you, but this is serious! You must go before dark. Tell Rose that I have a little foot already birthed, and I am bleedin' right smart. Ask Rose what she thinks we should do. Hurry and wake the girls. They will be better off over there with Rose. Get back quick as you can."

"Well okay, I'll go, give me a few minutes to get ready. I'll build up the far."

Mattie and Willie Joe's best friends were Rose and Leon Washington, descendants of African slaves. They lived about a half mile away. Over the years the Wainwrights and Washington couple had become the closest of friends. Rose and Leon had three adolescent children and a nursing baby. The two families usually spent their leisure time together. Those were the good times. Willie Joe would take up his fiddle and harmonica and invite Rose to harmonize with him. Leon was apt to do some tap dancing or keep rhythm to the music by slapping out some lively hambone. He had nailed homemade taps to an old pair of shoes and was always ready to entertain with a double shuffle.

Leon knew farming inside and out and usually had a good settlement check come harvest. He was capable of providing better but wisely opted to stay poor as the proverbial church mouse. Mattie had heard him say, "Not good for us darkies to get too uppity. It could get us a burning cross in our front yard or worse. Yep, they's still some white folk that hates us some 52 years after Juneteenth, even up here in Indian Territory." (Juneteenth refers to June 19th, the date news of Abraham Lincoln's Proclamation of Emancipation reached Texas, a date that is still memorialized by the descendants of African slaves well into the 21st Century).

Without Rose this story would have ended before it began. With the Lord's help and Rose's mid-wife'n skills, Mattie was saved from bleeding to death, no two ways 'bout it. The two women remained friends the rest of their days on earth. Mattie reaped other benefits from her association with Rose, an encyclopedia of frontier know-how.

The two women would pair up for sewing, canning, and gardening. They regularly scoured the area for medicinal plants and gathered wild food. When working the fields, the two families would stay within shouting distance. One of the older Washington children would sit beside the field on a pallet and watch over their baby Larry and little Ethyl, and later Cheatiebo. Annie Mae at seven was already old enough to work the rows.

The trek to the Washington's homeplace almost ended in tragedy. Darkness and poor visibility caused Willie Joe to lose his way. When he realized he was lost, his only option was to backtrack. By the time he and the girls found their way to the Washington's cabin, they were suffering from exposure and exhaustion. Willie Joe had tried carrying the girls, but that didn't last long, so he showed them how to step in his footprints. Finally, Willie Joe spotted a light and assumed it was Rose and Leon's place. "Girls we are almost there, don't quit on me now, just a little bit further, come on, can you see the light, we made it!"

When Rose heard a racquet on the porch she peeked out and yelled, "Look what the cat drug in! Get yourselves in here by the fire." Both Annie Mae and Ethel flung their arms around Rose, and she picked them up and carried them into the house. Rose noticed right off that the girls were acting like they were scared. They hid their faces in Rose's bosom and gripped her neck until it hurt. "Willie Joe, what's going on? Why you out in this weather? You got trouble?"

Annie Mae raised her head and sniffed the air, "Um, it smells good in here, like beans cookin'."

Rose responded, "Got plenty, let's get you warmed up, and then you can eat all the beans you want."

Chapter 3

BLUE NORTHER

Rose and Leon's Ben Franklin Stove took up much of one wall in their small cabin. The log structure was crudely furnished but clean and well organized. Willie Joe decided to set a spell and warm up before heading back to Mattie. It would take a few minutes to get the feeling back into his feet. First thing he removed his boots and socks and placed them by the stove. Rose poured warm apple cider for her guests. She helped a big plate of beans for Willie Joe and set out a wooden platter piled high with hog cracklings. Willie Joe wasn't bashful one bit and began wolfing down the food. Rose smiled and focused on the two girls. Rose held her finger over her lips to shush the girls. "Shoo, whisper when you talk, my youngins need their rest. You'ns can have a big-time tomorrow."

Rose removed Ethel and Annie Mae's shoes and stockings and gently massaged their feet. She could tell how hungry they were by the way they watched their father devouring his food. She decided against making them wait to eat. Rose sat the girls on a blanket facing away from the stove and placed a foot stool between them for a little table.

While the girls ate Rose got on her knees and continued gently kneading the circulation back into their feet. Rose stopped rubbing when it became painful. After the girls had finished their beans, Rose examined their fingers, ears, and nose, all the while singing, tickling, and hugging the laughing children. Rose looked up at Willie Joe and smiled in a way that told him they would be okay.

Rose didn't like what she was hearing in the girl's voices. They were both trying to tell her how scary the walk in the snow had been. Rose loved the two little ones like family, so she took them on to her lap and rocked them. Annie Mae leaned closer and whispered in Rose's ear, "Poppa got lost and, and well we was soooo cold we was thinkin' we might fall down in the snow and go to heaven. But I done like Momma and prayed."

Rose kissed Annie Mae and whispered, "You're safe now." Rose began humming *"Hold to God's Unchanging Hand"* and rocked from side to side.

Ethel first and then Annie Mae fell asleep in Rose's arms. Leon made a pallet near to the stove and helped Rose tuck them in.

"When your journey is completed
If to God, you have been true
Fair and bright your home in glory
Your enraptured soul will view.
Hold (to his hand) to God's unchanging hand
Hold (to his hand) to God's unchanging hand
Build your hopes on things eternal
Hold to God's unchanging hand."

Between chewing and swallowing Willie Joe said, "Gosh that stove does a good job, I wish we had one like it. How much do they cost?"

Leon smiled and said, "You settin' down? I paid 'bout $28.00 and that don't include the stove pipe. It took us a long time to save up enough, but it's worth it, sure gets the job done. Did you ever hear what ole Ben Franklin did to help po folk like us? That invention could've made him a lot of money, but he refused to take out a patent on the stove. He wanted to keep the price down. That Ben Franklin was a good man, cared 'bout people and a shore-nough genius. For my money he ranks right up there with George Washington."

Leon was wanting to visit, but Willie Joe was not his usual loquacious self. His response to Rose's question about his bandaged thumb lacked any detail, "Oh, hit it with the hammer."

Rose, reading Willie Joe's body language, sensed that he was near a breaking point, and started questioning him on Mattie's malaria attack. That is when Willie Joe threw out his hands in an exaggerated gesture of embarrassment and said, "Mattie's in a bad way, she wants me to tell you that the baby is coming early and not in a normal way. One little foot is hanging out, and she is bleedin' right smart. She wants to know what you think we should do. Alarmed, Rose got in Willie Joe's face and tilted her head to the side, showing her no-nonsense side, "You tellin' me our Mattie is in labor, two months early? It sounds like she is gonna have the baby breech. Oh, Laudy, you have to ride into town and bring the Doctor back with you. I'm not ready to handle a breech. Oh Lord, you got to git the doctor!

Leon said, "Calm down Rose, I can tell he's needin' t'go back, but he's got to warm up first."

It was rare for Rose to ignore Leon, but she exploded with emotion, risking waking her sleeping brood. "Willie Joe, don't you know what that means? She is having the baby feet first. You got to get the doctor!"

Willie Joe sputtered, "But I—."

"I cain't leave these youngins' in this blizzard but you got to ride into Millerton and get Doc. Simpkins. Before you go, build up the fire and make sure Mattie is covered up good. Wrap up really good yourself cause she's depending on you making' it through. Cain't let Mattie down. We'll take good care of your girls. Your whole family is depending' on you! We gonna be prayin'."

On the way back to Mattie, Willie Joe was battling a classic whiteout. Right away he was shivering and could not feel his feet. The predatory storm was now unloading its full fury, lashing out at any mortal challenger. Deep snowbanks formed against wind breaks while other areas were swept bare. A few slices of moonlight managed to break through the churning clouds. The howling of the wind became animalistic, and the land bore no semblance to Oklahoma.

Perhaps a sense of guilt convinced Willie Joe he was being singled out for punishment. The effects of hypothermia caused him to begin hallucinating. The storm borne demons seemed so real. Why was his top lip hurting? He removed his glove long enough to examine the area only to realize that his nose had grown a mucus icicle. Stepping carefully to avoid falling on the icy ground he paused due to drowsiness. *I gotta rest a bit.* Just then he bumped against a structure that he recognized as his outhouse, and that roused him back to awareness. As he trudged on toward the house he was thinking, *Thank God I made it.* One is left to ponder whether Willie Joe's reference to God was a profane utterance or perhaps a genuine appeal to some nebulous Creator that in his mind might or might not exist.

Willie Joe struggled to cover the last fifty feet to his porch. There was no light showing at the window. Fearing what he might find inside added to the heaviness of his feet. If Mattie died, he would blame himself. Suddenly he realized how much he needed Mattie. In the hidden recesses of Willie Joe's mind his love for Mattie was more like the affection a boy has for his mother. He had hurt Mattie in so many ways, and yet she remained loving and loyal. He knew he didn't deserve a woman like Mattie.

As he was stamping his feet to shake loose the snow, he heard a faint call, and threw open the door. There was Mattie with a blanket around her shoulders, trying to build up the fire. The flame in the table lamp was out. She had a handful of kindling to spread on the coals of the fireplace. Willie Joe lunged and stumbled toward Mattie almost falling over his numbed feet. He put his arms around her and hoarsely croaked, "Here, get back in bed, I'll take care of the fire. How is the labor pains, you still bleedin?" Before Mattie could answer Willie Joe continued, "Rose thinks I should go fetch Doc Simpkins in Millerton. What 'ja think? I hate to leave you alone again."

Mattie noticed Willie Joe's reaction to the dried blood around her mouth. She recognized the tell-tale signs of panic welling up in him and tried to brush the caked blood from her chin. "Just bit my tongue during a pain, but Rose is right, we need the doctor if we can git him here. Thank you can make it all the way into town? Look at you, you're already 'bout frozen. What you reckon we should do?"

Willie shook his head trying to clear his thinking, "First let me get some candles lit and build up the far in the cook stove."

Mattie made it to the bedside and said, "Willie Joe, I need to go. Quick, get the slop jar, oh no." A gush of amniotic fluid managed to leak past the tightly wedged baby. The cloudy fluid streaked with blood coated Mattie's inner thighs and pooled on the floor. Mattie turned around, sat upon the side of the bed and raised her skirt. There was no use trying to see past her belly. "Willie Joe, help me off with my skirt and bloomers. I need to see what is happening down there. Bring the hand mirror over here."

Mattie lay back and lifted her knees. Willie Joe held the candle and gave Mattie the mirror. They were looking at the little foot when a terrible pain coursed through Mattie's body, causing her to moan. The baby's leg advanced an inch or two and then retreated to its previous position.

Willie Joe took a deep breath and blurted out, "The baby is alive, the toes moved!"

Mattie had a chill and pulled the comforter over her half naked body. "Willie Joe, it must be the cord around the baby, it is holding the baby back. Bring me a towel and a pan of warm soapy water and hurrrrry!"

Willie Joe got the same pan Mattie had used for his hurt thumb. He sliced off a chunk of soap and added water from the iron kettle. To distract him from the fear of losing the baby, Mattie said, "Willie Joe, hurry and bring in more wood from the porch. Bring out some candles, get my big homemade candles, they burn longer."

Mattie rose to a sitting position and lathered up her hands in the pan of water. Then she lay back on the bed with her legs apart. She quickly realized that it was useless to probe her birth canal. She washed her hands and used the towel to wipe her face. She knew her situation was life threatening. When the next pain hit, she tensed her back and uttered a tortured prayer, "Lord if you are willing, help us deliver this little one safe and sound." Hearing Mattie pray with such desperation unleashed Willie Joe's hold on his emotions. He sat down beside Mattie and began weeping aloud.

Mattie placed a consoling hand on Willie Joe's shoulder and continued her prayer, "Lord, if you are willin' help Willie Joe to hold on and do what needs to be done. Lord, please keep our baby alive 'til Doc gits here." Mattie decided it would be better if Willie Joe left for town before his emotional state got worse. "Willie, hon, go ahead and git ready. Saddle Roany and ride to Doc's house. Tell him about the baby's foot."

Mattie was careful to use a soothing tone and said, "Everthang's gonna be alright, the Lord hears our prayers. Mattie took a big breath, "Dear God, Me and Willie Joe is ask'n for your help. Please, if you're willing, help us save our child. Help us to know what is best. Please be with Willie Joe on the trip into town. In Christ's name, A-Man"

Willie Joe finished stoking the fire and walked over to where Mattie lay. He gave her a tender look and brushed a lock of hair from her brow. Then he knelt and gave her a hug and said, "Mattie, I'm okay now. We'll let that prayer be from me too, you said just the right words."

Another terrible pain hit Mattie, "Oh, Lord help me! Wish Rose was here! Roany will help you find the way. He knows the road and animals have a second sense."

After almost freezing to death on the trip to the Washington's cabin, Willie Joe got serious about bundling up for the trip into town. Next to his skin he wore faded trap door long johns that had started out red. He layered three pair of woolen socks making it hard pulling on his boots. He tugged on a pair of heavy corduroy pants lined with flannel and a thick wool sweater. Over that he buttoned every button of a linsey-woolsey shirt. Still layering, he donned a buffalo hide vest and some leather chaps that covered the front of his legs. On top he wore a long, waterproofed canvas overcoat with a quilted lining. For his head he wore a felt drover's hat pulled down over a woolen Scandinavian cap with ear flaps and dangling ties. He wound a red wool scarf around his neck and tucked it into his coat. Finally, he tugged on two pairs of gloves, wool ones under the leather. He was decidedly stiff legged as he exited the cabin.

Willie Joe had finished lighting candles and the lantern. The fireplace grate was stacked as high as he dared, and the cook stove was full. He had hauled in more wood from the front porch. The snow would have time to melt off. There was nothing else to do. He flashed one last look at Mattie as he closed the door behind himself, grateful she had worked on the door latch. Mattie was better at fixing things. As he made his way to the barn, he was wishing he had learned to believe in Mattie's God. He decided right there that he would talk it over with Leon. There is nothing like a family crisis to make folks like Willie Joe "get religion," at least temporarily.

Now all alone, Mattie suffered another pain, stronger than the ones before. She wished for something to hold in her mouth so she wouldn't bite her tongue again. Was Mattie imagining the noises, maybe it was the wind? She wondered if the sounds she heard were coming from her own throat.

The unrelenting crescendo of labor pains exhausted Mattie. The interval between labor pains was so brief there was no time to catch her breath. The howling wind outside the cabin indicated that the storm was still intensifying. Mattie questioned whether the old cabin could remain standing in the face of such a storm. Within the space of three hours, the cabin's temperature plunged to well below freezing.

Chapter 4

"ALONE"

Mattie was having chills. She spoke to the empty room, "Gotta keep the far burnin'." She waited for the next labor pain to pass intending to use the brief interval to build up the fire. Mattie turned onto her side facing away from the bed's edge and backed off using her arms to push her body upright. When she tried to stand, her feet slipped on the frozen puddle of amniotic fluid next to the bed. On the way down she struck the edge of the mattress with her abdomen and fell crumpled upon the icy floor, unconscious. Only the colony of mice that lived in the rafters heard her scream. Flecks of debris rained down from their frenzied scurrying. Mattie lay sprawled on the floor, breathing but unconscious.

When Mattie revived from the stupor, she was prone. Her pain was so awful she became nauseous and vomited. A wave swept over her that blunted the pain. She experienced a strange peacefulness. Some unknown force gently lifted her from her body to hover near the rafters of the cabin. She had a panoramic view of the room and her own crumpled body lying upon the floor. Her fear and pain were gone. That is when she saw that the room was filled with creatures clothed in white, hovering beside her. She felt euphoric and protected. There were faint voices, familiar voices calling out. Mattie recognized them, first Annie Mae and then Ethel shouting, "Momma, come back, hold me, I'm cold." "Momma, hurry, I'm scared."

Suddenly, Mattie equated what was happening with death. She had to choose, stay or be carried away. The mysterious destination that beckoned to Mattie was peaceful and dazzling with indescribable beauty. Mattie resisted, and the trance ended. Suddenly she was back on the floor. The beckoning of her frightened children tore at her heart strings. She cried out for the Lord to postpone her one-way journey toward eternity. The Lord responded with love and grace toward sweet Mattie.

She raised her head and looked about the room. The cold air upon her face reminded her about the dying fire. When she went to right herself, she could not move her legs. Mattie moaned aloud, *oh no, I'm paralyzed!* Panic swept over her, and as she paused to catch her breath, she heard a faint gurgling noise. Could there be a small animal in the room? Then she heard a high-pitched cough and more gurgling. A most amazing thought occurred to Mattie. Is it possible that the pressure from the fall pushed the baby out? Mattie raised her head to peer over her shoulder to view her paralyzed legs.

What she saw was the miniature form of an infant not much larger than her hand. Lying next to the baby was what Mattie recognized as a placenta. The burgundy mass of tissue with the characteristic pattern of parallel lines looked just like the one she had seen at a recent birthing. She knew the cord should be tied-off quickly, so she grasped the bed rail with both hands and after two tries managed to turn over to her back relieving the pressure on her abdomen.

Bubbles of mucus had formed over the baby's mouth and nose, and only the slightest quivering movements animated the pencil like extremities. Mattie, now flat on her back lowered her head, grasped the bed side rail and maneuvered in an arc to reach the tiny child at the end of the cord. She turned the baby on its side and elevated its lower body. Some fluid drained from the tiny nose and mouth. Mattie, still naked from the waist down stretched her cotton camisole enough to insert the baby next to her chest. Mattie quickly twisted a knot into the cord and then positioned the infant's head over her mouth. She used the camisole to wipe the infant's face and quickly covered both the nose and mouth with her mouth and starting extracting fluid. When she turned her head aside to empty the suctioned fluid, the baby took a breath, not a normal breath, but it inhaled, making a raspy sound.

Mattie gently patted the tiny back with two fingers and repeated the suctioning.

The infant's second breath sounded more normal, and the baby began moving. Next Mattie tried breathing into the tiny mouth with carefully measured puffs of air. After three repetitions, the baby wrinkled up its face and began to cry. The sunken chest began rising and falling and the arms and legs flailed about.

Mattie's next thought was how cold it was on the floor. She was able to stretch her hand up to the bed's edge and pull a quilt to the floor. Still helplessly supine, she covered her chest with the folded blanket and secured it by tucking it under the bottom of the camisole. With the little peanut of a baby well covered she started moving toward the fireplace. As Mattie propelled herself across the floor using her hands, she noticed that the strand of umbilical cord was still attached to her vagina. Mattie was puzzled and carefully examined the dark red mass to confirm that it really was a placenta. Even in her weakened state she reached the correct conclusion.

Just as she said, "I must be having twins," Mattie's body convulsed with a contraction. The paralysis partly dulled the pain, and she looked down just in time to see another tiny baby slide onto the floor. The twin's umbilical cord was connected to the placenta already expelled. Mattie knew that identical twins share a placenta, and this second baby would be severely oxygen deprived. Mattie lifted the limp and lifeless infant to her chest and immediately applied suction to extract fluid. For what seemed too long the child appeared to be lifeless, but then a facial grimace rewarded Mattie's desperate effort. Soon the second baby was breathing and had turned from gray to creamy pink and was moving. She tied a knot in the cord and placed the second baby inside her camisole before continuing across the rough floor to the fireplace.

Mattie knew that she and the twins would soon freeze to death unless she could get a fire burning. Mattie pushed with her hands to advance across the floor, scraping her bare, numbed back on the rough floorboards. The tethered placenta was being pulled behind Mattie and was tugging on the two infants. Seemingly providential, Mattie spied a butter knife that had fallen to the floor and used it to sever the placental mass.

Suddenly Mattie felt a terrible pain pulse through her body that ended with tingling sensations in her legs. She figured the fall had further damaged her fragile spinal column. Mattie took a deep breath and tried to move her legs. They twitched a little, but the effort sent the worst kind of electrical impulses coursing through her body. She was consoled by the fact that her paralysis was not total. Mattie knew it would be best to avoid movement, but even more pressing was the cold. She continued moving across the floor toward the fireplace.

Mattie, surprisingly alert, was able to move tiny pieces of kindling to the coals of the open hearth and then gradually add larger splinters and sticks. The smoldering coals ignited the kindling. Within a couple of minutes, the fire was lively enough to add more kindling and a couple of split logs. From there she scooted to the cook stove and lifted the latch. She couldn't see inside the stove, but her hands felt the heat from coals inside. She managed to insert three small logs and lock down the door.

Mattie returned her focus to the twin babies as she propelled her way back to the bedside. Mattie had been too preoccupied to note the gender of the babies, but she knew they would be of the same sex if truly identical. She avoided the frozen puddle and umbilical mass staining the floor. The twins were not moving, so Mattie placed her hand inside the blanket to see if they were warming. She was alarmed at how cold they felt. Mattie pulled the feather tick and more covers from the bed; a pillow came along too. Next, she tugged until the corn shuck mattress fell to the floor. Mattie tossed a blanket over the mattress and then with the twins held to her chest with one arm managed to wiggle her way upon the mattress. Mattie knew her own body heat would transfer best with skin-to-skin contact. Mattie was curious about the sex of the infants and peeked under the quilt. Ah, the sight of the matching female genitalia brought a smile to Mattie's face. The gender was of no consequence, Mattie was so thrilled to have the little girls looking better, her preeminent thought was to express thankfulness to her Lord and Master for granting her prayer request.

Underneath the homemade comforter Mattie gently massaged the infants' bodies starting with their head and face. Mattie was instinctively mimicking the tactile stimulation of animal mothers' when licking their young. Mattie's efforts were rewarded with better color and increased movement. She covered her head with the comforter and exhaled several breaths of warm air. First one and then both newborns decided to register a complaint about the rigors of birth. The cries were indescribably strange, but sweet. Mattie had witnessed the hand of

God granting her supplications. She had never doubted God's control over His creation that no-doubt, included the natural laws.

Blood loss was causing Mattie to drift in and out of consciousness. Her heart rate was dangerously slow and irregular. Mattie's condition was ultra-grave, yet her life force refused to depart.

Mattie was startled awake by the sound of the door opening. A shaft of bright light hid the identity of the person entering. There was no mistaking the voice that spoke, "Mattie, it's me, Rose. Rode the mule over. Leon stayed with the chilins. Burr, it's cold in here!" Rose went to work building up the fires. The whites of her eyes registered her concern as she inspected the bloody smears and mass of after-birth on the floor. Rose brushed her hands off and put a tender palm on Mattie's forehead, "Hun, can you tell me what happencd here?" With a weak whisper Mattie said, "Look," and she moved the comforter enough to expose two tiny heads sleeping on her chest.

Rose gasped and lowered her voice to a whisper, "Oh Mattie, — two babies, oh my, so little! Mattie, they breathe'n okay?" Mattie was able to nod her head. Rose continued, "As soon as I gits it warmed up in here, I'll take a look at them." When Rose knelt over Mattie and lifted the bottom of the comforter, she saw the blood-soaked bedding.

Rose tried to hide her alarm. She knew Mattie was close to death. Rose encouraged Mattie to drink a large glass of water. What should she do about the blood loss? Then it come to her what must be done. She looked around the room for something to pack into Mattie's vagina. Rose decided that the cleanest cloth available was her own freshly laundered petty coat. Rose began ripping it into strips and Mattie shot her a questioning look. Rose said, "Mattie, sweet pea, we gotta stop the bleeding right now!" Rose moved a freshly filled lantern nearby and washed her hands. Next Rose used her gentle and dexterous hands to stuff the strips of cotton muslin into Mattie's birth canal.

At first Rose didn't understand why Mattie could not hold her knees up in a bent position, until Mattie whispered, "I'm paralyzed— my legs—the fall."

"It's okay Mattie; I will manage to do this with or without the help of your legs." It was tiring work, and being bent over made Rose's back hurt, but her love for Mattie gave her the stamina to finish the task without resting.

After a large portion of the petticoat had been packed inside Mattie, Rose turned her attention to the twins. Rose washed her bloody hands and arms and wiped away the perspiration on her face and neck. Then she thought to give Mattie more liquid. She finally found the tin of tea leaves and brewed two cups before getting back to the babies.

With the arrival of Rose, Mattie's chance for survival had improved. Short of having a doctor Rose was the next best person to snatch Mattie back from death's door. Rose decided to see if the infants would nurse. She quickly realized that Mattie's nipples were just too large for such tiny mouths. She fetched a teacup and expressed some of Mattie's colostrum. Using a spoon, she dribbled a few drops into each button sized mouth. At first the babies choked a little but then began swallowing. Nature's miracle liquid had a magical effect. The smacking noises brought smiles to the two women's faces. The milk turned out to be what the two babies needed. Rose grasped the mattress and pulled it closer to the fire. There wasn't a slack moment as she split her time between coaxing Mattie to drink tea, building up the fires, and feeding the twin girls.

Rose used the rest of the water in the bucket for brewing tea and was about to go to the well to draw more. While the tea brewed there was loud stamping upon the front porch and then Willie Joe's face appeared through a cracked door. Rose said, "Willie Joe, thank the Lord, you made it! Hurry and close the door before you let in the cold." Just when Rose was about to tell him he had twins, she heard Dr. Simpkins' voice complaining about his ice encrusted medical satchel. "Come on in here, Doc. Try to hurry ifn' you can. I'm tryin' to warm the place up. Mattie sure needs you! Praise the Lord, you'ns made it through the storm! Mattie, did you hear me, hon, Willie Joe is back with the Doc."

Dr. Simpkins looked at the preemies and shook his head. He said, "Good job Rose."

Rose interrupted him and said, "Po Mattie done this her-sef 'foe I got here. Mattie slipped on ice on the floor, and the fall put pressure on her belly. When she come to one baby was born, and she couldn't move her legs. Both babies was spit out on to the floor. Mattie did a good job taking care of them. She had to scoot on her back over to stoke both the fireplace and stove. That is what made the streaks of blood across the floor. I found her on the mattress covered up with her feather bed. I saw that she had lost too much blood, and the only thing I could think to do was pack her with strips of cloth to stop the hemorrhaging. I gave her water and tea. I am shore glad you'ns got through. Doc, Mattie's legs is paralyzed from the fall."

Doc. Simpkins helped Mattie roll to her side and looked at the bloody wood-torn flesh that extended the length of her lower spine. He ran his hand down the vertebral column and remarked, "Sure looks like you done yourself some damage when you fell. How is the pain, Mattie? Does this make it hurt more?" Mattie could only groan from the pressure.

Doc. Said, "Mattie, whatever you do, stay still, don't try to move. We will bring in something and get you lifted off the floor."

Willie Joe walked into the house with a load of firewood and announced that the snow had stopped falling. Blue sky was showing through the clouds. He said, "Rose, we would've been back sooner, but sure enough me and Roany got turned around and took the long way to Doc's place."

This is when Rose said, "Willie Joe, let me be the first to tell you, you got twins, two little girls." An emotional Willie Joe dropped to the floor next to Mattie's pallet and searched her pale face, and then as was his habit, he smoothed some sprigs of her hair. Mattie was unable to speak but returned his gaze. When he bent and kissed her brow, he heard the slightest of noises, almost like mice squeaking. Mattie motioned with her head for him to go ahead and look under the comforter.

Chapter 5

WILLIE JOE CAN'T TAKE NO MORE

What Willie Joe saw so shocked him that he reacted badly. "Mattie, they look like rats!" and he jumped back. He looked at Doc and asked between sobs, "Is they ah-life? His reaction caught everyone off guard especially Mattie. Tears formed and ran down her temples into her hair line. She thought to apologize but decided they weren't nothing to be sorry of. Willie Joe would have to get used to the way they looked. Rose hurried to comfort Mattie and drilled Willie Joe with a warning that could've backed off Satan himself.

Doctor Simpkins spoke up. "Calm down Willie Joe. The babies are alive and even took some milk. This is the way premature babies look, but with time they will or at least should develop into normal looking babies. Girls usually do better than boys. First, we must keep them alive these first few days when they are in the most danger. The cold will make them sick, so get all the firewood you can and do some chinking. These log walls are in terrible shape, I see light coming through right there, see it?"

Willie Joe said, "Sure, Doc, I been meaning to take care of the chinking, I need to buy some plaster, and money's been short."

Doc said, "Use what you got, even mud is better than nothing."

Doc switched back to the survival of the babies, "Now Willie Joe, I think the babies have a fighting chance for survival. Keeping them warm is your job, so keep the firewood coming. Do you think you can haul in another arm load? And we need a couple of buckets of water from the well. When we get it warm enough in here, Rose and I will bathe Mattie and the babies."

"Rose, can you put on more water to heat?"

"Mattie, dear, you need to drink liquids like tea and broth and maybe eat some scrambled eggs?" A closer look revealed that Mattie had fallen asleep.

Willie Joe hauled two armloads of wood to the porch, drew water from the well and fed the animals. He walked into the cabin, nonchalantly took a jacket from its hook, and used it to conceal his fiddle case as he left the cabin. Willie Joe needed a drink in a bad way. *I done my part and 'bout froze to death in the storm. Think I'll head into town and settle my nerves. I'll be back before they miss me.* "After a couple of hours Rose started looking for Willie Joe. She said, "Doc, I'm a mind to think Willie Joe has flown the coup, flat out left us high and dry." Neither Rose nor Doc was too surprised.

Confronted with Willie Joe's desertion Rose and Leon stepped up and took over as care givers. They packed up Mattie and moved her and the children into their own home. Rose improvised a bed for Mattie in the already crowded living room and each night spread pallets for Annie Mae and Ethel.

Willie Joe made a stealthy, keepin' to the shadows, trip into Millerton. He lost no time tying on an alcoholic binge that left him drunk out of his mind. The episode ended when his money ran out. The only way he had of prolonging his party was to organize a dance and pass the hat. He lost track of the days as he spent his time either drinking up the proceeds of the square dances or nursing a hang-over, broke and suffering withdrawal.

During the days he stayed in town he managed to find a heap of trouble. He started out as a spectator at the annual game cock fights on the outskirts of Millerton. Willie Joe's curiosity quickly turned to avarice, and his impulsive nature led to placing a bet. He picked a large dark red and black rooster with a lot of iridescent green in his tail feathers. A cock like him was sure to win with his aggressiveness. He was a fine-looking rooster that was so aggressive he slashed his own handler on the arm as he was being lowered into the arena. What appeared to be a sure winner was quickly dispatched by a lack luster solid black opponent owned by a couple of burly fellows out of Tulsa.

Caught up in the excitement, Willie Joe foolishly accepted a loan from the boys from Tulsa to stay in the game and maybe recoup his money. By the nights end he was deep in debt and was looking for an opportunity to sneak out on the debt holders. When the out-of-towners insisted that Willie Joe pay up on the spot, he used the next trip to the two-holer to slink away—like draining the sludge from a swamp…disappear into the night. Not many folks in Millerton knew the exact whereabouts of his farm, so he high-tailed it for home.

After two weeks with Rose and Leon, Mattie had gained back most of her strength. The rehabilitation exercises coupled with Mattie's determination to resume her life resulted in a quick recovery. Rose wisely prepared meals of calf's liver and iron rich canned mustard greens to speed Mattie's recovery from blood loss.

The evenings at the Washington home were pleasant. Mattie was engrossed with Leon's Bible studies and joined in hymn singing, storytelling, and games. Rose and Leon could not have been more loving and generous. Mattie hid her hurt and bravely prepared to resume her life. It wasn't the first time Willie Joe had let Mattie down. It was the bed she had chosen.

There was no keeping Mattie down for long. She felt like she was imposing on Rose and Leon and wanted to let them get back to their normal lives. Rose was looking haggard.

Mattie named the twins Cornelia Fannie and Delia Nannie after their grandmothers whose names happened to rhyme. Baby #1, Cornelia was off to a good start, but Delia was having trouble with swallowing and was listless. Rose was at a loss as to what should be done for the infant. She had instructions from Doctor Simpkins on rehabilitating Mattie's back injury but not much on caring for the two babies.

Mattie credited the Lord with keeping her and the twins alive, and she was determined to recover and take care of her family. Her concern for Rose was ever present, "Rose, hun, you need to kick back a spell." Mattie gave Leon orders for Rose to spend some time resting and volunteered to take the Washington children for a visit as soon as she got things in order.

As a testament to the innocence of childhood, and Annie Mae and Ethel were having the time of their lives playing with the Washington children, they had seemingly forgotten all about their absent Poppa. It was Christmas time, and Rose helped the children decorate a little spruce tree. Mattie began talking about getting back to her own home, "Rose, Leon, it's time for me to go home, I can take care of things now. I need to be home."

Rose said, "Oh Mattie, only if you're sure? Ya kin rest assured we will be checkin' in on yawl." Leon hitched up the wagon and took Mattie and her girls to their home on New Year's Day following a traditional meal of black-eyed peas, mustard greens seasoned with bacon drippings, and iron skillet cornbread.

As the wagon approached the Wainwright cabin, they could see smoke coming from the chimney. Willie Joe's head peaked from the partly opened door just as Leon parked the wagon near the cabin's entrance. Willie Joe was holding his shotgun at the ready, fearing that the Tulsa boys might have found him. He put the gun away and eagerly greeted the new arrivals. The grownups feigned normalcy for the sake of Annie Mae and Ethel.

Willie Joe's mouth erupted with the usual excuses. Leon ignored his empty words and set the atmosphere with the following response, "Not now Willie Joe, step out of my way, I got to get this wagon unloaded. I got to get on back home and take care of my family." Willie Joe pretended not to get Leon's pointed reference to a man's responsibility. Leon could tell it had registered. Willie Joe was looking sheepish and had guilt written all over his face. He turned to Mattie with outstretched arms, but she was even more dismissive of him. She abruptly shut off his nervous babbling and stopped his approach with an open palm thrust in his direction. As soon as Leon left for home, Mattie sent Annie Mae and Ethel out to look for eggs. Without making eye contact Mattie told Willie Joe, "We need to talk!" Willie Joe tried to hug Mattie and she shoved him away. He stormed out the door and returned a few minutes later with liquor on his breath and a bottle tucked under his belt.

Willie Joe said, "Mattie, before you have your say I want to apologize! I was needin' a drink bad, and so I bolted for town. I understand you be'n mad, you should be. I'm gonna try to do better, cross my heart and swear on the Bible. Can you give me another chance? How 'bout we start over and make this marriage work? Mat, you know I love you, always have. I think I love you more than you love me. If I mess up agin, I'll just disappear out of your life, and you can find yourself a better man, heaven knows you deserve better than me."

Mattie hid her face in her hands and began to weep. Willie Joe rushed to envelope her in his arms. Finally, she said, "I do want our marriage to work, and hard as you make it, I still have feelings for you. It's your drinkin' causin' the problems. How 'bout us start'n over by giving me that bottle?"

At first Willie Joe refused but decided to hand it over. "Okay Mattie, I'm gonna try to do better." Willie Joe was thinking, *she ain't gonna leave me, she's bluffin'.* He was comforted with the knowledge that he still had another bottle hidden out in the shed. Willie Joe's *new leaf* lasted a couple of weeks, just long enough to give Mattie a little false hope.

Baby Delia's fragile health continued to deteriorate, and at one month of age she came down with pneumonia and died on the second day. The funeral was heart breaking. Leon built a tiny casket and Rose sewed the infant a long white dress for the burial. Without exception everyone that viewed Delia's body thought she looked like a tiny China doll. Despite crushing grief Mattie found the will to go on with life out of consideration for her other three daughters.

Mattie recovered from the back injury and was able to fully resume her responsibilities. Only two months after the birth of the twins Mattie became pregnant again, this time with a boy. The pregnancy caused her breast milk to dry up thereby threatening the frail Cornelia's survival. Thankfully Rose was still nursing her own infant and volunteered to wet nurse Cornelia.

Chapter 6

TIME TO THROW OUT THE DISH WATER

We had an old rooster named Scarface. Daddy brought him home in a tow sack from the cockfights. In his former life Scarface had been a prized fighting cock. He was a big rooster and had dramatic plumage in iridescent shades of brown, blue, green, and black. That was the night Scarface lost the fight that left him blind in one eye and with a crippled leg. His tuft of tail feathers were almost two feet long. Once he had recovered from his defeat, he acted more like a peacock when he was strutting for our flock of hens. Bein' crippled up didn't slow his quest for romance. The attraction was mutual. Just the sight of him would cause the hens to ruffle their feathers. Scarface was a family pet, and we hoped we would never be forced to eat him.

One of my fondest memories of Daddy was the day we all played Indians. I was about seven years old. I remember that day like it was yesterday. He decided to give us girls Cherokee nicknames. For once he was all playful and affectionate. He pretended to be the chief. He decided to reward our bravery by giving us new names. Ethel was changed to Ahyoka, Cherokee for "She Brought Happiness." He named Annie Mae Tsistunagiska the word for "Wild Rose." My Cherokee name was Cheatiebo and was supposed to mean "Sweetheart," but later we learned he got confused, and Cheatiebo didn't mean sweetheart at all. We girls butchered the names and pronounced them Hoka, Siska, and Cheatie. The game we were playing called for the Chief to send us on missions, and we had to do as he said. We were having fun, but then Momma called us to eat lunch and then insisted we catch up on our chores. Momma was strict when it came to us doing chores, "You girls need to draw some water, gather the eggs, and pull some greens and carrots out of the garden, and I don't mean later."

There was this one special evening that sticks out in my memory. It was hot and sticky. After supper we kids was sitting around our oak pedestal table hoping Granny would tell us a story. The table had a brownish/black linseed oil finish that gave it a soft, matte texture that could be imprinted with a fingernail. The surface bore the scars of much use.

Earlier in the day I had finished my chores and took off hunting. I got dressed up in my homemade Indian garb and law, I bet'chu I was a sight. My coveralls had fringe cut into the hem, and I made a turban out of an old red and yeller scarf. Oh yes, I wore my rabbit pelt moccasins, made them myself. I was gittin' tired of vinegar dumplings ever night, so I went hunting for a squirrel for supper. I pocketed a couple of birdshot shells and hiked to the creek with Daddy's shotgun over my shoulder. Like all twelve gage shotguns, it had the kick of a mule. I had learned to brace the butt of the gun against something other than my shoulder. In this case I used the trunk of the tree. I didn't have to wait long before a squirrel darted about in a nearby tree. I waited for a clear shot and knocked the ball of fur from the limb with the first shot. My imagination got a whiff of the squirrel meat cooking. Momma was always worried about me using the shotgun, but she never put her foot down. I could tell she was relieved to have the squirrel meat. Annie Mae helped me clean the squirrel. We left the tail attached and nailed the hide to the barn wall next to the other skins we had curing."

That reminds me of going frog hunting. One evening me and Annie Mae got back from a two-mile hunt along the creek with a good dozen bullfrogs in a bag tied around my waist, we was feelin' purty proud of ourselves. Annie Mae was worried about the bag of frogs being too heavy for me to carry by myself, but I told her, "These frogs is light because of them jumping around in the bag, seein' how at least half of them are in the air at any one time."

Annie Mae laughed in my face and said, "Unk-uh, you made that up."

"Did not, it's according to science. Member the story about the Fig Newton man having an apple fall on his head. Ya 'member, he's the one that invented gravity."

Annie Mae said, "You think you're so smart. Well, it just so happens I don't like science, and I don't need to know it, so there." About then poor Annie Mae stepped on a sharp thorn. I removed the thorn, and she limped the rest of the way home. Right soon she soaked her foot in a pan of coal oil before going to bed. Everyone else was already in bed, and I had a job to do."

"Best I recall that was the first time I cleaned frogs by myself. I set a plank out on our back porch like I seen Momma do. I brought the kerosene lamp out and drew a bucket of water. I poured a little of the water in a pan and stabbed the first frog in the brain with my hunting knife, so's to put it out of its misery. Next I cut off the hind legs and used a pair of pliers to strip off the skin."

"Out of the corner of my eye, I noticed the top half of that frog was crawling away with its' guts trailing out behind and its long white tongue hanging out. With it be'n so late at night I was a little scared, so I stabbed it again. We needed the food, so I kept on cleanin' frogs. After stabbing him over and over I figgered ya cain't kill a frog. Instead, I pitched 'em out in the darkness where I didn't have to watch what they was doin'."

"By the time I was working on the third frog, I heard a swishing sound and suddenly something big flew down from the sky. After I got over bein' scared, I reckoned it was a bird. I didn't get a good look, but I heard it and decided it must be one of the big barn owls we heard most nights. Whew, it scared me so bad I was shakin'! The creature kept on comin' back after ever one of them frogs. When I was finished, it took two big cannin' jars to hold the big meaty legs. I put both jars into an extra bucket and lowered it into the well, just like Momma always done. Our well was deep and had good, cold water. That was the only way we had to keep our food cool."

I kinda got sidetracked about the frogs, but getting' back to the main story, "The only problem with the squirrel meat was that it had right smart birdshot. Of course, we never let a little birdshot ruin a good meal. Our faces looked funny separat'n out the shotgun pellets from the meat. We got the giggles, which caused me to get the "heecups." Before long a scuffle broke out when Ethel spit one of the bebes at Annie Mae, watermelon seed style. Momma jumped up from the table, upsetting her chair, and yelled, 'Stop it right now! Eth-thellll, say you're sorry! And Cheatie, (heecup) wipe that grin off your face (heecup)!'

With supper dishes cleared away, and the table set with a kerosene lamp on a crocheted doily, we were hoping Granny would tell a story. Story time always began as soon as Momma threw out the dish water.

Granny Delia's stories were sure humdingers. On this evening we settled down and waited for Granny to get started. We could hear the night sounds through the screens. I recognized the call of an owl, a whippoorwill, and crickets, lots of crickets. The sounds set the stage for Granny's continuing yarn.

Our little Momma Mattie was propped up on the rusty wrought-iron bedstead with her sewing basket beside her, working her way through a big stack of clothes that needed mending. As always, she wore her porcelain thimble with flowers painted on it. The dim lighting caused her to squint and hold the work at arm's length. Poppa had been kidding her about needing spectacles. Looking back, it seemed that Momma was always working, she fussed that there were never enough hours in the day.

Granny had an earnest look on her face, "Girls you know that we have Tsalagii Clan blood in our veins, somethin' to be proud of." Granny had our full attention. While she was reminding us where she had left off on her story, the rodent population was holding a jamboree above our heads. Our quilting frame was hanging above the kitchen table, and the fabric shielded our food from falling debris. Granny asked me to fetch the broom, so she could reach up and scare the critters away but, in the process, she tore a hole in the brittle wallpaper. Sure-nuf, a little mouse fell through the hole and landed on my head. When I slung my head forward, it went down the bib of my coveralls. When it fell down as far as my knees, it started trying to climb back out. I overreacted and panicked, "Oh, ow, it's biting me! Make it stop!" I jumped up and down, stomped my feet and screamed. I began unfastening my coveralls and dropped them right there on the kitchen floor. My stomping-fit struck Annie Mae as funny, and she started laughing at me. Ethel decided to join in the fun, and the little copycat began laughing too. I was experiencing my worst nightmare, and my own two sisters were laughing at me.

In the summer we loved to build a bonfire in the yard and tell tales. Annie Mae liked to see how scary she could make her tales about ghosts, rabid dogs, and the likes. One of her favorite stories was about monster rats that would attack children. She would describe how they would bite off toes and ears. She loved to imitate their sound, and at my age it was all too real. When that mouse went down my coveralls, I was experiencing one of Annie Mae's horror scenes in real life. If that wasn't bad enough, to have her laughing at me was too much to handle. And then worst of all I looked down at the puddle between my feet. I had wet myself. That struck my sisters as even funnier than my wild dance, and their laughter sounded just like witches cackling. Woe to traitor sisters!

As an adult the mouse-in-my-overalls scare makes me laugh, but at the time I needed some satisfaction along the lines of pay-back. I started plotting my revenge. I refused to speak or even look at either one of my sisters. I came up with a plan to booby trap one of Annie Mae's shoes by hiding a cocked mouse trap inside.

Momma noticed my brooding over the incident and decided to intervene. She set me down for a talk about forgiveness. She asked me to admit that my sisters didn't cause the mouse to fall in my coveralls and that they didn't realize just how scared I was. She pulled out her worn Bible and read Hebrews 10:30, "For we know Him that said vengeance belongeth to me, I will recompense." Being a self-centered child like most, I hoped God would come down hard on them, but after a couple of days I kept forgetting to be mad, especially when they was nice to me. Looking back, I figure they got a talk from Momma too.

Chapter 7

GRANDMOTHER,
THE FOLKLORIST

That night after Momma threw out the dish water Granny started her storytelling, "The Tsalagii are a little different from the other Cherokee Clans. I'll talk more about that later. When he was president, Andrew Jackson let our tribe down when he signed the legislation that forced us off our land. He ordered the military to march our people out here to Oklahoma under guard. Some were able to ride on wagons or horseback, but many were forced to walk. A General under President Jackson was put in charge of the march, in direct violation of signed peace treaties. The Supreme Court sided with the Cherokee but claimed lack of jurisdiction as far as enforcement. Andrew Jackson was being pressured by thousands of brave soldiers that had never been paid, and by nations like France, financiers of the war effort. Selling off Indian land designated as hunting grounds was the best and fastest means of amassing the revenue needed."

The trek West to Indian Territory was tragic due to wet, winter weather and unsanitary conditions. The physically exhausted "People" took the dysentery or consumption and died a terrible death. Most of the country favored President Jackson's plan to settle debts. In them days ships were arriving at eastern seaports daily loaded with white European immigrants in search of land. Arriving along with hardworking salt-of-the-earth families were unscrupulous land speculators, gamblers, and every kind of riffraff one could imagine. The American Indian was sub-human in the mind of many of the newcomers. Many of the Europeans dismissed the Indian Tribes' claim on their ancestral territory as a waste of valuable resources.

"In the late 1820s Legislators in the state of Georgia passed laws against Indians owning land and made it illegal for them to sue a white person in the courts. The Federal government had declared the various tribes to be denominated domestic dependent nations. Protection of the sovereign rights of Indian Territory made its way through the court system, but the Supreme Court refused to hear the case for lack of jurisdiction.

Granny continued, "Much earlier the Indian Nations with territory east of the Appalachian Mountains were encouraged to become civilized and many did exactly that. By the 1820s the Cherokee community of New Echota was as nice as any the whites had. After Chief Sequoyah came up with a Cherokee alphabet, and established schools, a library, and newspaper, many of our young people could read and write both English and Cherokee."

It was too much for the whites to swallow. The Cherokee's civilized culture became an affront to the whites. By mistreating Indian people, white society proved itself to be more savage than the people they called savages. Like whale oil dashed on a fire the discovery of gold in Georgia sealed the fate of the out-numbered Cherokee Nation. One of these days we will study the book, *Trail of Tears*. Cherokee history must be an important part of your education."

Suddenly Granny had to spit. Granny had a vice, poor thing, she dipped snuff. Her poor-folks cuspidor was a tin coffee can. Did'ja ever stop to thank how much smell has to do with memories? I will never forget how the very distinctive stench of the spit cans smelled up our house.

Granny Delia said, "Girls, remember that this Lion's Cave story began back in Georgia and Tennessee in the early 1800's." Granny's story telling appealed to us kids, and she used the right mix of suspense and humor to keep us hanging on every word. Granny's emphatic tone caused us to sit up a little straighter in our handmade chairs. Picture us three girls with alert looks, nervously dangling our bare feet. Granny said, "Getting back to my story, we'll call it *The Lion's Cave Story.*" Then Granny did the darnest thing; she looked directly at me and nodded her head the way she did when verifying some strange phenomenon. Her ebony eyes were so piercing I imagined that they could see right through me. It's a wonder I didn't git the hee-cups again. There was a moment of silence before she continued. My sisters got puzzled looks on their faces but said nothing.

Granny sure knew how to tell a story. She could have us laughing out loud one minute and then bawlin' our eyes out the next. Granny said, "This here story is mostly about my great grandma, who was full blood Tsalagii. It is quite a story about how she ended up married to a Scotsman named Patrick Larson. Patrick had curly auburn hair, a freckled face, broad shoulders, and stood about 6'2". A fine figger of a man he was. Patrick was someone to be reckoned with in a boxing match. He and his brother had trained as gymnasts back in Scotland. The boys worked as performers at the local circus thanks to their mother's brother. He was ring master of the local circus. The money the boys earned from employment at the popular attraction often kept the family from the discomfort of poverty. Uncle Jaime loved his sister and did not hesitate to look out for their welfare despite some resentment from the towns' people. He made sure the boys were trained in several venues.

Patrick had a playful nature and didn't have a mean bone in his body. He was ruggedly handsome with his red curls and eyes the color of robin's eggs. Patrick and his brother, Rory, hired on as shipmates in exchange for passage on a cargo ship bound for Virginia. The boys were in their early teens when Uncle Jaime took the plague and died suddenly. Less than a week later the boys' parents fell ill and passed away. Since their parents were tenant farmers, the brothers were left without property or belongings of value. They were too old to be fostered by their protestant church, but the owner of the circus that employed them took mercy on them and helped to find them employment as kitchen-mates in exchange for passage to the New World. Unusual for them times, both Larson boys could read, write, and do a little ciphering'. Later in life, Patrick's schoolin' caused him a heap of trouble, but I'll git to that eventually. The Larson boys arrived in the new world at Baltimore Harbor and settled in the Chesapeake Bay area.

When Patrick was about 19, Rory asked, "What's wrong with you Brother?"

Patrick said, "I'm feeling a mite restless." Rory was already married and had a young child. He and his wife had settled into a comfortable life operating a little country store for an old couple. Patrick decided that Rory's lifestyle was too civilized for him. He hungered for adventure. The great-unexplored expanse to the west beckoned. Everyday Patrick sought out travelers and searched written articles for information on the frontier. He liked to read the "pulp fiction" novels so popular at the time.

After some planning, Patrick said his farewells and struck out on the westward trail that would merge with the Cumberland Trail. He got rid of what he couldn't tote along. Anyhow, his belongings didn't amount to much. His knapsack held a bedroll with a water repellant cover, a small tent, a change of clothes, and a winter coat. In the bottom was a tin cup and bowl that doubled for cooking utensils, a jug for water, an extra knife, and a whetstone. Slung about his neck was a bag of lead balls and a black-powder horn. A leather strap secured his smoothbore muzzle loader over one shoulder. The weapon was heavy and not very accurate but was what was available to him.

The downside to Patrick's wilderness adventure was leaving Rory behind. Patrick knew that separation would be painful, but he wasn't prepared for the massive void it created. They had never been apart.

The route Patrick chose would lead through the Cumberland Gap, an 800-foot-deep natural break in the Cumberland Mountains, located close to where Virginia, Tennessee, and Kentucky all come together. The heavily traveled road meandered through the Great Smoky Mountains, home to the Cherokee nation.

Early into the trek Patrick struck up a conversation with a half breed Shawnee named Path Strider LeBlanc. At first Strider was standoffish, but Patrick was hard not to like. Patrick's penchant for joking and playing pranks chipped away at Strider's introverted temperament thereby paving the way for a friendship of sorts. Though Strider was only a few years Patrick's senior, he seemed older. He had experienced hunger, exposure to the cold, and cruel neglect. Before long Strider was playing his own version of practical jokes on Patrick. From there on it was a contest of one-upmanship.

Though Strider's life had been full of disaster and loneliness, he was intelligent, talented, and ruggedly handsome. His survival as an adolescent was evidence enough to his resourcefulness. Odds would normally have been against an orphaned 14-year-old alone in the wilderness, but he was no ordinary boy. His parents had prepared him to fend for himself. In the event of food shortages orphaned half-breeds were often the first to be expelled from the clan. Fortunately, Strider's parents had foreseen the possibility of such a fate. Strider was grateful for the small cabin his parents had built on the banks of the Clinch River, but Strider rarely spent more than a few days per month at the cabin due to his restless spirit.

Patrick and Strider were well matched in wit and physical strength, but emotionally they were opposites. Strider was cynical and had a violent streak. He was a wounded spirit on the inside, one that kept his own council. He was both a white man and an Indian and was comfortable in either community.

Strider, for some unexplained reason, had developed an interest in human behavior. He routinely looked beneath a person's public persona. There was something appealing about Patrick, and Strider decided to delve into his character. Strider began instructing Patrick on how to find wild edible herbs and vegetables and how to stalk game. That Patrick had managed to survive in the wilderness as long as he did was remarkable. Strider recognized his ineptness immediately. He invited the big red head to hang around and learn to forage. Right away Strider and Patrick became friends. As for Patrick, he was in awe of Strider. Within a couple of days Strider realized that Patrick was a quick learner.

The excess food from the hunts they went on was divvied up between needy white families and the orphaned Shawnee children. Having Patrick around was unsettling to Strider. It took him a few days to pinpoint the reason. It seems that Patrick reminded him of his white father.

A while before Patrick had arrived on the scene, Strider had a chance encounter with a traveling preacher named John Raccoon Smith. Strider was invited to share the man's campfire and partake of the rabbit he had roasting on a spit. Strider saw an opportunity to probe the mind of the preacher man and settled in by the fire for the evening. After the meal of rabbit meat and a hard tact biscuit, the two men lounged by the campfire. Bro. Smith introduced himself as John and admitted that some called him Raccoon John because he lived near a place known for its large population of the ring-tailed raccoons. A friend gave him a hat made of a raccoon pelt and any place he went folks recognized him as Raccoon John Smith. He eventually accepted the moniker. A man that saw the humor of life, he enjoyed the recognition that came with standing behind pulpits wearing a cap made from a coon pelt, but it was his knowledge of the Holy Bible that brought him the respect of church goers and made him so successful in converting sinners to Christ.

Raccoon John responded to Strider's questions in a gentle and slightly amused manner. Strider began, "Just what do you see in your mind when you think of God? Can God see and hear us here now? How did Satan come to be?"

Bro. Smith said, "Hold on, please ask your questions one at a time. The discussion was just getting going by midnight. The preacher described the "one true God" as exceedingly frightful to the sinner but loving and kind to those that obeyed Him. According to the preacher God required "turning the other cheek" and "loving one's enemies." By the end of the long conversation, the preacher had covered the basics of the gospel of Christ. He spoke of the virgin birth of Jesus, the Lord's ministry, and sacrificial death on the cross, and His resurrection and ascension. When the preacher asked Strider if he would like to be baptized for the remission of his sins, his response gave the preacher a chill. Strider said, "It wouldn't take too much to convince me, but I'm not ready right now, I will mull it all over and maybe someday."

The Preacher sat up-right and removed his raccoon cap and said, "That is what King Agrippa told the Apostle Paul. It's in the 26th Chapter of Acts, verse 27-28: 'King Agrippa, believest thou the prophets? I know that thou believest.' And Agrippa said unto Paul, 'With but little persuasion thou wouldest fain make me a Christian.'"

"My young Strider, I will leave you with one last scripture found in the book of Hebrews 4:12-13 – 'For the word of God is living and active and sharper than any two-edged sword and piercing even to the dividing of soul and spirit, of both joints and marrow, quick to discern the thoughts and intents of the heart.'" At daybreak the two men waved farewell, but the preacher's words had taken root in Strider's memory.

Strider was a handsome fellow and enjoyed the company of the fairer sex but opted to keep the courtships casual. Patrick was inexperienced when it came to girls, so Strider set out to remedy that condition. He figured to initiate the fair-haired boy at a barn raising and square dance being held at Sweet Spring Holler just a mile or so from his log cabin.

The components of a top-notched shindig all came together. The young single ladies outnumbered the gents two to one, and the home cooking turned out to excel most community spreads, a rare treat for the two bachelors. The home-grown musicians featured a banjo, two guitars, a fiddle, and a homemade percussion instrument made up of a tambourine mounted on a mop handle along with a washboard. Once Patrick had eaten his fill and complimented the ladies on their cooking, he found a seat on a straw bale in the shadows and was looking forward to some people watching.

About once per hour while the band took a break the stage was open for anyone to engage the audience. A very old gentleman took the opportunity to tell s few jokes and warmed up the crowd for more impromptu displays of talent. A ten-year-old girl all dressed in a frilly frock recited the Lord's Prayer.

Patrick noticed Strider speaking to a young woman who then approached him in a coy manner, obviously hoping he would ask her to dance. She was nice looking, but a little too forward in her manner. Patrick decided to take her for a turn around the dance floor and enjoyed himself. A surprised Strider was standing back and watching Patrick's fancy foot work on the dance floor. Patrick's mother had taught him to waltz and fox trot at an early age, just part of educating a boy in merry Old Scotland. As he danced Patrick was concocting a challenge for Strider.

Patrick was normally shy around the opposite sex, but he was a trained performer. The dance provided the perfect setting to even the score with Strider, the self-proclaimed 'Ladies Man.' First off, the normally shy Patrick visualized himself as a ladies' man and assumed the posture of a confident, devil-may-care charmer. One by one he asked the ladies in attendance to dance, even the grey-haired granddams. He caught sight of Strider smiling and fanning himself. Strider recognized the changes in Patrick's demeanor and felt a tinge of suspicion. The red head had more surprises in store for Strider. He was just getting warmed up.

Patrick jumped into the square dancing, smiling and clapping to the lively music. All eyes were on Patrick, unsure what to expect from him next. Things got a little rowdy when the inebriated square dance caller got his *tang tungled up* as he shouted allemande star and promenade back to your partner.

The dance switched to waltzing, and after a full set of songs, Patrick approached the band. He asked if they could play the Kavkaz song, and only one of the guitar players knew the song. He started out solo, but the other members of the band soon joined in.

Patrick walked to the center of the dance floor and crossed his arms across his chest. He began dancing with varied cross stepping and stamping of his heels. After several variations he dropped to his haunches and began the signature Cossack stepping that featured springing up and down while extending one foot at a time. He encouraged everyone to clap their hands. Patrick was beaming with a most appealing smile, and several of the ladies were seen speaking to one another behind hands.

Patrick had full participation from the energized audience who were yelling 'hey' and clapping in time. The crowd got even more excited when Patrick did the squatting steps. He switched to a cross stepping Greek dance that included bending down and slapping the floor with his hand on the forward step. Patrick concluded his performance with a backward somersault and landed bowing to the audience. He stood and located Strider and beckoned for him to approach.

Patrick pantomimed that it was Strider's turn to entertain the gathering. For once Strider was caught off guard and shook his head in refusal. He quickly read the mood of the crowd and stepped to the center of the floor. He responded to the applause with a smile or at least as close to a smile as he could muster.

Strider's dancing experience was limited to the Shawnee version of hoop dancing and the common ceremonial dancing around a bonfire. Strider decided to accept the challenge by singing a song. From childhood folks had complimented his singing voice, so he decided to get past the awkward moment by singing a sad lament called *The Unfortunate Rake*. He spoke to the band members and determined that they were familiar with the old folk song. (The melody would one day be the tune of the song *The Streets of Laredo* in North America.)

"Folks, I'm not a dancer, but I like to sing, least to myself, out in the woods. I can't let him out do me so here is my reply to his challenge."

As I was a-walking down by St. James' Hospital,
I was a-walking down by there one day,
What should I spy but one of my comrades?
All wrapped up in flannel though warm was the day.

"Don't muffle your drums and play your fifes merrily,
Play a quick march as you carry me along,
And fire your bright muskets all over my coffin,
Saying: There goes an unfortunate lad to his home."

The audience was thrilled with his performance giving him a standing ovation. Before the applause could die down, Patrick hurried to congratulate Strider by slapping him on the back and commenting, "Great job! Wish I could sing like that." The hour was late, and folks were departing a few at a time. Strider decided to call it an evening, and Patrick agreed. Before leaving the dance floor they both bowed at the waist and thanked the locals for their hospitality, food, and music. "Good night to you all." The ladies responded by waving handkerchiefs and batting their eyelashes.

Patrick and Strider sang, laughed, and told and re-told the evening's events on the trek back to the little log cabin. Strider asked, "Did you eat any of the deviled eggs?

Patrick nodded and said, "Yup, I ate several, excellent! I was partial to the bread pudding. It reminded me of my mother's, God rest her soul. That roast beef with potatoes was seasoned just right, I had seconds."

Strider said, "Oh, the roast beef, umm. I had seconds too. Pat, old boy, where did you learn to do all that fancy dancing and flips and stuff? How come you never told me about your special talents?"

"My brother and I worked for a circus back home in Scotland. I don't perform anymore, but I do like to stay in practice. The circus owners took me and Rory under their wings and taught us dancing, acrobatics, and we got to perform with the trained circus animals. It was a lot of fun for us kids, and we got a good education in the bargain. We got to know circus entertainers from Russia, Greece, Spain, and well, all over. It is nice to have something to pull out of the hat at gatherings; once a showman always one."

Strider said, "Well, I think the folks enjoyed having us there and are likely to invite us back. As far as attracting the ladies you are ready to go that alone. Hew, I'm tired tonight. How about you? Look at those stars, beautiful—" Yawn. Responding yawn. They were both silent the rest of the way home.

Strider's reward for the wild game that fed the village orphans was access. He could walk among them without arousing suspicion. Strider liked to visit with relatives and friends, but preferred going it alone, at least until he crossed paths with Patrick. The two of them were comfortable living in the wilderness, and both treasured their freedom. They were constantly pulling practical jokes on each other and sometimes unsuspecting strangers. It kept the long days interesting. A day didn't pass without Strider marveling that Patrick had so far managed to hang on to his scalp and avoid starvation. Strider concluded that Patrick was a lucky cuss.

Strider was smarting from Patrick's latest prank. The lunatic redhead had ingeniously sabotaged Strider's tunic while he took his daily dip. While Strider completed his daily ritual of hygiene in the icy creek Patrick inserted a few baby Northern Water Snakes into a front pocket of Strider's garment. Patrick had been looking for a good prank. The telltale hole next to a rock led him to discover a den of sluggish hibernating serpents. The species was a type of harmless grass snake that was easily mistaken for the deadly copperhead. Patrick rubbed his hands together and thought *this is going to be a good one.*

Strider slipped his feet into the leggings and had them up to his waist before he noticed the movement in the pocket. His reaction to the squirming creatures was quite entertaining. He violently jumped from the leggings that had fallen around his ankles. He took a stick and carefully lifted it off the ground and into the small campfire before noticing Patrick's gleeful smirk. Strider had been one-upped for sure. Wearing only a loincloth made for a chilly trip home.

This last prank of Patrick's called for payback, big time. Not just any old prank would do. The plan came to him in a dream, but he wasn't too sure how it would play out. It would take some planning. The next day Strider killed a large rutting buck with a big rack. He removed the tarsal gland of the animal when Patrick wasn't looking and extracted the oil. He smeared the pungent gel upon a piece of rawhide and wrapped it in leaves and then several layers of hide to disguise the scent. While Patrick rested by a small campfire, Strider pretended to trip over his legs presenting him the perfect opportunity to rub some of the musk on Patrick's buckskins. Patrick sniffed and thought Strider needed to take a dip in the creek.

Strider said, "We need another deer, so let's stalk one on the way back to camp." The two of them began walking through the woods about fifty yards apart, hoping to flush out a bedded down buck. Patrick was shocked when a huge buck walked out of a gully and stood facing him.

Patrick yelled, "Strider, got a buck here, look at th—," suddenly the animal lowered his head and attacked what his olfactory sense identified as a competing male. It was fall, in the middle of the rut. When Patrick tried to evade the buck, he dropped his gun and was reduced to fending off the beast with his bare hands. Strider hurried toward the frantic cries coming from Patrick.

Totally off guard, the big red head failed to react in time to avoid the flailing hooves. He punched at the deer's snout, but landed a glancing blow to its neck. He tried to drop and run from under the rearing beast, but that tactic got him trampled by the hind feet. He grasped the large rack of antlers and twisted hard enough to throw the animal to the ground. This placed Patrick in an awkward position. He was lying on his back with the buck on top, struggling to gain the advantage while engaging in arm to antler wrestling. Patrick dared not turn loose of the antlers but ingeniously mounted an offensive attack by using his teeth to bite the deer's nose. The spectacle was even more entertaining than Strider had anticipated. Patrick being highly motivated to survive, proceeded to grind and rip at the vulnerable organ until the pain-maddened herbivore indicated a notion to flee.

Patrick released his grip, and the thankful buck made a frantic dash for freedom. When the blood soaked, adrenaline flooded Patrick who looked up, and there stood Strider convulsing with laughter. He was pointing to Patrick's waist, suggesting that he should have used his knife to dispatch the buck. Patrick's response was, "Hey, you saw me, it's not like I had an unoccupied hand. Why didn't you jump in and help me?"

Strider ignored Patrick's comment and said, "That was a nice buck, too bad you let him get away?" Patrick groaned and lay back on the ground to catch his breath.

Finally, Strider extended a hand and lifted his compadre to a standing position. He helped Patrick check his bodily parts and remarked, "Looks like you'll survive, but like me you need a new suit of buckskins."

Patrick growled, "Yes, no thanks to you," His face and chest were contused, abraded, and bleeding. His buckskin leggings and tunic were slashed and torn. The poor redhead's mouth, chin, and upper chest were crusty with the blood from the animal's nose, and Patrick's eyes revealed a terribly wounded ego.

"I was trying to decide if that high-pitched noise was coming from you or the buck. My ears are still ringing." Strider's behavior was out of character for such a mishap unless it was contrived. Suddenly it dawned on Patrick that he had been the butt of a joke. He stood glaring at the prankster and said, "Now I know what I smelled, deer musk, right?"

Strider nodded, and Patrick lifted Strider's right hand above his head and announced as though to an audience, "I proclaim you, Path Strider, the winner of the best practical joke ever hatched. I will not even try to top it." The two men walked back to their camp laughing and rating their long list of practical jokes for most original and inventive.

The camaraderie continued for a little while longer. No more than a week had passed when Strider invited Patrick to visit the Shawnee village of his deceased Mother. The celebrated clairvoyant known as Tecumseh would be speaking before the clan. Patrick had little interest in the chieftain but gladly accepted the invitation because he could eat as much as he wanted, and the pow-wow was an opportunity to kick up his heels Patrick style.

The much-revered Tecumseh was a dignified man known for his humility. His great love for the Shawnee People was beyond question. His familial affection extended to all the North American Tribes and even some individual white people. He was famous for his rhetorical argumentation and unparalleled eloquence. His audiences were held spell bound to the very end. The scheduled visit from Tecumseh created much excitement. Tecumseh's brother, Lowawluwaysica often acted as his spokesman, but on this occasion the clairvoyant would be speaking from his own mouth.

It was rare for the Clan to be visited by such a renowned person. The preparation exceeded normal pow wows. There was an overwhelming sense of anticipation as well as dread considering the inevitable bloodshed and upheaval the message was rumored to be organizing. Tecumseh stressed that the exact nature of the campaign must be kept from the whites.

Strider had heard that Tecumseh and an entourage had been visiting every Tribe that would accept his request to speak. He sent runners ahead with advance notice. He spoke out of compulsion as he was directed by visions from the great spirit. His urgent message became the mission of his life. That evening Tecumseh spoke, the amphitheater was filled to overflowing. Strider told Patrick to find a viewpoint high in a tree where he would be out of sight. The language barrier kept Patrick in the dark, but he enjoyed the spectacle of it all. According to witnesses Tecumseh's delivery went something like this.

Hear me, my fellow Shawnee, brothers and sisters, we of common blood and ancient tradition. Many seasons I have served as your prophet, and you know my powers. Still yet do I have your allegiance, shall I continue as your seeker of divine direction?

Tecumseh cupped his ears with his hands as he waited for their response. The roar of approval that traveled to the heavens exceeded his expectation. His face glowed with gratification as he delayed silencing the uproar.

In order to enlist the spirit world's support, we must observe certain laws and unify with the many other tribes into a massive war party! But first we must purify and purge ourselves of all wrong practices. We must exhibit only honor and kindness to each other; Feed the hungry and clothe the old people among us. As a people we must dress in the skins of animals, never using wool, or linen. Eat only wild game, and never cattle or sheep. By the lives we lead we must prove that our people were created superior to other peoples of the world.

I pledge to walk rightly so that you can follow me in a life of devotion. There is none superior to the Shawnee! So that you will know that Moneto speaks through me he will send signs. Your eyes will see, and your heart will be filled. Moneto has told only me the time of his signs, and now you will know. I will distribute a sacred slab and a bundle of red sticks to each tribal shaman with orders to burn a stick at each full moon. The sticks will count the time. The writing on the slab will instruct and prepare you for what is to come. When there is only one stick left, your seer will cut it into thirty pieces and burn a segment per day. The signs will happen when the last one is burned. The signs sent to us will confirm my message. Doubt will be no more. All Indian peoples will join together into a great and fearful army ready to march on the white Europeans. Their lives will be spared only if they leave our lands. I have spoken!

Immediately after Tecumseh's speech the feast began, to be followed by an all-night dance. Too late Strider learned that the speech was not intended for the ears of whites. He knew he must sneak Patrick out of the camp quickly while his scalp was still in place. Patrick didn't understand why Strider insisted that Patrick cover his head and shoulders with a blanket. But, with a good-natured shrug Patrick went along, figuring that Strider had his reasons.

Patrick was disappointed over missing the feast. The darkness of the night masked Strider's reaction to the speech. The half-breed was immediately spell-bound with the logic and wisdom of Tecumseh's eloquent plea. The majority of his male clan members were pledging to support Tecumseh's mission on that very evening.

Fully committing to Tecumseh's campaign to cleanse North America required Strider to sever all ties with white people. On the hike back to Strider's cabin Patrick noticed the change in Strider. When Patrick attempted to give Strider a pat on the back, his reaction was to coldly duck away. As soon as the two reached the cabin, Strider stood in front of Patrick and said, "Patrick, I have something to tell you. Something has changed, we can no longer be friends. You must leave here; you are no longer welcome. Go now!"

Patrick assumed he was joking and laughed it off. Strider crossed his arms, turned his back on him and entered the cabin.

Patrick shook his head and asked, "What happened at that village tonight? What did that old man say to turn you against me?"

Strider walked to his bed and lay down, facing the wall. Patrick followed him inside and began piling his belongings on the table. With a shrug Patrick acknowledged that the friendship was over. Shortly after sunup he was ready to strike out on the westward trail. More than a year would pass before Patrick understood what had occurred to change his relationship with Strider.

Chapter 8

GRIZZLY ATTACK

M other started by quoting Granny, "Patrick pressed on westward along the Cumberland Trail all alone and traveling light. For weapons he carried a fixed blade hunting knife and the old flintlock musket that had belonged to his father. But thanks to Strider, Patrick was better prepared to survive by living off the land."

Patrick tended to get a mite lonely and looked for the opportunity to share campsites with other travelers. He looked forward to the fireside conversations and benefited from the safety that numbers provide. Many of the migrant expeditions routinely used the evening campfire gathering as an opportunity to rosin up the bow and pluck the stringed instruments. On the evenings when they were not too exhausted, dancing would spring up. Another activity was yarn spinning. Patrick was always ready to join in. He became quite popular with the travelers. Patrick liked to stay in practice with the dancing and acrobatics, and he was always looking for boxing partners to spar with. The mostly hospitable travelers gave young Patrick advice and even let him dip into their soup pot.

A few weeks after parting company with Strider, Patrick came upon an inviting stream. Then he spied the pond, obviously dammed by a beaver family. The glassy surface of the pond was shaded with towering cottonwood trees. Beneath them clumps of shorter dense willow trees spilled over the water's edge. Trail weary, Patrick found the water irresistible and stopped to cool off in the pond. Patrick was aware that his shirt felt tighter across his shoulders, but his belt was cinched up two notches. The trek had transformed Patrick into a trail hardened frontiersman.

With gear safely stowed on a large bolder, a naked Patrick gingerly picked his way to the water, hopping from one river rock to the next. Out of his line of sight, Patrick heard a twig break. His head turned to peer in the direction of the sound. The relaxed moment quickly changed to one of horror. Only a few yards away a gigantic bear made eye contact with Patrick. The head was stretched forward and the ears laid back. The animal was obviously stalking him as prey.

Once the element of surprise was gone, the bear transitioned from stealth to intimidation and made a guttural growling noise. Patrick froze in place unsure what to do. Suddenly the bear reared on hind legs and belched forth a terrible roar. A moment later the massive creature charged straight for Patrick. The athletic redhead whispered a quick appeal for the Lord's intervention. No doubt the she-bear had chosen Patrick for her next meal, and she wouldn't even need to rip off his clothes before eating him.

Patrick's rampaging heart moved up into his throat. His adrenal glands secreted enough of the fight-or-flight hormone to fuel a trip to the moon. Impersonating Granny Delia, Cheatie said, "Patrick sprang into action. After looking around he made a running leap for the lowest branch of a large cedar tree and started climbin'. Patrick remembered readin' that grizzlies cain't climb trees. Unfortunately, this bear was not one of them, this one could climb anything she could get her claws sunk into. The she-bear was gaining on him as she pulled herself from limb to limb. The beast was using her long claws and teeth to pull her bulk up the tree. So much for what bears cain't do, depends on how hungry they are I reckon." Granny stammered in a frightened manner. "Just as the animal was pawing at Patrick's kicking feet, his limb snapped off."

"The falling limb struck the bear between the eyes and musta dazed her for a moment, causing the monster to fall to the ground. Happenstance appointed that poor scared Patrick land on top of the creature. The fall knocked the breath out of him, but catlike, he sprang away and bounded up the bank. He dashed behind the bolder where his gear was stowed. Quick as lighting the bear took out after Patrick.

Once again, the bear, as bears do, reared up on hindquarters and roared so loud it made the leaves on the trees quake." (Granny gave us her best bear growl, which startled the sleeping Stella Ruth. The baby's crying suspended the story telling for a good two minutes.)

"As the bear got closer, Patrick prepared for the battle of his life. With knife in hand, he sprang to the top of the bolder. Yelling at the top of his lungs, Patrick waved his shirt and flung it onto the bear's head. While the bear clawed at the clingy fabric, Patrick launched himself onto the hump of her back. This caused the bear to sling her head from side to side and start bucking. After a wild ride, she dislodged Patrick. As he lay on his back, the bear bit down on the left arm that protected his throat."

Too scared to feel pain, Patrick went to work with his adrenaline-fueled right arm, stabbing and slicing at the animal's throat. Luckily, his knife was sharp, and the blade was able to penetrate the thick fur and muscle just below the base of its skull.

Just when the beast was about to finish Patrick off, she jerked backward in a spasm and released her hold on Patrick's arm. The blood from Patrick's arm mingled with the blood spurting from the sow's jugular. Her awful stench was so foul it stung the lining of his lungs and made his eyes water. Patrick's ear drums were still vibrating from the animal's roar. The now lifeless bulk pinned him to the ground. Patrick moved his head to the side and saw an arrow sticking from the animal's upper back. Patrick was addled, and it took a second or two to get his wits about him. It took every ounce of strength he could muster to push the animal aside.

Granny with her most excited tone said, "Boy howdy, was Patrick ever surprised to be alive! Like folks say, his short life flashed before him as he prepared to face his maker." A fog of confusion made the struggle surreal and it was all he could do to stay conscious. After catching a few deep breaths, he looked around for the source of the arrow.

It seems the sounds of the commotion had attracted an audience. A group of women had been picking berries just upstream. Rushing to the source of the racket, they were riveted by Patrick's fight for survival. One of the girls, who would eventually play a big role in Patrick's life, had expertly fired an arrow and severed the animal's spinal cord. As soon as the bear died, the girls started whooping with laughter. When Patrick looked up to see the six buckskin-clad girls, about ten feet away, he started to stand, but faintness caused him to fall back upon the ground.

As the gawkers gathered around Patrick, he remembered he was naked and tried to cover his privates. Where Patrick came from nakedness was disgraceful. The Indian girls had no such concerns over nakedness. To them Patrick's modesty was a novelty. Patrick was mortified. As the laughter died down, one of the girls inspected Patrick's mangled left arm. Even in such dire straits Patrick noticed how beautiful she was. The most serious wound spurted blood with each beat of his heart. Two of the girls moved Patrick away from the dead bear and helped him to lean against a boulder. The most prominent of the girls shook out the shirt and used it to bind the worst of the wounds. She understood the importance of applying pressure to the wound to slow blood loss. Though he couldn't understand what she and the others were saying, it was obvious that they meant him no harm.

Granny whispered in a mysterious tone, "The congenial atmosphere didn't last long, cause, right away a group of braves stepped out of the forest, and there was nothing friendly in their attitude. The band of men sported long leather-bound braids and a single, large brown feather standing from the crown of their heads. The bucks were naked, wearing only loincloths and moccasins. Upon their chest they each had a large scar in the shape of the symbol of a lightning bolt and their limbs were covered with scars. Their swarthy, hairless skin gleamed with a heavy coat of oil. Two of the meanest looking fellers took Patrick by the arms causing enough pain to cause him to black out very briefly as they drug him to the stream. He was told to wash in the pool of water. Patrick complied by fully immersing in the stream. It felt good to wash off the dirt caked blood. The cold-water shocked Patrick back from faintness and in his moment of clarity it occurred to him that he was a prisoner. After a brief soak, a brave helped him out of the water."

When Patrick's gaze returned to the dead bear, he noticed that the women were busy dressing out the meat. Later he would learn that the pelt with its attached head and claws was being made into a rug as a memento of his heroic battle. The bear pelt became one of Patrick's most prized possessions and would be displayed on his wall.

Granny continued, "While the bear was being butchered, Patrick motioned that he needed help pulling up his trousers. Because of their indifference to his pain, Patrick decided to forget asking these fellars for help. Patrick re-wrapped his mangled arm with his blood-stained shirt himself. Waves of faintness swept over him and he was forced to rely on the braves to get back to where his gear was stowed."

After a brief pause the same two braves grabbed Patrick by the arms, causing him to cry out in pain. They mocked Patrick's outcry and had a good laugh at his expense. Ignoring his discomfort, the three of them struck out through a meadow on a path that Patrick reckoned to be southeast. This is when Patrick remembered an article, he'd read warning that some of the wilderness tribes were known to be cannibals. That must be why they want me washed. Patrick took note of how thin and underfed the men looked.

"Panic swept over Patrick, and he decided to fake a fainting spell, in hopes they would leave him alone long enough for him to sneak away and hide. But, no-sir-ee, that only got him hog-tied and transported on a makeshift stretcher. After what seemed like an eternity of discomfort bouncing upon the stretcher, Patrick heard sounds, human voices, barking dogs, crying babies, and then through smoky air, he saw the destination, a bustling village."

"Patrick was carried into the town along a route lined with gawkers who stared at him with curiosity or was it hunger? Patrick was untied and laid upon a pallet inside a dome shaped mud hut. When he raised up on one elbow enough to look around, he saw that a brave was posted at the door."

"Within minutes of Patrick's arrival an aged medicine woman, a bit haggard and crippled, came to consider treating Patrick's wounds. She consulted with the spirits by sprinkling what smelled like tobacco on the gray coals of the fire-pit located beneath a roof vent. As the woman waited to see if the tobacco ignited her body froze in the posture of a bat in flight. A small puff of smoke was followed by a tiny tongue of orange flame. Her body remained motionless, but her eyes following the drifting smoke. Patrick, at this point could not have been more alert. He reckoned, correctly so, that the wafting smoke was the go-ahead sign. The Medicine Woman made eye contact with Patrick for a brief moment, gave a quick nod of her head, and then began to examine his wounds. She placed a leather satchel beside his pallet and removed several bundles."

"Patrick was so tense he was perspiring and suffering from muscle spasms. The old woman saw how frightened he was and rose from her crouch and began to rhythmically shuffle her feet and chant in a deep contralto. She accompanied her dance by shaking an embellished gourd. She appeared to be chasing spirits by fanning them from the hut with a bird's wing fan. Then she turned toward Patrick and gave him a nod and resumed treating his injuries. First, she sprinkled an orange powder directly into the deepest lacerations and punctures. The orange color of the substance changed to brown when it came in contact with blood. She opened a bag of singed prickly pear pads that had been split and dried. They were softened until pliable in warm water and placed over the most serious wounds. She bound them in place with strips of rawhide.

Finally, she helped Patrick rise to a sitting position. She signed for him to calm down. She immobilized his injured arm by placing it in a sling. She applied a sticky salve to his other cuts and bruises.

Next, she held a clay bowl filled with a strong-smelling liquid to Patrick's mouth. The warm tea quickly sedated Patrick, and he relaxed to the point of slumping to his pallet.

He was hardly aware of the dance the woman performed before leaving the hut. She stamped her feet in a slow rhythm while swooping around the fire with arms outstretched, repeating the chant with her unique vibrato that sounded masculine in range. A gourd rattle set the tempo for her dance. Patrick was sound asleep before her dance ended. Sometime later he learned the old woman's name was Dancing Spirit."

"When Patrick awoke, he decided it was a good time to pray. Lordy, did he ever pray! He wished he had been paying more attention when his mother held the nightly scripture readings. *Yea though I walk through the valley of the shadow of death, I will fear no evil.* Yes, a good verse and then he recalled one with a happy ending, "So Daniel was taken up out of the lion's den, and no manner of hurt was found upon him, because he had trusted in his God." Yes, this was another good verse to remember. Patrick's faith comforted him. Patrick would eventually learn that this particular group of Indians was not cannibalistic in the strictest sense, but they did believe that one could capture strong medicine from consuming a portion of the liver and heart of one's adversary, be it animal or human.

According to custom the village began preparations for a celebration in honor of their red-haired guest. This group of Indians had broken away from the larger Cherokee tribe long ago. The dispute had partly healed but kept the two groups separate, but tolerant of each other. The dissenters were classified as Tsalagii and called themselves "The Thunder Clan." With time the religious beliefs and cultural practices of the Thunder Clan evolved, and by the start of the nineteenth century the differences were numerous though the language had hardly changed.

Patrick Larson's rescue from the bear attack by an armed woman of the Thunder Clan was a stroke of good fortune. To "The People" Patrick's auburn hair and freckles were a mark of distinction bestowed by the gods and therefore, entitled him to special regard and hospitality compared to most white men.

The Thunder Clan as a collective group had special characteristics. They were fun loving, altruistic, deliberative, but carefully planned ahead for unforeseen crises. They promoted a sense of community by holding frequent celebrations like feasts and all-night dances. Patrick's rescue provided just such an occasion. Immediately the women began scurrying about organizing the food preparation. The adolescent boys readied the fire pits located in the ceremonial amphitheater for the dance that would follow. The celebration would honor the white man's bravery. An integral part of every ceremony held by the Thunder People included offering prayers to their version of deity including gods named Kanati and his wife Selu. At the appointed time the convocation would pay a rousing tribute to the slaughtered she-bear."

Granny's theatrical style for spinning her yarns added to the entertainment value. She continued, "After, who knows how long, Patrick awoke from the gosh-awfulest dream. In his dream, he was being cooked whole, in a clay cauldron. It took a while for him to realize that it was only a dream conjured up by a magazine cartoon, he had seen years before. The heat he felt was not from being cooked but was due to a raging fever. Patrick, struggling to focus his thoughts, looked up from the pallet and thought he caught a fleeting glimpse of the beautiful young woman that had treated his wounds."

Much later, when he could understand the language, Patrick would be told the story of "The Principal People" (or Tsalagii, the name the Thunder People called themselves), and their relationship to the bear family. The Tsalagii believed that long ago some of their brothers had failed to honor tradition, and consequently, long hair began to grow on their bodies. To escape the shame, these ancient ones moved deep into the forest and eventually started to move about on all fours. According to legend, these unfaithful ones became the creatures called

Yo-Nv, or bear. They roamed the countryside and were required by the Spirits to provide meat and fur to their brothers, the Tsalagii. Failing to properly honor the slain beast would show disrespect and carry the possibility of suffering a like fate.

That evening the "Thunder Clan" feasted on roasted bear, venison, bean bread, and a large variety of squash, nuts, and fruits. The same braves that had carried Patrick to the village appeared and helped him onto a pole stretcher and moved him to a skin-covered bed padded with evergreen branches. A log was placed behind his back, and the men helped him to a sitting position. Spirit-Woman handed Patrick a gourd filled with a strong drink. It had been thickened and smelled of menthol. After the first sip Patrick's tongue was instantly numbed, and his entire mouth and throat tingled. He placed the container on the ground and shook his head. The Medicine Woman re-appeared and put the drink back into his hand. He shrugged at the woman and held back his head and tossed the drink in one gulp. Almost immediately, Patrick felt relief from the pain in his arm. Within the space of two minutes an inebriated Patrick yelled much too loudly, slurring his words, "thank jou, thank you slowo much!" and gave the healer a smile that was so silly looking the medicine woman cracked a slight smile and acknowledged his appreciation with a nod of her head.

Patrick as the honoree, with his ring side vantage point was first to be served a bark platter with a generous amount of unfamiliar looking but delicious smelling food. There was a whole roasted bird the size of a dove, a rack of extra-large ribs covered in a brown sticky sauce, and what looked to be chunks of steamed squash, roasted corn on the cobb, and a mussel shell filled with berries and honey. On the perimeter of the plate were several round balls of what looked like boiled cornmeal. Patrick would later learn that the bread was Tsu-Ya-Ga, or bean bread, a Tsalagii staple. Patrick started to eat but was warned to wait until all were served. He thought, "*These uncivilized natives have better manners that we white people.*" Once the eating began, Patrick eagerly consumed the food, and when he was offered more bean bread, he accepted.

Following the meal, the dance began with a slow, rhythmic drumming. Despite his medication-altered mind, Patrick watched the event unfold with great interest. The largest drum was constructed from a section of tree trunk. It was sealed to hold water and was covered with a tightly stretched animal skin. The drummers stood in a circle and with great showmanship, raised their arms above their heads with each strike. They held wooden clubs in each hand and created intricate flourishes of percussion. A second instrument was a thin vertical slab of Bois d'Arc wood inlaid with brightly colored stones designed to be struck with a variety of clubs each of which produced its own unique sound. This instrument was the invention of the Thunder People. It was capable of closely mimicking distant thunder. Another instrument used for the dance was borrowed from the Cherokee. It was constructed from hollow turtle shells filled with pebbles and was usually strapped to the dancer's ankles.

Patrick was invited to participate in the dance, but as soon as he stood, his knees almost buckled. Patrick was forced to decline the invitation. The same young girl that had been so attentive handed him a gourd of cool water. He quickly drank the water and returned the vessel indicating that he desired more. The girl nodded and reappeared with a larger container of water. Then she quietly sat at Patrick's feet, facing away from him.

Patrick's pallet was within six feet of the dance arena. As the ceremony progressed, the drumming grew in intensity, and the dancers appeared to be under a hypnotic spell. Patrick suspected that the dancers were having some of the same pain medicine he had been administered by the Healer. The athleticism exhibited by the male dancers was impressive but as a gymnast he felt confident that he could hold his own with them. The Thunder Clan's leaping and strange gyrations were stored in Patrick's memory for future reference.

After a half hour, the Medicine Woman appeared with more of the fermented drink. This time Patrick needed no coaxing. He shook his head and made a guttural noise and said, "This is good stuff!" Patrick felt very little pain from his badly injured arm. The events of the evening would be indelibly imprinted on his memory. It occurred to Patrick while in his chemically induced state of heightened awareness that he was living his dream. It was exactly the kind of adventure he had dreamt of in his former life.

Granny drawled, "Things could have been a lot worse for ole Patrick, at least he wuddn't bein' parboiled." Sometime before daylight, Patrick was carried back to the hut where he had spent the previous afternoon. The drumming and dancing had gone on all night, and as dawn approached, many of the dancers slept where they fell in total exhaustion.

As Patrick healed from his wounds, the villagers made sure he felt welcome with one exception. The head Shaman's attitude toward Patrick was outwardly hostile. Most of the time the people of the village ignored the senile relic of a man. He had grown out of favor because of his extremism. Patrick decided to ignore the old man too, a decision he would later regret. The title Witch Doctor seemed to fit the old man better than shaman or medicine man. He was shriveled, snaggle-toothed, and potbellied. His buckskin garments were faded, terribly worn, and stiff with layers of filth. His head dress was a wooly Bison skull with the horns still attached. Underneath his tunic, the old man wore leggings supported by cords connected to the band that held his loincloth in place. It was common for the shaman to go about his daily routine with a coiled snake about his neck. The serpent's scaly skin was shiny black. The head of the serpent was constantly moving, testing the air with a darting, forked tongue. When Patrick inadvertently passed near the old shaman his gaseous odor was enough to trigger his gag reflex.

Patrick found himself analyzing the attire and actions of the old man. Around his neck hung a necklace strung with a variety of animal teeth and claws. When Patrick's eyes dropped to below the old man's waist, attached to his binding hung what looked like a light brown human scalp. The decrepit old man's slow-motion movements reminded Patrick of a giant tarantula. Patrick decided to nickname him "Old-Spider." The hyper-vigilant Old-Spider saw Patrick inspecting the scalp and derived considerable gratification from Patrick's shocked expression. In the weeks that followed, "Old-Spider" seemed to be shadowing the movements of the red-headed stranger.

An incident occurred a few days after Patrick's arrival that almost sent him on down the trail. He awoke from a sound sleep in a state of fear, thinking he was not alone in his small hut. He detected a putrid stench. It took a moment for him to recall where and when he had encountered it before.

The ancient Healer awoke Patrick when she held a cup of tea to his mouth. He was quickly sedated and began drifting into a dream state. Patrick whispered, "Who's there?" No response. Again, he asked, "Speak up!" Patrick rose from his bed and lit an oil lantern with a coal from the fireplace. He heard footsteps outside his hut, and he knew the old man had been there in his hut. The odorous fumes dissipated after a few minutes, but it took more than an hour for Patrick to calm himself. When he returned to his blankets, he left the lamp burning? After daybreak Patrick almost stepped on a pyramid of carefully arranged bones strategically place in his entryway. Then he realized the reason for the old man's visit. The Thunder Clan was a superstitious people, and the old man was obviously practicing some sort of magic. Had Old-Spider placed a hex or curse of some kind upon him? He took comfort in his Christian faith that rejected all such notions of the occult. When Patrick exited the hut, he caught a glimpse of Old-Spider about a hundred feet away sitting cross legged partly hidden by a bush. Patrick made sure he was watching and angrily gathered up the pile of omens and tossed them into the surrounding forest in plain sight of Old-Spider. He knew there were no gods, but the one true God and superstition belonged to the devil and his followers.

Wathena was the name of the girl that had saved Patrick's life. She stopped at nothing to make Patrick's visit pleasant. Wathena was quick to anticipate Patrick's every need. He concluded that she must be the acting welcome committee.

Even before Patrick's wounds healed, Wathena began teaching him her language. Patrick observed Wathena's independent nature; she rarely joined the other girls her age. Eventually Patrick learned that Wathena was a "Ye Ho-Nawa" or Warrior Woman chosen by the spirits.

The designation of Ye Ho-Nawa placed Wathena in a special class with special privileges. She was expected to learn to function as a clan woman and a warrior both. Her female relatives were responsible for teaching her the core skills of Clan women while her uncle Falls-From-Heaven would oversee her proficiency training in hand-to-hand combat, tracking, stalking, and wilderness survival. As part of her horsemanship training, Wathena was awarded a beautiful white on black dapple mare to train. Her Ye Ho-Nawa training was mostly complete by the time Patrick came upon the scene.

Wathena's history was both tragic and triumphant. She was orphaned as a six-week-old infant when both parents died of smallpox. Her unlikely survival added to her mystique. Perhaps there was intervention from the spirits or merely the protection that newly borne infants receive from their mother's colostrum.

Chapter 9

THE PLACE
OF BLUE SMOKE

Wathena had her parent's intelligence and looks. At the time of his death, her father, Leaning Oak, served as the Supreme War Chief of the Thunder Clan. The clan's period of mourning was prolonged due to the dire loss of the renowned battlefield tactician. Time was needed to conjure up the strong medicine that could choose a successor. The clan elders under the guidance of Stands-Alone hand-picked Leaning Oak's younger brother, Falls-From-Heaven to succeeded him as War Chief. Falls-From-Heaven adopted the orphaned infant Wathena.

Wathena's mother, Earth Woman, had been a distinguished medicine woman. Her powers were legendary. Word about her knowledge of medicinal plants had spread throughout North America. Even more remarkable was her psychic power. During tumultuous times Earth Woman was said to communicate with the primordial spirit world. She credited a great deal of her healing power to the indwelling of supernatural deities. Telling and re-telling the stories of those she had healed was a favorite pastime around village fires throughout the Shaconage (the Smoky Mountain range called 'place of blue smoke') region. Not only was Earth Woman a gifted healer, but she had been loved for her deeply held compassion for all living creatures.

Shortly after the birth of Earth Woman's daughter, a deadly epidemic had spread to the Thunder Clan. A clan hunting party happened upon a feverish French Trapper. It is likely the trapper had traded with the tribe in the past and was seeking to make contact. True to their benevolent nature the hunters carried the sick man back to Earth Woman for treatment. Earth Woman held nothing back in her effort to save the man. In the case of the trapper, her powers failed, and he died within a day.

The Smallpox organism was even more of a threat to the American Indian than it was to Europeans. The whites had the advantage of hundreds of years of acquired herd immunity. After a few days, Earth Woman fell ill with a throbbing headache and high temperature. The early symptoms were quickly followed by painful pustular eruptions that covered her body. She was the first to die, and by the time the contagion had run its course almost half of the clan had died. It took years for the Thunder People to recover from the tragedy.

Earth Woman's only child was a beautiful healthy girl and was adopted by her uncle, Falls-From-Heaven and his wives. The wives were all barren, and Wathena remained his only off-spring, appointed by the gods to fill a great void and perpetuate the bloodline.

Falls-From-Heaven recognized Wathena's precocious traits at an early age. This was a child abundantly endowed with inquisitiveness and brilliance. Despite holding great promise her precociousness often clashed with tribal traditions and took liberties with cultural taboos. There was a downside to permitting her to be such a free spirit. Historically the Thunder Clan encouraged the barest of discipline and allowed children to grow up without stifling their creativity and curiosity, especially in Wathena's case.

A prime example occurred when "Ye Ho-Nawa" was about ten years of age. Wathena was high in the branches of a tree when her limb broke. The mud hut just below cushioned her fall but caused the dome top to implode. Housed inside was a trio of Creek men being held for ransom. The captives were bound hand and foot, but hopped away intent upon escape. The assigned guard had stepped away and did not notice the child playing in the treetop. A council meeting currently in progress near the scene of the accident heard the crash and yelling. The braves poured from of the hut with weapons in hand. It was a chaotic scene for the few minutes it took to subdue the hobbled prisoners.

Wathena was scratched and bleeding, but not seriously hurt. Once she regained her wits the elders surrounded her with the prisoners in tow. Their scowling expressions revealed their irritation for the foolish child's carelessness. Wathena was determined to redeem herself before her uncle. But what could she do to smooth over the incident? Quickly she lowered her gaze and said, "Please forgive my carelessness and the damage I caused. I will help with rebuilding the hut." Her quirky ingenuity took over, and she thought of a strategy that employed confusion.

Wathena raised both hands above her head and began an extemporaneous chant while stomping out a bizarre dance step. She circled the elders and captives where they stood frozen in place. The chant morphed into a plaintive song of warbling. Wathena's behavior was so unexpected the elders were bewildered, with each of them waiting for someone to take control of the situation. Even the most senior council members were totally flabbergasted. By default, Wathena had taken control. Her next move was extremely presumptuous for a child but ingenious.

The ten-year-old asked a warrior to help her bind each captive to a separate tree, and he did so without questioning. To the elders she said, "Now we clear the crushed dome." She hefted a large section of the roof to her head and carried it to the edge of the grounds. She energetically returned for another load of debris. Suddenly she stopped and looked at her audience and said, "I need help. Here, you stack the pole rafters ready for using in the new hut. Wathena pointed to a young man and said, "You, take these to the wood pile." A dumbfounded crowd had gathered and was looking at Wathena's uncle Falls-From-Heaven to see how he was reacting to the child's authoritarian behavior. Surprisingly Falls-From-Heaven had his chest out and was flashing an adoring smile at his protégé. It was obvious he was delighted with her initiative and budding leadership qualities. He gave her a pat on the head and said, "That's my girl!"

Just as Wathena was about to suggest that Falls-From-Heaven carry the other end of a heavy timber one of her aunts grabbed her by the hand and led her to the family hut. Wathena's cuts were cleaned and doctored; the aunt handed her a moccasin beading project, but she said no, not now. Then she was handed a bowl of dried berries and nuts and a cup of water. Wathena pushed them away and shook her head. She was pouting. As soon as the woman left the hut, Wathena fled into the woods where she spent the afternoon among the treetops, practicing her bird calls.

Other than the wounds she suffered in the fall, there was no evidence that anything unusual had happened. The People's permissiveness had covered over the incident. Due to her special status Wathena's future antics were part of clan politics.

One rainy autumn afternoon, Patrick was frustrated by his inability to reproduce a certain utterance, and Wathena attempted to assist him by demonstrating the correct position of his tongue. The session disintegrated into a playful scuffle but ended in a long passionate kiss. Patrick felt a rush of emotion that attacked his religious conviction. The state of *Being in love* had always been described as something that happens when a boy and girl like each other. That sounded so understated to Patrick. Full of desire, he held Wathena at arm's length while looking into the depths of her eyes and whispered "I love you! I really love you; I am crazy in love with you!"

The scenic beauty of the Thunder Clan's territorial grounds captivated Patrick. He was convinced he had found his utopia. The territory of the Tsalagii was called Shaconage, which meant Place of Blue Smoke; white folks called the area the Great Smoky Mountains. Patrick had settled in with the Thunder People for two main reasons. The second reason was the Eden-like locale of the Tsalagii homeland. Of course, Wathena was the over-riding motivation. Patrick couldn't imagine living without having her beside him.

Cultural differences were many but not necessarily grievous. He learned to practice willpower from eating only twice per day. The common diet though different, was nutritious and fueled his stamina while sharpening his wit. Unlike the majority of Caucasian men, the Tsalagii bathed daily, year around. Patrick was one that appreciated cleanliness more than most having grown up with a steadfastly fastidious mother. There were several of the Clan's attributes that white people could do well to copy, cleanliness being one.

From the time he could comprehend what was being said, Patrick found the stories about the little people called Nunnehi humorous and equated them with fairy tales. The story about the transformation of some of the ancestors into bear people was also entertaining. To Patrick the stories were mere folklore, and he was amazed that the Thunder People appeared to believe them.

Old-Spider's constant surveillance was Patrick's fly in the pudding. Chance encounters with the beady-eyed curmudgeon were awkward for Patrick. The old man would display open hostility toward Patrick by breaking into what was intended to be a dance accompanied by a chant and gourd rattling. Patrick had known some crotchety old men in Britain and a few on this side of the Atlantic but none as disagreeable as the old chanter.

From the day of Patrick's rescue Wathena sensed that he would become her soulmate. The physical attraction she felt for him was problematic. A Beaver Clan family had spoken to Falls-From-Heaven about a union between their warrior son called Crow and Wathena. An agreement was sealed, and the pipe was passed. Area wide pow-wows provided Crow and Wathena the opportunity to become acquainted. Wathena was immediately repulsed by Crow's personality. She was waiting for the right time to tell her uncle that she wished to reject Crow. It would be a messy business. But then Patrick showed up and really complicated the matter.

In order to be a worthy mate for Wathena, Patrick was required to train as a warrior. Patrick did not totally understand that he was being adopted and would be expected to conform to the lifestyle and customs of the Thunder Clan. What mattered to him was his relationship to Wathena. The spell Wathena had cast over Patrick transformed him into human modeling clay ready for the potter.

By the time Patrick's arm was healed, he and Wathena were practically inseparable. Their strides at learning each other's language was moving along quickly. The shady glades and shadowy stream banks became a perfect incubator for their blossoming romance. As soon as his fluency allowed the question, Patrick asked about the Old-Spider. Wathena looked around and found a soft grassy spot by the stream they were following and pulled Patrick down beside her. In a serious tone she painted an elaborate word picture of the aging shaman. Wathena began by saying, "His name is Stands-Alone." Her detailed narrative stretched on past sundown. Woven into her reflection was a matter-of-fact explanation of the old man's connection to the supernatural world. She went into detail about Stands-Alone's mystical powers.

According to Wathena, Stands-Alone justifiably feared the recurrence of moral corruption and dangerous communicable disease due to contact with White Men. Wathena said, "Patrick, one of those white-man diseases is what killed my parents. It was a terrible disease that covered their bodies in pus filled sores." Patrick was able to comprehend most of what Wathena said about "Stands-Alone". But what Wathena had just told him about the death of her parents really struck a chord because of the similarity to Patrick's parents' demise. Patrick struggled to choose the correct Tsalagii words as he spoke of the tragedy they held in common. After the lesson on Stands-Alone's background, Patrick vowed to esteem the revered tribal elder.

Once Patrick's wounds healed, he was moved from Dancing Spirit's convalescing hut and relocated to a long building that served as a dormitory for housing the young men in training. The training began the following day, and it was surprisingly rigorous. He would be required to learn the ways of the Tsalagii along with other young men. Patrick was more than willing to pursue the training being offered.

With the passing of each day Patrick acquired the attitudes, disciplines, and skill set of a young Tsalagii man. Would he be able to meet the high threshold and successfully compete with his dark-skinned cohorts? Due to Patrick's age and larger size, he had a slight advantage.

Patrick had become a toughened version of his former self. As autumn changed into winter, the daily trips to the now icy stream became part of his daily routine. He accepted exposure to cold weather, hunger, and fatigue as part of the Tsalagii experience. His innate tenacity and romantic attraction for Wathena made the discomfort worth it.

Wathena appeared one late winter afternoon and interrupted Patrick's stalking lesson. She took him to a brush arbor where the village elders, male and female, were seated in an open sided circle around a small fire. Wathena walked to the open space of the circle and motioned for Patrick to sit beside her upon the ground, thus completing the circle. The process of endlessly passing the ceremonial pipe forced Patrick to control his impatience. Finally, Wathena was asked to speak. She arose from her seated position and respectfully greeted each council member before revealing the nature of her request. "I have come here today for the purpose of nominating my friend Patrick for adoption into the Thunder Clan. I watched how he battled the great she bear with great courage. Our clan will benefit from his endowment of skill and diversity of attributes." She took Patrick's hand

and had him rise to stand beside her. The group responded with nods and soft exclamations, "aye, aye."

In order to be adopted into the Thunder Clan, Patrick would compete for the honor with other young men. It all depended on becoming proficient in three areas, hunting, warfare, and a game know as ball. The French Trappers called the game La Crosse. Patrick had a few advantages over the other trainees. He was larger in stature and a couple of years older. Patrick's ultimate advantage was his superior eye-hand coordination, balance, and physical agility.

A quick glance in the direction of Stands-Alone revealed that the old man wished to defer to the other elders. Patrick did not yet appreciate the great honor that was being bestowed upon him. The fact that Wathena was openly promoting Patrick's adoption would go in his favor, especially since Stands-Alone would not be voting.

Wathena was keeping a secret from Patrick, and it was causing her some sleepless nights. She had postponed telling him about her betrothal to a young man named Crow, arranged a few years earlier by Falls-From-Heaven. Unbeknownst to Wathena, Crow was a member the Beaver Clan La Crosse team. The previous year Wathena, out of curiosity, had attended a dance at the Beaver Clan village all for the purpose of scoping out her future mate. With her identity disguised, she was able to observe Crow during the visit. To Wathena's disappointment, she found Crow to be overtly flirtatious with all the young women. She was present when he provoked a fight over some trivial matter and when reprimanded by the Tribal Elders, reacted with hot-headed contempt. Wathena went back to her village determined to reject the betrothal. Crow's obnoxious character was detestable, and under no circumstance would she marry such an overbearing brute despite any political discord.

When Patrick's training period came to an end, he was confident that he had met the skills standards. The big question was whether Stands-Alone would try to influence the final vote. The long list of rules in place during the training period were merely minor obstacles along the way to claiming Wathena as his true love. Avoiding the forbidden foods and keeping his distance from all females, fighting off hunger, and suffering through the many physical challenges would be easy if he kept his eye on the target, the stunning Wathena.

The training began in earnest immediately. From the start he managed to meet or exceed the challenges. Patrick's natural competitive spirit served him well during the weapons training period. Partly, thanks to Strider's lessons, Patrick passed the survival training and weapons proficiency without a hitch. His mastery of the tomahawk, bow, spear, and blowgun caused the elders and his peers to take note.

By this point in Patrick's training, he was growing over-confident. The red head had forgotten his mother's admonition taken from Proverbs 16:18, "Pride goeth before destruction and a haughty spirit before a fall... God resisteth the proud, but giveth grace unto the humble." He was in danger of becoming overconfident.

Patrick kept overhearing the other young men whispering about the scratching rite, a test of pain tolerance. Ignorance of the future can be a blessing.

"What is this scratching?" Patrick asked his cabin mates. "Why are you being so mysterious?" By their reaction to his question, he could tell it was a set-up of some kind. He rightly guessed that they were worried about competing with him. Their scheme was to frighten Patrick into withdrawing from the ball game thus derailing his apprenticeship.

When the training period ended, the elders announced plans for the naming of the successful candidates. An all-night dance would emphasize the importance of the occasion. With only three days to prepare for the feast and dance, the village was bustling with activity. The women coordinated menu items and assigned cooking tasks. The men took to the forests with bows and spears searching out the forest's gifts of food.

Finally Stands-Alone was ready to announce the successful novice warriors by their childhood names and then speak the new name. A rumor had been circulating that all seven had met the requirements. Speculation about what their new names might be was the topic of conversation. Names carried great significance and could affect one's relationship with the spirit world. The naming council had met earlier in a remote place and spent the preparation period consulting with the tribal historians and calling upon the spirits for guidance.

The evening before the scratching rite the boys were all bedded down in the darkened dormitory when they began describing the pain involved. Their description was graphic to the point of being ghoulish. Patrick sensed their motive and pretended to be frightened.

The day of the induction ceremony the entire village gathered in the ceremonial arena. The newest warriors formed a line before Stands-

Alone. True to tradition the Shaman hand signed each new name and then pronounced it clearly and loud enough to be heard throughout the arena. Patrick was the last to receive his name. Stands-Alone made rare eye contact with Patrick and after a pause cleared his throat. He placed his right hand upon Patrick's head and with his raspy voice shouted Yo-Nv-Ayastigi (Bear Wrestler).

Another tradition was for each new warrior to receive a new set of clothing from his family, to be worn for special occasions. Patrick was prepared to skip that part of the ceremony, but Wathena stepped forward and handed a stack of folded garments to Patrick. Patrick's mouth dropped open when he saw the exquisite artwork. The tan colored doeskin tunic and leggings were edged with long fringe. An upright grizzly bear was painted on the front of the tunic and embellished using a special beading technique that gave the image the illusion of three dimensions. The moccasins were decorated with the same beading. Patrick was astonished at the tedious detail and intricate design of the beading. The buttery soft garments were literally works of art. Patrick would treasure them. The sparkle in Wathena's eyes told him what his gratitude meant to her. Now he knew what had been occupying much of her time while he was in training.

The wildness of the dance seemed to cast a spell over Patrick, and he behaved with primordial abandon. He mimicked his attraction for the beautiful Wathena by tracing her figure with his hands and then placing both hands over his pulsing heart.

The induction ceremony for new warriors had fallen on a full moon. The trappings of the dance included turtle shells anklets, wooden flutes, and handheld disk drums. The sound of the dance carried for miles. In attendance were relatives and friends from surrounding villages.

The time for scratching came, and Patrick was called forward first. He stood with outthrust chest. Patrick wondered if Stands-Alone had gone through scratching. Patrick made a mental note to ask Wathena about the matter. The instrument Stands-Alone used was a comb with seven sharpened turkey quills the length of a tack, designed to slice into the flesh.

Both upper arms were punctured at the shoulder, and the comb was dragged to the elbow four times leaving 28 parallel cuts in the skin. The same was done to the upper legs. Lastly the old man took a flake of flint and carved the shape of a lightning bolt centered over the sternum. Patrick managed to avoid grimacing or flinching during the mutilation, expending considerable self-discipline.

The day of the scratching rite was a memorable day. Not one of the inductees showed cowardice. Once Stands-Alone finished mutilating the group, they were allowed to cool their pain by diving into the river. The water of the slow flowing stream took on a pinkish tint from the blood. The candidate's faces reflected relief to have the scratching rite behind them.

Late into the night, Patrick left the dancing to relieve himself and drink from a gourd. Wathena, ever conscious of his whereabouts, followed him into the darkness. The two of them embraced and stood staring at the unusually bright full moon. Patrick was dressed only in a loincloth, and Wathena gently ran her hand over the swollen, puss filled scabs that covered his chest, upper arms and legs. Heat radiated from the infected wounds. Wathena admired the badge of bravery the cuts represented and then whispered for Patrick to sit on the grass. "Stay here, I will bring medicine."

In less than five minutes, Wathena returned with a mussel shell of thick salve. The concoction smelled of camphor and menthol. As soon as medicine was applied, the pain subsided. Being alone with Wathena was so charged with desire for Patrick, he struggled mightily with temptation. Patrick wanted to wait to consummate their love, following a wedding ceremony. As a youngster he had promised to wait for marriage before his mother and God. He nuzzled Wathena's ear as he whispered how much better his wounds felt. Speaking in a hushed tone she responded with, "I will need to repeat the treatment once per day for a week. You will have nice, prominent scars that will forever speak of your bravery." They were both trembling with desire when they broke their embrace and returned to their own blankets.

The day after the naming ceremony, Bear Wrestler was attached to a raiding party. The platoon, twelve in all, boarded two dugouts, and paddled down the rain swollen Greenwater River. Their mission was to spy on a Creek encampment, notorious for raiding the Thunder People. They cautiously approached the camp only to discover that it was recently abandoned leaving behind smoldering fires. Patrick and his fellow braves returned to the Thunder village triumphant, convinced that the cowardly Creek had fled the territory from fright.

The special feast and dance, an all-nighter, set the stage for the main event, a highly advertised La Crosse game. Gamblers from surrounding villages were arriving to wager on the outcome. Before the actual ball game began, the athletes were allowed a brief time to nap. Stands-Alone awoke the team at first light. It was a beautiful morning with no sign of rain or strong wind.

The Thunder Team walked to where the Beaver team lay sleeping. The Thunder Team invited the guests to share a special, high calorie breakfast. At least three of the Beaver Clan contestants had fresh scratching wounds. Patrick noticed that he was of particular interest to a Beaver team member. One of Patrick's fellow teammates whispered, "Watch out for the scar face named Crow." He assumed he was being singled out because of his Caucasian ethnicity, but it was that and much more. An indignant Patrick decided it would take more that this arrogant brute to back him down. Perhaps the competitors equated red hair and fair skin with weakness. Patrick heard the big one being called Gogv, the word for Crow. He had a jagged scar across his chin and was unusually tall and muscular. His eyes were intense and seemingly full of rage. Patrick thought, *why is he so angry with me?* That is when Wathena approached the staging area, and of course all eyes were instantly fastened on her. Since she was prohibited from speaking to Patrick until after the ball game, they gazed at each other with unmistakable affection. Crow bristled at the sight and called out for Wathena. She tried to ignore him, but he persisted. He looked at Wathena and then Patrick, Wathena and back to Patrick, back and forth a couple of times. His suspicions were confirmed. His already sullen countenance was glowering at Patrick.

Crow was surprised at the Thunder Clan's breach of trust. Had Wathena forgotten that Crow's father had spoken to Falls-From-Heaven about a betrothal more than three years before? The woman he desperately wanted was courting another, a disgusting white man. Wathena read Gogv's thoughts. She looked directly at him and stamped her foot, before dismissing him with a wave of her arm. She turned toward Patrick and mouthed, "Do well, I will be cheering for you." She wisely left the scene before her presence caused a disturbance.

Crow's family had spoken for Wathena, and he wasn't one to relinquish what was promised without a fight. Inflamed with jealousy, he purposely collided with Patrick, shoving him aside like one would send a dog scurrying. Patrick knew nothing of the betrothal, but picked up on the looks and reactions between Wathena and Crow. A strong possessive urge swept over Patrick, but he reacted like a thoughtful, self-controlled man of intelligence. Instead of attacking he chose to settle the provocation with finesse. His response was totally unexpected and so novel that he was left with the upper hand.

A crowd was starting to surround Crow and Patrick. Crow was surprised that the anemic, comical white man would dare to challenge him, The Crow, Beaver Clan wrestling champion. The crowd of gawkers were eagerly waiting to see what was about to happen. The audience was thinking that a fight to the bloody end was about to materialize.

The two men continued staring each other down. Their nostrils were flared and eyes narrowed. They began to rotate in a circle. Patrick seized the initiative and edged closer to Crow. He assumed the stance of a boxer and began shadow boxing. Crow flinched and sprang back a few feet. Patrick's appearance became more menacing as his scratching scabs broke and began to bleed. Crow was confused by the unusual movements. He expected to wrestle this strange acting man that was reportedly moving in on the woman he had publicly claimed. This was the perfect opportunity to show Wathena that he was the superior suitor. He could quickly send the white man away in disgrace if only he would stand still long enough to engage in a wrestling match. The normally threatening Crow just stood and stared at the darting figure called Bear Wrestler.

Patrick's plan was to settle the confrontation without resorting to violence. He figured to do some intimidating but in his own unique way. He began demonstrating the bobbing and weaving style of a trained boxer. The unfathomable aspect of the quick-time foot work and lightning-fast punches was that the barrage was aimed at a phantom opponent. (The British boxing champion of the day called Tom Cribb would have been proud of Patrick.) Each jab, upper cut, and punch was accentuated with an audible grunting sound. Patrick, now streaked with drying blood, danced over to the big drum and punched the skin membrane so hard it was torn away from its moorings. Then Patrick pummeled the vertical slab with his closed fists in a quick staccato, making the air reverberate with cracking noises. Patrick turned back to the aggressor, stood with his arms crossed, and nodded his head. Crow appeared to be frozen in place and incapable of reacting.

So Patrick continued. He was searching his repertoire of tricks from his circus performance days. He paused for dramatic effect before dropping to the ground and performing twenty of his rapid hand-clap push-ups. Then he sprang to a backbend and encircled the Beaver team with a series of backward flips. They stared with wide-eyed amazement as they might have appeared when seeing a ghost. The Beaver team had formed a tight outward facing circle much like a heard of buffalo fending off a lone wolf attack. Patrick performed a circular run of tumbling, and for the finale he walked about on his hands and finished by balancing himself aloft on one hand. Patrick waited to see if he had successfully defused the situation. He walked in a small circle with his arms widespread before approaching the stunned challenger. Patrick gave Crow and his team mates a nod that invited a response. The humbled brave stood facing Patrick slack jawed. This was not the reaction Patrick had been going for. He wanted to defend his honor but without ramping up the hostility.

During the course of the performance, a large crowd had gathered, and after a moment of silence a great swelling chorus of trilling and clapping rang out. Patrick acknowledged the crowd's amazement by bending at the waist in a flamboyant bow, and then with a big smile on his face walked over to his antagonist and made the hand sign for 'peace' before grasping Crow's right hand and shaking it in the manner of white men.

Barely within his range of sight, Patrick caught a glimpse of Stands-Alone speaking with Wathena. The old man had a big toothy grin on his face, and Wathena was smiling. Patrick suddenly began to second guess himself. As a novice to Tsalagii society, it occurred to him that he might have gone too far and shamed this man named Crow. But then it would have been cowardly to let Crow get away with his intimidation. Patrick was confused and suddenly embarrassed. Had he successfully diffused the crisis or made matters worse? His question was quickly answered. His teammates hoisted him to their shoulders and began walking in a circle while chanting. A crowd surrounded them and cheered for the Thunder Team by stamping their feet and making the high-pitched trilling.

Patrick had set the bar high for the game to follow. Would it be a bone crunching, flesh ripping contest as everyone hoped? The Beaver Clan Team had blinked. Wagers on the game were now favoring the Thunder team.

A supporting contingent from the Beaver Village had been arriving all day and many had witnessed Patrick's demonstration. In a show of neighborliness a few Beaver Clan leaders complimented

Patrick on his athletic skill. The dance began, a little delayed while the drum membrane was re-stretched and secured. The women took to the arena first and scooted their feet to the beat of drums while singing the traditional ball game songs. While they danced, they did not smile. They sang in the minor key with a plaintive tone. At the proper time the men began dancing. The women remained apart from the men as they danced. The shuffling back and forth went on for hours. The singing was punctuated by shouts from the men appealing to the Spirits for victory. Most of the dancers wore the traditional pebble filled turtle shell anklets. The participants included the very old down to the infants, strapped to the back of their mother in a cradle board. The dancers revolved around the fire, crooning to the beat of the accompanying drums, pebble filled gourds and other noise makers, the noisier the better.

The ballgame field was surrounded by forest. On the way to the playing field, in accordance with tradition, Patrick and the other players were allowed to cool off by diving into the river. Stands-Alone exhorted the players to do their best, assured them the omens were favorable, and reminded them of the high stakes and glories to be had. The old mystic promised to use his powers to drive their opponents into a state of fright. Stands-Alone certainly owed Patrick some credit for his role in intimidating the opponents.

The game began early morning. The novice players began the game with scant rest, weakened from blood loss, and fatigued from dancing. They wore only a loincloth that was tied at the waist by a cord that would break if tugged. Wathena had a boy deliver an ornamental necklace decorated with an eagle feather, deer's tail, and a snake rattle. After a dip in the river the players re-applied a coating of bear grease or the slippery elm to their bodies.

Each end of the playing field had two upright poles that served as the goal posts. A point was scored each time the ball went between the posts. The first team to score twelve points would win. After the ball was in motion, it could only be picked up with the playing stick, although after having picked up the ball with the stick the rules allowed the player to transfer it to his hand. Then he could pass or toss it to a teammate. The game could last for days, but most games lasted two days. The bodily contact was brutal and violent. Players that were injured too badly to continue were unceremoniously dragged from the playing field. Crow and his friends were out to send Bear Wrestler to the sideline. They tried to trip him several times, but he saw it in time except for once when he went sprawling.

Late on the second day Patrick feigned injury, but then scooped up the ball and managed to score the winning point by thrusting the ball between the goal posts. The Beaver team played rough but with considerable skill. When Patrick scored the winning point his team members were half expecting a brawl to break out, but the losers were dispirited by that time and merely gathered for the trip back to their village. The Thunder Team raised Patrick to their shoulders and paraded him around the arena. Patrick could see Wathena waving at him and cheering from her seat under the cooking arbor.

A post game feast followed and offered great platters piled high with the foods that had been forbidden. Custom called for the players of both teams to be celebrated as heroes. Over the next few days as the La Crosse players healed from their wounds, they did no work, and the women waited on them. Patrick was reminded of the stories he had heard about the ancient Roman gladiators.

Time passed quickly, and life with the Thunder People was becoming routine to Patrick. After the seven-month period of training, he was scheduled to stand before the elders. His adoption would go forward, or he would be forced to leave the village. The decision would be absolute and final. It was a tense time for both Patrick and Wathena. What if Patrick was refused? In such matters, the elders usually respected the will of Stands-Alone, who was careful not to give any advance indication of how he would vote. The council sat with lowered eyes, and blank expressions. The seemingly endless period of passing the pipe tested Patrick's patience. Patience, a treasured attribute, forced Patrick to sit without obvious expression.

Finally, Stands-Alone approached the fire and sprinkled tobacco upon the smokeless, gray bed of coals. After a long moment a slight puff of smoke rose from the coals, indicating that an answer was forthcoming. The tiniest flame reached around a partly burned stick and sent a thin string of smoke upward and then with the help of a puff of air drifted to the north. An audible sigh emanated from the circle of elders. Kanati, the great spirit had sanctioned Patrick's induction as a warrior. Stands-Alone turned to face Patrick and Wathena and motioned for them to stand. Stands-Alone felt an uneasy sensation deep in his gut, but he kept his foreboding private.

Patrick was unsure of the verdict until he saw the smile on Wathena's face. Next, Stands-Alone reached out and raised Patrick's right arm toward the sky. Comments from observers was positive and welcoming. A sense of relief and accomplishment flooded over Patrick. He stood, exhaling his pent-up suspense, and then Wathena took his other hand and raised it above his head. That is when Patrick let out an ear piercing, "Ha! tald-gwu!" The elders flinched with surprise and then accepted Patrick's unorthodox outburst with amusement. Bear Wrestler's impulsiveness was overlooked and that wouldn't be the last time.

Two of Bear Wrestler's favorites that had been on the forbidden list was fried frog legs and roasted rabbit. He managed to get his share before the bowls were empty. Many of the Thunder People placed small gifts into Patrick's hand, items to be cherished, and suitable for his medicine bag. One look at Wathena's facial expression made words unnecessary. He felt her say, "I knew that you could do it."

Springtime brought on summer, and the days were hot. Patrick had just finished felling a birch tree that would be burned out and carved into a canoe. Exhausted, he leaned against the trunk of a big tree to enjoy its shade and cool off. As he gazed up into its branches, he thanked the Lord God for his new life, for the bounty of the forest but most of all for finding Wathena. Still, something was missing. Not even his new existence could replace the longing Patrick felt for Rory. The mystical connection he felt for his twin dogged his thoughts. Patrick was determined to entice Rory to follow him. Time has a way of working out such matters but not always one would expect. To repeat an earlier observation lack of knowledge of the future is a very good thing.

Patrick and his squad of warriors settled into a routine. When meeting with Falls-From-Heaven to strategize future campaigns, Patrick began feeling conflicted. Their sorties were usually to keep other tribes from encroaching on special hunting grounds or capturing slaves. Two of the sub-war chiefs voiced the need to step up attacks on white wagon trains full of homesteaders in search of farmland. The European intruders had out and out rejected Tribal Sovereignty. A poll was taken, and it was decided to include white immigrants on the enemies list along with the Shawnee, Creek, and Catawba. Patrick's junior position as a warrior kept him silent but emotionally disturbed. He decided to speak to Wathena before refusing to join in the war on white people. Trouble was brewing, and for the first time Patrick sensed the approaching storm.

The bad blood between the Creek and Cherokee went back more than a century. Patrick's squad had previously reconnoitered a small encampment about two days away by canoe. Due to expert stealth the Thunder Squad successfully invaded the Catawba camp, whose sentries had fallen asleep. The raiders discovered four captives, gagged and bound and loaded them into canoes. The four boys were Chickasaw, about 12 years old, and were perfect candidates for adoption. The Thunder Clan elders engendered the boy's loyalty with kindly living circumstances. The boys would introduce genetic diversity when they took Thunder Clan wives. Marriage among clan members was taboo, but that did not apply to adoptees. Patrick's raiding party was hailed as heroes. Ah yes, the newest warriors were fine indeed. The capture was a big coup against the pesky Catawba.

The white race had many good God-fearing people, but the damage done by droves of small minded, greedy, criminal types casted a shadow over the influence of the good people. The population of American Indians had been victimized too many times, and the resulting hatred made them receptive to the message of the great messenger Tecumseh.

Publicly, Patrick had managed to gain acceptance from "Stands-Alone," but the shaman had been receiving bad omens while communing with the spirit world. Bear Wrestler would bring tragedy, he was sure of it. The Thunder Clan valued Patrick and had great affection for him. The conversations went something like this, "What a handsome couple Wathena and Yo-Nv-Ayastigi make. They will have strong children. Bear Wrestler has brought us good fortune."

The young lovers were obviously overwhelmed with the blush of love. Patrick, a novice at romance was eager to follow the dictates of his biological longings, and to him that meant marriage. Patrick decided to speak with Falls-From-Heaven.

According to Tsalagii tradition, when a man is bound to a wife, he is expected to reside in the dwelling of the bride's family. "The People" are a matriarchal society meaning that the wife possesses the family hut, the children are hers, and the mature women of the tribe are the decision makers in matters involving everyday life. This bit of information had been largely omitted from Patrick's orientation.

At some later time, Wathena would find a good time to discuss such matters with him.

At this point in the Lions' Cave Story, Granny took a few minutes to teach a history lesson to us girls. Before that we girls were bored with history, but after Granny explained the relevance it had for our recent ancestors, it clarified the big picture and made it more interesting.

Granny with her thick-as-honey southern drawl launched into the history lesson, "At the time of Patrick and Wathena's betrothal and wedding, the Thunder Clan Village was thriving. Things seemed to be much as they had been in the recent past. Unbeknownst to Patrick and Wathena political upheaval was about to destroy their utopian existence. The triggering event was the discovery of gold on ancestral land."

Granny's eyes were bright, and she used her hands to express the intricacies of the history lesson. Her vernacular was mesmerizing to us kids. She removed a couple of history books from the wall shelf and read aloud a few excerpts. After the reading she summarized the passages to be sure we got her lesson. By the late eighteenth century, the European Continent was an inhospitable place. The available farmland was inadequate to support the population. The soil was so depleted of minerals the crops lacked critical nutrients. The European monarchies were tyrannical and largely outlawed all but state sanctioned religion. The countryside had been denuded of timber, and the cities were pits of contagion like black plague, typhoid, and chorea.

Farmable American land was cheap and plentiful. The timber and fur trade were lucrative. Great waves of Europeans responded to the abundant raw resources and relocated to North America. Land speculators, many of whom were criminal opportunists, flocked to the American East Coast. They managed to gain influence over the Congress with favors and if necessary, threats. The land promoter's sales pitch whipped desperate immigrants into a frenzy. Ship after ship arrived loaded with migrants, many of whom had spent the last of their money to purchased land sight unseen. In some cases, the same tract of land was sold more than once or didn't exist.

Though freedom of religion attracted huge numbers of immigrants, they and many more came to settle on cheap tillable land. The immigrants largely rejected the notion that the sub-human, nomadic indigenous population could be proper stewards of the land?

The hospitable nature of the Thunder People exposed them to many threats including foreign diseases. Unlike the people of Europe, they had no herd immunity to the diseases that came across the Atlantic. Entire villages were devastated by the pox and dysentery. The tribal people were tricked into trading for worthless trinkets. The white man's firewater played havoc with their unique endocrine and metabolic systems.

The year of 1814 would see the beginnings of a battle over sovereign territory that would doom the once gentle, trusting American Natives to forced relocation. President Thomas Jefferson was a strict Constitutional constructionist and supported the newly formed Republican Party, formerly known as the Anti-federalist. He favored states' rights over a strong central government, and his opposition to the Alien and Sedition Acts of 1798 won him the presidency. Once in office he drastically cut federal spending, downsized the federal bureaucracy, and began funding the federal treasury with revenue from land sales and customs duties. The costs associated with the War of 1812 added to the debt burden. Eventually under Andrew Jackson's administration, legislation was passed to rid the land of the savages.

The Indian Removal Act was signed into law by President Andrew Jackson on May 28, 1830, a dark day in the history of our nation. The Cherokee Nation filed suit in the Federal Court system, but the Supreme Court rejected ruling on the case citing lack of jurisdiction. The removal act was followed by the Treaty of New Echota of 1835 that specifically applied to the Cherokee Nation. President Martin Van Buren was left to implement the Treaty of New Echota and placed Major Winfield Scott and a force of 7,000 troops in charge of moving the thousands of Indians west to land that already supported a large population of Indians. Many Indians including some Cherokee opted to relocate voluntarily, well ahead of the forced marches. Those that resisted were captured and held in stockades to await the next forced trek westward. Many died before departing due to the inhumane stockade conditions. Thousands more died on the trip westward, and the incident became known around the world as the "Trail of Tears."

Granny said, "Girls, our Cherokee history is important to know. Yawl ready to hear more?"

"Yes! Please, Granny, keep a'goin." Cheatie squealed.

"It's gonna cost each of you a hug." Granny almost fell from her chair because of the mugging she took disguised as hugs. "Easy girls, yore ole Gran ain't what she used to be."

Wathena was diligent in seeing to Patrick's needs. The other young maidens knew that the Bear Wrestler was spoken for. One afternoon, as they strolled along the riverside, Wathena pointed to first her chest and then Patrick, "Soon you, me, my man." Patrick stopped in his tracks and looked at her. Then he smiled, and said, "Where I'm from the man proposes marriage."

Wathena stood on tiptoes and touched her nose to his. "You here now, Bear Wrestler, you and me. You, mine."

Patrick threw back his head and laughed, "Only if you can catch me." He sprinted toward a patch of heavy undergrowth and hid. He was confident that Wathena would have a hard time finding him, but she walked to the general area and began looking toward the sky and tree tops. The last thing she did was walk in a circle looking at the ground for tracks. In less than three minutes she was staring at Patrick face to face. She started to spring away but Patrick said, "Wait, tell me how you found me so fast."

There remained a lot to learn about being a Tsalagii, but his new community was patient. They overlooked Patrick's frequent faux pas, except once, when he ate some banned food before a ball game. Stands-Alone gave him a verbal flogging. The second stickball game lasted four days, and several of the athletes suffered serious wounds including cuts, broken bones, and one young man lost a tooth. Patrick got off with a badly scraped knee and a cut above his left eye. With the scratching rite behind him, Patrick was able to enjoy his new status. The very visible scaring would serve as a testament to his bravery for the rest of his days.

Chapter 10

THE WEDDING THAT CHANGED WEDDINGS

It took considerable time for Patrick to summon the courage to ask Falls-From-Heaven for Wathena's hand in marriage. The beloved uncle viewed Patrick's request as a mere formality since their betrothal had been a matter of public knowledge for weeks. Wedding preparations didn't happen overnight much to Patrick's chagrin. Patrick asked Wathena to move up the wedding, but that wasn't possible. He was told to be patient. The villagers all assumed the wedding would adhere to Thunder Clan tradition, or that was the plan. As the wedding date grew near, Stands-Alone and one of Wathena's cousins took Patrick aside and instructed him on his responsibilities. He was eager to be a proper groom. Because Wathena had been orphaned, and raised by an uncle and aunts, the ceremony would have to be adjusted. The day of the wedding, tradition required Patrick to furnish a freshly killed deer to the bride's family for the wedding feast.

The wait had seemed longer than it really was. Long before daybreak on the actual wedding day, Patrick awoke earlier than necessary, too keyed up to fall back to sleep. He dressed, took up his bow and spear and silently slipped into the dark forest. He knew of a place where deer liked to graze. From behind a natural blind, he seated himself on a limb and waited with his bow at the ready. Green River valley was teeming with all kinds of wildlife, except for deer. The noise made by a family of playing squirrels all most drowned out the chirping birds. Every movement caught Patrick's gaze. A motionless Patrick watched two half grown cottontails frolic, and even spotted the field mice darting about. But where were the usual deer?

Patrick had expected at least two or three to be at the stream's bank. When he was about to move to another place, Patrick saw something moving on the opposite side of the creek. As he watched a lone buck stepped from cover and drank from the flowing water. The animal was alert and held his head high, testing the air. The large ears were spread wide and moved independently, alert for danger.

The white underside of the tail flicked from side to side. Patrick slowly drew down on the buck, sending the carefully carved arrow forward in a blur of motion. It struck the buck in the neck. The wounded animal sprang behind the cover of brush. Patrick jumped to a standing position and hurried toward the prey. Patrick's vision was inhibited when peering into the shade from bright sunlight. Patrick splashed across a wide, shallow section of the stream. Blood marked the spot where the deer had been standing. He followed the trail and found the animal lying on the ground only twenty yards away.

At close range Patrick sent a second arrow into the dying animal. As he approached the magnificently antlered buck, it struggled to stand. Patrick came from behind, distended the neck by grasping an antler and slashed the jugular vein. It was painful for Patrick to watch the frightened eyes became dull and sightless as the life force drained from the neck wound. Killing had always distressed Patrick but there was something especially traumatic about killing this splendid animal.

Opening the belly of the deer caused his hands to tremble. Wathena would expect him to thank the deer for the gift of meat and hide, bone, and antlers. Patrick did not recognize the deities worshipped by Wathena and her tribe. Still, he refused to be disrespectful of Kanati or Moneto. Patrick knew of only one God, the God of the Holy Bible. So far, he had avoided discussing the topic with Wathena. He wanted to wait for the right opening. Patrick said a brief prayer of thankfulness before building a small fire and cooking the tongue to demonstrate his gratitude to the great buck. While the tongue roasted, he bowed on one knee and sang a quick song. The exact lyrics failed Patrick, so he substituted his own.

> *Thank you, Sender of this fine buck for our feast,*
> *And your gift of a wife, one to share my life,*
> *Gratitude fills my heart for this home among the People,*
> *Bless our wedding feast with baskets of strawberries,*
> *Bless our shared paths with combs of honey.*

The rack of antlers would make a fine trophy, so Patrick preserved the head with the carcass. He could hang them beside his bearskin rug. He wrapped the skinless carcass in the hide and hoisted it onto his back. The day was warm, and the walk back to the village of about two miles would have tired a lesser man, but Patrick's physical conditioning had him feeling his virility. He had forgotten that pride precedes a fall.

When Patrick reached the village, he washed the deer carcass in the river and delivered it to Falls-From-Heaven's wives. The early hour would allow sufficient cooking time. Wathena walked out of the hut, and feigned surprise at the gift of the venison. Patrick watched as Wathena sliced off several choice roasts and carried them to the food preparation arbor so that they could be spitted over a cooking fire.

Patrick rushed to bathe in the stream and donned his new buckskin garments. He kept repeating to himself *"relax, breathe."* Patrick put grease on his Mohawk to help it stand up. He cleaned his teeth with a chew stick, and then rinsed his mouth with a tea made from cedar berries. Finally, Patrick summoned his most dignified demeanor and hiked the short distance to the brush arbor in front of Falls-From-Heaven's hut. As Patrick traveled the path to Falls-From-Heaven's dwelling, villagers stopped what they were doing and greeted Patrick with great affection. He felt proud and very happy. Patrick arrived for the wedding ceremony thinking he had fulfilled the instructions.

Stands-Alone met Patrick as he was about to be seated in the shade. The shaman took Patrick to a short, hide covered hut called a sauna. There was just this one last tradition Patrick was told. The steam would purify Patrick's being, both body and soul. Patrick was instructed to undress and crawl into the steam house. This wasn't his first experience with a sauna, but this one felt different. Without understanding the longer effects of the steam bath, Patrick went along and hunkered down inside the little hut. Following the ritual Patrick went to the river and dove in for a swim. He was told that steam purification would assure a successful marriage.

In the kitchen area, Wathena had fussed over choosing the seasoning and firewood that would produce the best flavor. A wife's cooking skill was an important wifely qualification, and Wathena wanted to impress her groom. Nothing in the preparation of the venison was left to chance. She had summoned the advice of the very best cooks.

The sun was casting long shadows by the time the wedding party sat down to eat. Wathena withdrew and walked to bathe in the stream before dressing in a colorful tunic. She would don her wedding garments when the meal was finished. Since early childhood, she had dreamt of this day. Never in memory had a bride's trousseau compared to Wathena's in terms of ornateness and artistic expression. She was breathless and jittery with anticipation. The bridal tunic and accessories were the sewing project of half a dozen female members of her extended family, a monumental task that represented hundreds of hours.

Weeks in advance of the wedding the doe skin for the wedding garment had been harvested by Wathena using her own bow. She chose a pair of very young does. An aunt called Spotted Leaf supervised the tanning process. The basic hide preparation methods mimicked that used by the Cherokee for eons and was essentially the same process used around the world for thousands of years. Spotted Leaf rehearsed the steps involved in tanning and added a few secret techniques that yielded a better outcome.

Wathena was so grateful to have Spotted Leaf's expertise she made a point of listening carefully. Spotted Leaf went through the steps, "Wathena, we start by soaking the skin in a solution containing a large amount of brine taken from the salt lick. The skins need to soak for several days. I have everything we need like my big clay pot stored under my table, and my scrapers and stretchers. The next step is to soak the pelt in lime made from pouring water over wood ashes. Then it is time to remove the hair and fat by scraping the hide on both sides. Bleaching comes next. Start saving your urine in a jar. Tradition calls for only the bride's urine to be used. The gods will smile on the processing, stay true my child. We will need enough aged and decomposed urine to completely cover the two hides. The longer the hide soaks the lighter the color. After a good washing in the river, we rub the hide with a paste made from the animal's brains. It is important that the hide be tightly stretched so that the tannin from the brain mixture will fully penetrate. The longer it is rubbed the softer the hide will be. The brain paste is washed away, and the hide is hung up to dry. Once dry it is treated with cedar oil. The pleasing aroma will last for years and help preserve the beauty of the garment. At this point we can cut the garment to the right shape and size."

Wathena's emotions overflowed. She hugged Spotted Leaf and said, "Beloved Spotted Leaf, your doe skins are legendary, thank you for sharing your secret formula, I hope I can make you proud." Wathena hugged the aging woman a second time and peered into her eyes for as a prolonged gesture of endearment.

Spotted Leaf said, "Wathena, be assured, the doe skin will be very pale and ever so soft. Your wedding garments will be beautiful enough for you, our lovely Wathena!"

A cousin named Singing Frog offered to help Wathena cut and sew the garment. She was an expert at stitching and beading. The hide was cut with traditional stone knives and sewn using bone needles strung with thin strips of animal sinew. Four cousins helped with the beading. The garment was decorated with row after row of multicolored beading sewn in elaborate designs. Still more beading was sewn into geometric shapes on the upper sleeves and around the hem. The bottom of the tunic was finished with a lavish fringe. The garment was finished with a week to spare, a definite relief to the bride.

The wedding feast was held in a brush arbor in front of the family dwelling. Stands-Alone, with hands held toward heaven, addressed the Great Spirit, offering thanks for the food. As usual it was a long and grandiose prayer. In honor of the occasion, Falls-From-Heaven wore ceremonial dress topped with a leather turban, decorated with semiprecious stones. Falls-From-Heaven's demeanor was one of appropriate dignity and authority.

Wathena carried the first platter of food to Patrick. Then she sat cross-legged next to him, and the aunts finished serving the meal. As the family eagerly consumed the feast, Patrick was the butt of much joking. Food was the last thing on his mind. The playful, bawdy comments unnerved poor, blushing *Bear Wrestler*; it would be a relief to get beyond this part of the wedding.

Once the meal was over Wathena went to don the bridal garments. When she exited the house, it was as though a lightening charge had changed the atmosphere. Wathena's appearance was otherworldly, strikingly beautiful, truly a vision from heaven. An audible sound emanated from the guests' so striking was her appearance. Neither the Cherokee nor English terminology was adequate to describe the angelic creature that floated toward Patrick. Her attributes were paradoxical. Her trim, tall, yet curvy build radiated aphrodisiacal qualities, yet her musculature predicted kinematic strength. A fitting symbol for Wathena is a honeybee: yielding the sweetness of honey, but capable of warding off attackers with a painful sting.

Wathena's creamy wedding garment was form fitting. The skirt was split revealing an athletic right leg perfect in every dimension. The tunic was finished at the hem with pebble tipped fringe. The fringe touched the tops of her beaded moccasins. Her sun-streaked hair framed her symmetrical facial features. The hair part that divided right from left was painted crimson. Long braids woven with brightly beaded strips of leather fell forward of her shoulders.

Patrick had every intention of following tradition, an important aspect of being Tsalagii. Thanks to the orientation lessons he knew to lavish complements on Wathena's food preparation. It was during the meal that Patrick began to feel ill. Why was it taking so long? He felt nauseous and dizzy. He tried to eat, but was forced to excuse himself. When the meal was over Stands-Alone accompanied by several of Patrick's warrior comrades, rose and walked to the dormitory where Patrick's normally slept. With a dignified posture, (Old-Spider) Stands-Alone and the young roommates spread the groom's bedding and held it open by the upper corners and waited. Next, Falls-From-Heaven approached with Wathena's bedding, and the coverlets were folded together and handed to Patrick.

Patrick shook his head. What was happening to him? Maybe it was dehydration from the sweat bath or lack of food. He staggered a little when he walked. He concluded it was a case of nerves. Together Patrick and Wathena arranged the bedding at their feet, but Patrick's end was messy, and Wathena was forced to refold his end. She summoned an attendant and asked her to place the bedding in the honeymoon canoe.

Spirit-Woman recognized Patrick's symptoms and rushed to her pharmacy hut to concoct strong medicine. The medicine woman waited until the procession began the walk to the amphitheater and caught up to Patrick. She fell into step with him long enough to hand him the gourd filled with her tonic. Patrick swigged down the elixir without a second thought and hugged the woman. Within five minutes the tonic transformed Patrick into a cavorting, loudmouth. He was suddenly devoid of normal inhibitions. The new Patrick was about to take considerable liberties with tribal tradition. Wathena asked if he was feeling better, and he found the question inappropriately funny and made a silly noise laughing. The wedding procession was far from traditional.

The march began with Stands-Alone playing a handheld drum. It was an ornately painted hide-covered disk. He beat upon the drum with a leather covered stick, alternating the strikes between the membrane and the wooden rim. The result created the percussive flourishes reserved for weddings. Then the old man began singing the ancient wedding chant accompanied by his own drumming. Once the matrimonial warble ended the wedding party fell in line behind Stands-Alone as he led the wedding party along a quarter mile long serpentine pathway to the amphitheater where the larger population of Thunder Clan residents waited.

Patrick was as surprised as everyone else when he became giddy and was unable to control his impulses. The first sign of Patrick's altered state was a bad case of hiccups. Each hiccup tickled his throat and led to a combination giggle and hiccup that sounded a little like braying. The procession paused long enough to identify the source of the noise. Shocked expressions changed to smiles, and the marchers resumed marching to the drumbeat. Patrick knew his actions were inappropriate, but by this point he might as well have been a marionette on strings. Thunder Clan weddings emphasized the solemnness of the occasion. The marriage of Bear Wrestler and Wathena didn't measure up to the solemnness.

Wathena had seen Spirit-Woman administer the relaxant and moved forward to the head of the line and told the leader of the problem. Stands-Alone continued to walk, but indicated that Patrick must maintain self-control. He would not be excused for any misbehavior. Wathena, with an alarmed expression on her face dropped back to fall in beside Patrick. Patrick shouted much too loudly, "Oh there you are, my lovely bride, I love you."

Patrick's antics were totally undignified, far from tradition, but so, funny, hilariously funny! Patrick was marching by throwing one leg and then other straight out in front and slamming it down hard on the path. He was swinging his arms in like manner. Wathena began to laugh and asked, "Patrick, what are you doing?" Patrick's eyes were sparkling, and he looked so happy. He was smiling and laughing. He replied, "This is the stabbing-step march done by European soldiers. It started in Prussia. Nowadays folks call it the goose step. Here try it." Patrick resumed counting in German as he marched:

"Eins, zwei, drei, vier, funf—"

Wathena stopped and looked at the happy expression on Patrick's face and quickly cast propriety to the wind. Why spoil the fun? She hugged the big clown, slipped her arm through his and began the stepping in unison.

That was all it took for the strange marching to spread throughout the procession. The sound of feet hitting the path was loud enough to compete with Stands-Alone's drumming. After some false starts the two sounds were synchronized. Wathena knew Stands-Alone would disapprove of the break with tradition, but opted to ignore the old man. What mattered most was to mark the occasion with happy memories. As often happens lightheartedness is contagious and spread.

Most of the wedding guests remembered Patrick's challenge at the La Crosse ball game. It was happening again. What would he think of next? Spirit-Woman hurried forward and spoke to Stands-Alone on behalf of Patrick. After some serious coaxing she was able to convince the old man to forget tradition and allow the joy filled celebration to continue. Spirit-Woman took Stands-Alone's arm and commenced the crazy stepping at the head of the procession. Stands-Alone shrugged his shoulders in defeat and commenced a modified version of the march that resembled the gate of a chicken. The old man was too arthritic to do the full goose step had he been so inclined.

Only hindsight would reveal the extent to which Patrick Bear Wrestler would eventually impact the Thunder Clan Village. The crazy marching had just inadvertently created a new tradition for future Thunder Clan Weddings.

The public phase of the wedding began with a traditional fire lighting ceremony. Other than a few minor chuckles, Patrick managed to behave until the urge to hug each member of the supreme council swept over him. The spontaneous show of affection was tolerated and even welcomed. By this time even the leaders understood that Bear Wrestler had fallen ill and was medicated to get him through the ceremony.

Each phase of the ceremony symbolized two becoming one. Patrick and Wathena approached three stacks of wood ready for the torch. Stands-Alone handed Patrick (Hiccup) and Wathena each a small flaming torch. First Wathena moved to light the small fire on the south side of the fire pit. Then Patrick, grinning and swaying, rose and lit the fire on the north. Once the two small fires were fully engulfed, the bride and groom were instructed to rake the two small fires to the larger center stack of wood. At this point Falls-From-Heaven summoned the guardians entrusted with safekeeping the treasured white ermine cape. The Thunder Clan's prized ceremonial robe was made of hundreds of white ermine pelts all pieced together. Stands Alone and Spirit Woman took the oversized cloak and displayed it for all to see. The cape was spectacular with each black tail hanging like a tassel from the surface. Falls-From-Heaven, Spirit Woman, and Stands-Alone encircled the bride and groom in the cape, obscuring them from the crowd for a matter of minutes. Cheers and applause rang out. Patrick took full advantage of the moment of privacy. Everything was left to the imagination of the on-lookers. At this point the cape was removed and Stands-Alone raised his arms signaling that the marriage was finalized.

Patrick Bear Wrestler, recalling some of the Scottish wedding celebrations he had attended as a boy, decided to inject some of his tradition into the celebration. After all it was his wedding too. The wedding guests were seated, and Patrick surprised the crowd by walking to the row of drums. He spoke to the percussionists at length using hand motions. He said in his far from perfect Tsalagii, "Watch me and play a rhythm that matches my dance steps." The drummers smiled and agreed to try. Patrick extended his arms and walked in a circle in the middle of the arena and then paused for dramatic effect.

The observers were mesmerized as Patrick began to dance. Wathena stood with her hand over her heart, and gestured that she was as surprised as everyone else. Patrick started the dancing with a lively Irish jig. The jig soon morphed into a Slavic dance characterized by stepping forward and backward while crossing his feet over each other. The drummers were right on tempo. Then he picked up the pace and crossed his arms over his chest and bounded sideways and then forward and back in a bouncing dance step that included tricky cross over stepping, high splits, and kicking out to each side. He altered the stepping by reaching to the opposite side with one hand and then the other, bending low and slapping the ground while punctuating the ground strike with a loud, "Hey." As the dance continued the pace accelerated.

The assembly of hundreds looked on spell bound. Since the day Patrick stood down the La Crosse opponent with his gymnastics display and the shadow boxing routine, it was no secret that he was an entertainer and showman. His drug induced euphoria served to enhance his dancing to the delight of his audience.

Patrick was having the time of his life. As a youngster he had learned to perform the Russian folk dance of the Cossacks. He wasn't sure if he was doing the dance exactly as taught, but it really didn't matter. What did matter was that Patrick was expressing his joy over finding Wathena. In Patrick's culture weddings were cause for full-blown celebration. Patrick took a moment to encourage participation from the audience with hand clapping in beat with the drums. It took some arm twisting, but Stands-Alone actually joined the clapping. The aged shaman became fatigued and had to sit out the rest of the festivities. He almost smiled when he noticed the crowd's delight with his participation.

The spectacle of the dance step called 'Hopak' that featured Patrick squatting on his haunches and bouncing as he kicked out one foot at a time while staying stationary was a huge crowd pleaser. Crowd participation was spirited and loud. The signature movement of the Cossack dance left The People in awe, smiling, and highly entertained. Patrick's knees quickly felt the strain, so he ended the dance by springing upright and standing on his out-thrust heels while throwing out his arms and yelling a final "hey!" He bowed at the waist, sweeping his arm in a great ark. Patrick ended the dance by signaling the drummers to resume the traditional program.

Patrick walked toward Wathena, and she ran and jumped into his arms. While he spun her around, they kissed in full view of the audience, eliciting a deafening roar of approval. Weddings would never be the same for the Thunder Clan. Patrick Bear Wrestler had made his mark once again.

The head drummer began a livelier version of the wedding staccato. Bear Wrestler and Wathena returned the white ermine blanket to the aunts in charge of preserving it for future generations. Then, holding hands Patrick and Wathena, facing outward, began to revolve around the fire pit stomping the ground with perfectly timed steps to match the rhythmic drumbeat.

Patrick and Wathena's faces looked ethereal as they danced. After three complete revolutions, immediate family members joined them in the dance. As the drumming built to a more intense tempo and singing became livelier more of The People joined the dance. Additional drummers joined the percussionists resulting in sound that could be heard miles away.

The line of dancers grew until the entire assembly joined the circling mass of well-wishers. The circle of dancers became so large that the outward facing circle was forced to morph into a serpentine wave. A rested Stands-Alone managed to dance and shake his gourd rattle one complete circle before being escorted to his hut. The effects of Spirit-Woman's elixir had worn off leaving Patrick drained of energy, and he and Wathena sat out a few of the dances. Wathena took the opportunity to pop some nuts and berries into Patrick's mouth. There was a procession of guests filing by to express their wishes for wedded bliss.

More and more people abandoned the dance and lounged by the fires. The children were chasing each other, and one older group of pre-teens had lined up and was doing a goose step while doing a clipped version of counting in German. After a couple of hours, Patrick was told by Falls-From-Heaven that the time had come to escort his bride to their honeymoon hut. Patrick received directions to the hut whispered into his ear. It was hidden in a secluded cove downstream. A canoe lighted with torches and decorated with sunflowers and vine garlands was waiting to carry the honeymooners away amid great swelling cheers.

Chapter 11

CHEATIEBO'S EARLY YEARS

A t this point in the story, Granny (Delia) stood up and said, just think girls, Patrick and Wathena's blood runs in our veins. Then Granny said, "I think I'll take a trip to the outhouse." I quickly stood up and declared that I needed to go too. Even a trip to the outhouse with Granny was an adventure. The story about the bear and talk of an actual sighting of a mountain lion in our neck of the woods the previous week made the dark shadows in the yard look scary, and I squeezed Granny's hand as we walked the well-worn path. I even passed up a chance at a lightin' bug.

After dark we sometimes used the slop jar or as some people called it, the chamber pot, but Granny was fearless, and I felt safe with her. As always, before entering the outhouse, Granny held the rusty old lantern above her head and inspected the inside for unwanted visitors. "No snakes or polecats tonight," she whispered. While seated next to Granny in the two-hole privy, I said, 'I thought this story was about a lion's cave.' As Granny tore out a couple of pages from the tattered catalog and handed one to me, she said, "Patience, child, that part will be coming up 'fore long. Cheatie, I've been meaning to talk to you.

Hows about we go for a walk real soon? I've had something on my mind, and we need to have a nice long talk."

"Oh, Granny, can we do it tomorrow? Please, Please! I have something to show you. You will be real surprised."

"Seated back at the table, Granny yawned and announced that it was getting too late, and promised to continue the story the following night. More sounds of the night drifted inside. "Shu- listen, them coyotes are close by; we better keep our ears open for any noise coming from the hen house. Mattie, make sure the shotgun is loaded." We all knew that it would be better if we were asleep when Daddy got home. And that was a big if, because many times he stayed out all night.

Annie Mae, Ethyl, and I all slept together in the abandoned, homemade bed pushed up to the wall clost to the wood stove. The bed had been slammed together out of scrap lumber and was no more than a box with legs. It sure weren't much, but it beat sleepin' on the floor. The mattress was pieced together cloth fabric filled with corn husks. One end was easy to open 'cause we changed out the fillin' real often. Mother (Mattie) had a big bag of feathers and down saved that would one day make another down comforter. We usually had one down comforter under us and one for on top in the winter. No feathers ever went to waste around our place. The bed was too narrow for all three of us to sleep side by side, so, since I was the runt, I had to pile in with my head in the middle between Annie Mae and Ethel's feet.

Mother interrupted her story and said, "Honey, you 'member that song by Little Jimmy Dickens, "Sleepin' at the Foot of the Bed"?

I (Glenda) nodded with a smile and said, "As a kid I recall seeing him on television." Neither of us remembered the lyrics, but I looked them up. Here are a couple of verses.

"A-Sleepin' At The Foot Of The Bed"
By Happy Wilson – Luther Patrick

Did you ever sleep at the foot of the bed
When the weather was whizzin' cold
When wind was whistlin' around the house
And the moon was yeller as gold?

Or cold toenails a scratchin' your back
And the footboard Scrubbin' your head

I'll tell the world you ain't lost a thing
Never sleepin' at the foot of the bed.

Even in summer we covered up to hide from the mosquitoes and falling things. We pretty much made our bed covers from old rags. Momma (Mattie) and Granny (Delia) made quilts from squares cut from castoff clothes, and in between the two layers was cotton batting or sometimes down and feathers. Folks called comforters tickens or a feather bed and sometimes feather ticks. We had summer quilts and winter quilts. Purty much year round we kept the quilting frame suspended from the ceiling. Any time we got in to Millerton we always checked the local used clothing bins at the Indian Center. Sometimes we brought home a big bag of ripped and worn clothes perfect for cutting into squares for quilting. I 'member how Granny and Momma took pride in their quilts. Law they loved quiltin', and they was quick with a needle. Granny could come up with some beautiful Cherokee designs. Sometimes they was in a hurry and just made checker-board quilts.

Before daybreak the following morning, Granny woke me with a soft touch to my shoulder. She was standing near my head with her finger to her mouth. I slowly crawled out from under the quilt and stepped into my coveralls. Granny had the shotgun in her hand and led the way out the door. Momma was the only one to rouse and gave us a wave before going back to sleep.

Granny was a sight in her sunbonnet, made from a floral print flour sack. She wore a white long sleeve cotton waist that buttoned in front, an ankle length blue denim skirt, and an apron with big pockets. For shoes she wore a pair of blue canvas slippers. Her long gray hair was in a single braid, which trailed down her back.

After walking a few hundred yards Granny and me walked past a wild blackberry vine and decided to stop for breakfast. The vine was loaded. Granny whacked me on the back and said, "Can't beat this for a fine breakfast." This is when Granny asked what it was I had wanted to show her. When she asked my mouth was full, and I had purple juice running from the corners of my mouth. I said, after swallowing, "Promise that you won't tell on me?"

She lowered her chin and said, "We'll see, it all depends on what it is."

I was bursting to clue her in on my secret so I blurted it out: "I found a baby mountain lion, and I been taking care of it."

Granny staggered a little and had to find a rock to sit upon. She said, "Start over, what did you just say about a mountain lion?"

"I heard a faint peeping sound almost like a baby chick or duckling would make. The sound was coming from a hole way up in the side of the creek bank. I climbed up the steep bank by holding on to the bushes and grabbed a big stick to shake around in the hole. Vines was growing everywhere and covered the hole, so after waiting a minute or two I stuck my head in the cave. Granny, I was not expecting it to be a mountain lion. When I brought the little critter out in the light, I could tell she was starving. She had dark spots all over her back and was all squinty from the bright sunlight. As soon as she could open her eyes, I saw they was blue. The poor little cub was cold and skinny and shaking all over like this." Granny got tickled at my shaking.

When I first went to pick her up, the little rascal showed some spunk and hissed at me, but I went ahead and picked her up anyway, and then she started sucking on my finger. Oh Granny, she was so cute! Before, when we took care of orphans, Momma always said to mix milk with beaten egg. I put the baby down and ran all the way back to the house and started to look for a way to carry some milk and egg back. Then I saw an old worn-out leather glove under some old rags and junk. I put some hay in the milking stall, and Nanny went in. I only milked out about two cups of milk and then got two eggs out of a hen's nest. I poured the eggs and milk in a jar and stirred it with a stick. It only took about five minutes to run back to the baby."

That's when Granny interrupted and said, "Child, what was you thinking? If the mother lion had come back and found you—." Then Granny broke off talking and tilted her head to the side and said, "You know, I remember hearing hunting hounds at bay and gunshots down this way a few days ago. Those hunters must have killed the mother lion. Oh, and Mario was warning about a lion in these parts: said he was keeping his shot gun handy."

Mother (Cheatie) said, "Don't think I ever told you about Mario. He was a tinker this Mario, had moved to the area from across the ocean. He had a strange accent, supposed to be from some place called Czechoslovakia. He liked to dress in bright colors, wore a shiny scarf tied about his head, and had one earring. He had a deep voice that carried and he liked to sing opera. We could hear him coming a mile away. Someone in town called him flamboyant and said he was an itinerant huckster. Those were new words to me. We had heard rumors about a troupe of Gypsies living over toward Paris and Texarkana.

We liked Mario, and it didn't matter to us if he was a Gypsy. He was friendly and made an honest living. On the road he pretty much lived in his wagon. We looked forward to Mario's regular visits. Sometimes we would invite him to camp out and let his mule graze on our pasture. He knew what folks like us needed and purty much had it on that box wagon. He carried a big box camera and took pictures with a cloth thrown over his head. He even carried along the equipment to develop them on the spot. They didn't cost much, and he was always ready to barter for stuff he could sell. We had him take our family picture and paid with eggs and goat cheese. We laughed til we was blue in the face when we saw the picture."

"Mario shoed horses for his clientele and was able to repair machinery, a real jack-of-all-trades. He was our main source of news and carried a big stack of magazines and newspapers. Sometimes we got to look at them for free. Another service he offered was mail for a modest fee. We grew to depend on Mario bringing the goods to us instead of the all-day wagon trip into Millerton. We bought or bartered for most of our staples like sugar, flour, coffee, and Granny's snuff.

Childlike I would get excited when I heard the pots and pans and the horse tack banging together as Mario approached along our bumpy road. Every once in a while, the tinker would give us kids a treat. Once he gave each of us an orange and another time a piece of hard candy. That was my first orange. Oh, after that I became obsessed over the fantastic taste. Once when we needed our mule shooed, he camped in our yard for the night and shared our evening meal. Momma brought the food outside and we all ate around the campfire. Daddy pulled out his fiddle, and we had a really fun time with Daddy playing jigs and Mario dancing around playing a tambourine and singing."

I (Glenda) said, "Mother (Cheatie), thank you, thank you a million times for telling me about your early life and what it was like back then. I know I'm not that good at writing, but one day I just might try my hand at putting it all down on paper. It would be nice to share these stories with the rest of the family."

Then Mother (Cheatie) got back to the story about her pet lion. "Well, anyway, I rushed back with the milk and egg in a fruit jar. The old leather glove was full of holes, except the little finger didn't have a hole, so I took my knife and cut a tiny hole at the tip. At first the baby wouldn't take the glove in her mouth, so I tricked her by putting my finger in the milk and letting her lick it off my finger. Then I dribbled some of the milk into the side of her mouth. She perked up and started smacking, so I squirted some milk into the side of her mouth, and she started some loud smacking real loud and licking her whiskers. Then she took the finger of the glove into her mouth, and I squeezed some more milk through the hole into her mouth. The smacking got faster, and then she got strangled a little, so I quit squeezing so hard. Then I got worried that she might get sick if she had too much all at once. I took the glove out of her mouth and tied the little finger off so no milk would be wasted. I laid her on her back on my legs and took a while to play with her. I gave her a good rub down, and I could tell that she was a girl. In a few minutes I fed her the rest of the milk. Next, she curled up in a ball and went to sleep on my lap. Granny, it has been hard keeping my secret and sneaking down here to feed her at least twice a day. I was afraid to let anybody know what I was doing, except you. You are the first to know about my baby. A neighbor gave me a baby bottle supposedly for my dolly. Feeding her is a lot easier with the bottle."

"To make a long story short I took Granny to see the little lion. When we got to the cave where I left the baby, she was gone. She had fallen down to the creek and was creeping around scared and hungry. It's a good thing we found her when we did because she was in the open, and with the red-tail hawks around she was in danger. Granny stayed with her while I went to get her bottle. By the time I got back, she had the baby up in her arms, petting her little head. The baby had latched on to her little finger and was sucking away. After I fed the hungry ball of fur, Granny said, "Cornelia, we need to talk." When Granny called me Cornelia, I knew she was about to say something important, and I paid attention to what she had to say."

Granny continued, "Hon, according to the ways of nature, this little animal should have died. I know she is sweet, and you love her, but she will be too dangerous to keep as a pet when she is grown. The only way to save her is to teach her to hunt and survive in the wild on her own. I will try to help you with that, but the chances of it working ain't too good. If we are not successful, she will have to go to a zoo. The zoos in Oklahoma City or Dallas are a long way off, and I don't know how we would get her there. Besides, zoo livin' ain't much of a way for a lion to live."

Granny was silent a while and then turned her head to the side and smiled at me before continuing, "Ya know, hun, to us Cherokee, mountain lions have strong medicine. Trying to save her is worthwhile because every single lion is important to preserving the population. I worry about them being hunted out. My Granny, Twyla, loved to tell stories about the puma. She studied the habits of all wildlife, and she would gather us kids around and teach us all about the animal world. Her lessons were interesting and most of the knowledge I have came from her. Sometime the topic would be on the black bear or the grizzly bear. She really knew a lot about bears. Other times she would teach us about snakes, frogs, birds of prey, and my favorite, the puma. She always called them pumas. The word in Cherokee is Klandagi and means "lord of the forest."

"Granny, you know what a good hunter I am. I can teach her."

Granny said, "You don't know what you're biting off. It will take up a lot of your time, and she could turn on you. Mountain Lions are animals of instinct and are unpredictable. I'm gonna have to keep a close eye on the cub as she matures and watch for danger signs. Cheatie, look at me. I am serious now, I want you to promise me that when I say "no more" you will give up on training her. I don't want you hurt; do you understand me?"

I thought about Granny's warning and decided to take her advice if the time came. Then I said, "Granny I been wantin' to give her a name. What did you say the Cherokee word for mountain lion is?"

Granny replied, "Klandagi."

I said, "That is a good name for her, yes that is her name, Klandagi. I like it!"

Then Granny lowered her voice and grew intense, "Child, that leads me to what I've been wantin' to talk to you about. You, my dear, are a throwback, sure as shootin', a Cherokee girl; a throwback to Puma-Woman, Wathena the woman warrior and a "Ye Ho-Nawa" as has ever been born. I've heard that family characteristics can skip several generations, and now I believe it. There ain't any doubt in my mind that you are a child of Granny Wathena. This lion den and this baby puma are giving me the most eerie feeling. This has got to be more than just happenstance. You'll know what I'm talking about when we get back to the story about Wathena, the Puma-Woman."

I broke the quiet of the moment and asked, "Granny, when will Klandagi need to start eating meat?"

She replied, "In the next few days since she doesn't have her mother's milk. You need to mince it into a paste and add to the goat milk and egg mixture. Use your knife and make the hole in the nipple larger so the meat can go through. Cooked meat is better at first and start off with a teaspoon full and gradually increases the amount of meat. After a month you can start feeding the meat separately from the milk."

I scooted closer to Granny, and the three of us sat quietly and relaxed. Then Granny said, "Law, law, Cheatie, you give me goose bumps." as she smoothed my hair and then pulled me to her bosom. I will never forget the faraway look on her face. Granny's secret was revealed. I knew the reason for her always paying such clost attention to me. Granny could be mysterious, and all of this about me being a throwback was way over my head. Understanding what she meant would take some growin' up.

Before we started back home, I stacked up some limestone slabs across the entrance of the den to keep the baby from wondering away. As Granny and I walked back home, hand in hand, I asked her to tell me about the night I was born, again. She said, "Oh my, not now, all of this is taking too much out of this old woman." The walk back home was hard on Granny, and she had to sit and rest ever so often. We was resting when I told her about the catfish. I held my arms out and said, "It's about this long and lives in a deep hole downstream from our farm. I've seen it several times. Do you think we could catch him?"

To this she replied, "Why, I reckon. I have some ideas on how you might catch him." When we got back home, Granny dug through a dusty wooden box on a shelf in the barn, and pulled out a three-prong fishhook. Then she told me the best catfish bait is animal entrails, especially liver, and we set out fixing up what she called a trotline. Granny found some leftover close line rope and said that it would be perfect. She said the way to catch catfish is to let the baited hook rest on the creek bottom, since catfish are bottom feeders. Amazed, I decided that Granny knew about everthang.

Granny said, "I can already taste the fried catfish."

That night Granny continued the Lion Cave Story. Only now it was more real to me and Granny. It was fun having secrets only Granny and me knew. How I loved that old woman. Several months passed with me continuing to hide the young mountain lion. With Granny's help I built a pen across the front of her cave. At first the pen was to keep Klandagi safe from meeting the same fate as her mother. The front side of the cave was made secure with scrounged steel re-bar, pieces of left-over hog and chicken wire, tin roofing panels and lots of left-over baling wire. Some of the tin was buried into the ground to prevent Klandagi from digging under the barrier. So far Klandagi had not tried to break out of the cage and considered it her lair. I had never let her down and left her penned up too long. Me and Granny took her hunting and spent endless hours exercising her.

One day on the way to the lion's den Granny said, "Honey, the mountain lion is a very special animal to us Tsalagii. Tribal legend says that Kanati blessed them with an extra measure of intelligence, power, and cunning. They are beautiful and it is up to us to protect them from being wiped out by hunters."

Over the months Granny had been helping Cheatie care for the wild creature. Now, approaching a year of age it would be dangerous for anyone other than Cheatie or Granny to touch the cub. Granny gave Klandagi regular check-ups by feeling her ribcage for body fat, and looked into her eyes, ears, and mouth. She checked for parasites and looked at her fur to make sure she didn't get mange or ringworms. So far the playful animal was healthy and learning to do mountain lion things. Klandagi loved to hide and jump out and surprise Cheatie and Granny. Klondagi had a short high-pitched whistle. Her peeping and chirping noises were changing to a deeper tone. Granny said that pumas cannot roar like African lions, but when looking for a mate or on rare occasions, they do an eerie scream.

By the time Klandagi was a year old, she had lost most of the spots from her pale buff coat, and the color of her eyes was changing from blue to yellowish-green. In size she now dwarfed Cheatie. It was around this age when Klandagi started to exhibit signs of dominance by standing and placing her paws on Cheatie's shoulders. Granny recognized trouble, and she was heart sick. The Klandagi project was failing. Cheatie was having a hard time explaining her scratches and cuts to her Momma and Daddy. When chickens began disappearing throughout the region, Granny and Cheatie figured Klandagi was finding food the easy way.

"What to do, what to do," said Granny. Something would have to be done about the cub before someone got hurt. I heard about a neighbor that had slaughtered his barren milk cow, and I asked for some of the bones and unused parts. I took them to Klandagi and low and behold, Annie Mae decided to spy on me and find out what I was doing during those times when I disappeared. Annie Mae always did have a suspicious nature.

Annie Mae's curiosity exposed my secret. When she found me, she approached from some bushes, and blurted out, "Cheatie, what are you doing out here?"

I jumped up from my seat on a log and held my palms out to Annie Mae and urgently shouted, "Stay there and be quiet. Don't you dare move a muscle!"

Then I called, "Klandagi come." Out from behind a boulder cautiously crept the lion with eyes fixed on the stranger. Klandagi walked over to me and rubbed her torso against me, as she did when she felt threatened, almost knocking me over. I always carried a long piece of clothesline for a leash, and I slowly placed it over Klandagi's head while petting and cooing to her. Under my breath I said to Annie Mae, "stay still and quiet until I get her in the pen." Next, I walked over to a tree where I had suspended the toe sack of cow remains and lowered it to the ground. I took out a big bone with some meat on it. Klandagi's ears perked up; I never saw a time when she wasn't hungry, and tame as a kitten she followed me into the den. I sat for a moment and praised her for being such a good girl before leaving her to enjoy her snack. Once the latch was fastened, I hurried over to the awestruck Annie Mae. I took her by her sweaty hand and brought her to the camp fire, and we sat on the log. She was white as a sheet and bug eyed. I added some wood to the fire and offered her a drink of water from my canteen. Suddenly I felt a little guilty for holding out on her.

I said, "I been thinkin' bout telling you my secret, but I was a little worried you might tell on me. Now you know and Granny knows about Klandagi, by the way that's her name, but nobody else knows. Do you think I should tell Momma and Daddy?"

I waited for Annie Mae to say something. When she found her tongue, she started asking questions, lots of questions. She said, "I ain't ever been so scared! How did you tame the lion? Is it your pet? You need to warn all of us! What if it attacked one of us? What are you going to do with it?"

I said, "Wait a minute and I will explain. I found her in that cave almost dead. She was just born, about this big, and so cute, you should have seen her. Big blue eyes and she growled at me at first, but when I picked her up, she started sucking on my finger. I could tell she was starving, so I got an old glove and put goat milk in it, and she drank it all down. For sure she would have died if I hadn't found her. Granny knows all about her and is helping me get her all growed up healthy."

"Me and Granny think hunters killed her momma. After I started feeding her, she got better right away. I really, really love her and for the most part she has been a sweet little girl. Annie Mae kept looking at the cage and finally asked, "Do you think she would get used to me and let me pet her?" I considered the request and said, "I better ask Granny first cause she said to keep other people away, or she will get too tame and not be able to live in the wild."

Then Annie Mae said, "Cheatie, ya got to tell Momma and Daddy. They might git eat up or hurt." I agreed, and we headed home.

Me and Annie Mae arrived back at home just before supper time and announced that we wanted to tell everyone something after supper was over. Daddy was preoccupied with perfecting a new hoedown song on his fiddle. I went over and kissed him on the cheek and said, "That sounds real purty Daddy." Then I gave Stella Ruth a big hug and took the toddler up into my arms to dance around the room to the fiddle music. Stella Ruth was a beautiful child, and we all doted on her. "Momma, let me guess what's for supper; um, smells like rabbit stew, I am starved." Annie Mae was sittin' on the bed with a silly look on her face.

Momma asked, "Annie Mae, why are you acting so strange?" Annie Mae just shook her head and grinned and then stared at me, sending me the message that she wasn't taking any blame for having a dangerous animal.

After supper Momma and Granny cleared the dishes and quickly washed them in a pan of steaming lye soap water. The scraps went into a dish pan to be fed to the chickens. Next Granny pitched the dish water out into the yard and set the lamp on top of a crocheted doily in the center of the old pedestal table. Everyone pulled up a chair except me; I preferred to stand. I straightened my back, elevated my chin, and searched Momma and Daddy's faces before I spoke my piece. Just then Annie Mae blurted out, "I only found out about the secret today, so don't blame me none." The nervous tension in the room was thick enough to cut with a knife. Granny was sitting at the table and sent me a nod of encouragement, and that sure helped having her on my side.

Everyone had concluded that I was about to plea for mercy for some big flub.

I started with, "I was north of here on Breakneck creek scouting for game. The woods and brush is heavy with lots of thorns and stickers down there. You know how I am always rescuing some little orphaned animal and taking care of it. Well, that is what my announcement is all about. I heard a peeping noise coming from a well-hidden hole halfway up the steep creek bank and inside I found a tiny newborn puma cub." The only sound was that of "aw" being inhaled collectively. After a pause I went on with my story, "Annie Mae discovered my secret today, so I decided to tell the rest of you. I named the cub Klandagi, the Indian word for Puma. She is getting big now, and it is time for her to starting fending for herself. I have been teaching her to hunt and take care of herself.

Granny has been knowing my secret for a while and gives me pointers on getting her used to living on her own in the wild. She said the more Klandagi is around people the less chance she has to survive in the wild on her own. I been real worried about her having to go to a prison for animals cause that's what a zoo is. Now, yawl know my secret and I hope—." Cheatie covered her face for a moment and ran from the cabin. Granny gave her a chance to think before following her. After an hour or so Granny and a red-eyed Cheatie returned and got ready for bedtime. Nothing more was said until breakfast. Momma and Daddy said, "Cheatie, we will talk to Granny and let you know what we decide about the lion." After two days Willie Joe gave the answer. "That lion can have one chance to prove she's safe to run loose in these woods.

The time had come to leave Klandagi's pen open. She would taste freedom for the first time. Delia and Cheatie's goal for the beloved feline would be tested. Granny and Cheatie held hands as they walked away from the open pen. Klandagi was free to roam the forest at will. Cheatie knew her hunting skill was improving but not perfect. Cheatie found her playing with, rather than eating a captured jackrabbit. Klandagi had developed into a powerful wild puma. Cheatie still checked on her daily and summoned her with a turkey bone whistle. This continued for a few weeks, but then the danger signs began appearing. The last straw came when Klandagi went after the laying hens. It was evident that Klandagi would have to be caged. Buying new material for the cage was not an option so the salvaged material from the original cave was hauled to our place. The whole family, except for Willie Joe spent a day and a half building a pen. I used the barn wall for one side.

Willie Joe and Mattie laid down the law. Klandagi would only be allowed out of the cage on a leash handled by either Cheatie or Granny. Even they were having trouble controlling the rambunctious animal. Since the plan to habituate the cub to live independently had failed, they would look for a zoo to take her. The whole family agreed that it would be tragic to destroy such a beautiful animal.

One day when Klandagi was being playful she took off running across a field, dragging Cheatie at the end of the leash. The "grass sledding" incident was innocent enough had it not been through a prickly pear patch. When Willie went after Cheatie and carried her back home looking like a pin cushion, he threatened to shoot the lion. "Poor Cheatie was picking cactus needles for a month of Sundays," said Granny. And then Klandagi decided to practice her hunting skills on the laying chickens. It only took a moment and 4 dead chickens littered the garden. Klandagi responded to Cheatie's call and tried to appear innocent. The cub unknowingly provided ample crime scene evidence: chicken feathers sticking out of her mouth.

The lion began displaying signs of dominance over Cheatie. Her play was increasingly rough and once Granny saw her push Cheatie to the ground and stand over her. Another time Granny witnessed Klandagi rare up and place her paws on Cheatie's shoulders. Delia pulled Cheatie aside and said, "I'm so sorry, but I can't allow you to be alone with Klandagi. Until we find her a home with a zoo, she will have to stay penned up, except when I am with you." Cheatie covered her face with her hands and wept. Granny placed her arms around her, and they consoled each other. The writing was on the wall; Klandagi would never be a natural wild lion. Granny and me was heartbroken.

While hoeing the garden Granny and Cheatie heard the approach of Mario's clanging pots and pans accompanied by a favorite operatic aria. They both ran to make sure Klandagi was securely locked away in her pen.

The usual greetings were exchanged, and then Mario announced that the Hagenbeck-Wallace Circus was coming to Millerton. Mario's uniquely European accent was a little hard to understand. He was accustomed to being asked to repeat what he had just said, so in this case he carefully enunciated, "Admission costs a dime so save your money. Now, down to business, I need to buy some laying hens. Folks hereabout have been losing chickens, some kind of predator. Say, about 6 if you have them to spare." Mattie spoke up and said, "A critter has killed several of our chickens too, and we need to replace them; got none to spare." Then Mattie yelled for Ethyl and Cheatie to go to the garden and pull some carrots, radishes, and turnip greens to barter for a couple of items. Mattie traded 3 jars of wild honey for a two gallon can of kerosene. The garden produce was exchanged for a bag of flour and a small bag of cane sugar. Granny approached Mario about buying a can of snuff, all on the "QT" of course. Mario was a savvy bargainer and according to Granny, was known to cut us Wainwright women some slack. He had a big heart and felt badly about the poverty daddy's drinking problem brought on us. Once he said, "How you six womenfolk are able to survive so well amazes me."

Mario was all excited about the circus. "It is scheduled for next week, and we'll set up in an open field on the edge of Millerton." Mario described the circus in great detail and answered questions. We all admitted to him we'd never been to a circus before.

According to Mario, "There will be a main tent for most of the entertainment including the animal acts. Inside the biggest tent is a ring laid out on the ground and surrounded by bleachers for crowd seating. To the side of the center ring is a wire cage for the big cat show. There will be rigging for a trapeze act high up over the ring. The center ring is where the elephants, trick riders on horseback, dogs, and lots of clowns doing all kind of pranks perform. Beside the big tent will be a row of booths all lined up next to the road." Mario described freak shows, games of chance, and a boxing arena. According to Mario, a young man named Clyde Beatty would be performing in the cage with lions and tigers."

I asked Mario about photographing me with Klandagi and he agreed. The picture turned out to be a good likeness of the two of us. I was sitting on a log with Klandagi standing with her paws in my lap and rubbing her head against my extended arm. He claimed he just happened to be having a sale on photography and only charged me a dime the exact amount of money I had at the time.

When something big like a circus came along, not even we Wainwrights could resist seeing the spectacle. Daddy's face lit up and he said, "I reckon we all orta go, might be fun."

Before daylight on circus day Daddy harnessed the mule to the wagon, and the whole family piled in. We kids each had a dime tucked into a pocket. Our impatience with the long wagon ride was a testament to the excitement we kids was feeling. We were all spiffed up and smelling good. I hated bathing in the galvanized tub inside the house and took my bar of soap to the spring. Birth order prevailed in determining the order of bathing and I chose to suffer the cold creek water instead of bathing in the disgusting lukewarm soapy water that would leave me with soap scum on my skin and feeling dirtier than before the bath.

Clean and modestly attired was good enough for me. I dressed up as Cheatiebo the Woman Warrior outfit. That way nobody would git me mixed up with any other kid. I was all decked out in my turban, the newest pair of fringed coveralls and my handmade moccasins. Momma and Granny looked at each other and winked, but said nothing when they saw what I planned to wear. They reckoned it was alright for me to be me. Annie Mae and Ethel were mortified and wanted to avoid being identified with me. This shunning fit into my plan perfectly. I had an idea and the family need not know until it was a done deal.

Daddy dropped us off near the entrance and went to park the wagon beside the nearby creek, so the mule could graze and drink from the water source. I noticed from a distance that folks were recognizing Daddy, and he stopped to greet them as he walked toward the Circus entrance. From his body language, the people were asking if he would be performing. He told them that he was not on the docket and did not have his fiddle with him, but he might borrow a fiddle or guitar. Daddy was always ready to rosin up the bow if enough folks were interested in cuttin' a rug. I was hoping there would be a shindig because that meant we would be staying until late. The showman in Daddy craved the limelight and organizing a spur of the moment square dance would keep him occupied while I took care of business. My plan was to convince the circus to take Klandagi but something unexpected happened that turned out even better. I struck out on my own as soon as I was inside the admission gate.

Right off the bat I come upon the boxing ring Mario told us about. It was an elevated platform with two ropes strung around it. I got there just in time. The crowd started yelling and cheering as soon as two men sprang over the ropes and started dancing around and throwing jabs at phantom opponents. Those boys were putting on a show; Mario had described it to a tee. The crowd was choosing sides, and money was changing hands so I figgered they was gambling.

The crowd was egging the two men on with shouts and jeers, and the whole bunch got real worked up. A third man was dancing around the platform trying to stay out of the way. The two doing the dancing around were hopping mad at each other. The man the crowd called the "Ref" had the two boxers meet and touch gloved hands and then he sent them to opposite corners.

As soon as a bell rang, I realized that it was a contest staged for the entertainment of the audience who appeared to be enjoying the awful scene. I couldn't figure out why the fighters were willing to git beat up like that for the pleasure of a pack of bloodthirsty gamblers. Right away one of the fighters was knocked out or maybe dead and was carted off on a stretcher. He looked dead or close to it. The ref held up the winner's hand and walked him around the arena a few times. Then the next contestants jumped into the ring and began springing around the arena. They were doing that same dance routine while striking out at the space in front of them. The taller of the two, a black man, entered the ring with a huge snake around his shoulders. Later I found out it was a boa constrictor. Upon a signal from the "Ref" the contestants, that's what Mario called them, met center ring and touched gloved hands just like the previous pair."

While the two men stood touching gloves, the serpent hissed and struck at the other fighter. When the man dodged the darting head, he lost his balance, stumbled backwards, and fell flat on his back. The raucous fans roared with delight. I used my elbows to gradually edge closer to the front until I stood right next to ring. I was spell bound and watched as the black man's trainer took the boa from the ring, and then the bell sounded. The meaner black fighter was bigger, but the other fighter was real good at dancing around and dodging punches.

The audience was mostly pulling for the white underdog. The tricky white man would bounce off the ropes and whirl around to come from a new direction, flicking his gloved hands with lightning speed to land his punches that should have hurt. But the black fighter shuffled around the ring in pursuit of the dancer. The blows of the smaller man seemed to have no effect, and the black man just stood his ground and kept advancing. The snake man missed a couple of blows and then landed one to the nose of the dancing fighter. The punch caused the man to stagger but he was able to continue his in and out dancing. Then in a split second the Black fighter got the opening he was waiting for; it was lights out for the Dandy Boxer. The Ref bent over the flattened man and started counting aloud. When the unconscious man failed to stand up, the frenzied crowd went crazy with about as many boos as cheers. The excited audience continued cheering as the black man preened for the crowd, posing and flexing his massive muscles. Then it was time for the Ref to raise his right hand and parade him around the arena. The handler made a great show of handing the serpent back to the black man before he left the arena.

The loser was able to rise to a sitting position but had rubbery legs and needed help leaving the arena. I had seen enough and decided to move on. I had trouble shoving my way through the milling circus goers, and I ducked behind a shed to find a short cut over to the big tent. I just happened onto the poor battered fighter that was knocked out; he was sitting on a chair at the entrance to a small tent. I decided to have a few words with him.

The man, with one eye swollen shut, asked, "Well, who do we have here?"

I said, "That was some kind of show you fellars put on; ain't ever seen nothing like it. How come you are a boxer?"

The man responded by saying, "Money, it pays right good win or lose, more if you win."

I said "Oh now I understand. My name is Cheatiebo." The man asked, "Cheatiebo, what kind of name is that for a purty little girl like you?" I told him, "Cheatiebo means sweetheart in Tsalagii Indian, my Momma is part Injun. What's your name?"

While they spoke Cheatie was noticing the man's deformed ears. She asked, "What's wrong with your ears?"

The fighter grinned showing some missing teeth and answered, "Ain't you ever seen cauliflower ears b'fore? All us fighters get them sooner or later, comes from being hit on the ears. They don't hurt or nothing."

I changed the subject and asked, "You know any fighter that is looking for a mascot to take into the ring?"

The man looked surprised and asked, "You got one?"

Cheatie said, "Yep, sure do, got a puma cub. Her name is Klandagi, and she is almost a year old. She is getting into trouble out at our place, and I am looking for a good home for her. She needs a strong man that can control her. I found her almost dead after hunters killed her mother. She was just a few days old, bout this big, so I took her for my secret pet and nursed her back to health on goat milk and raw eggs, kept her hid in a little cave that I boarded up. A few days ago, Klandagi got excited and drug me through the brambles while I was trying to take her on a walk. My daddy is threatening to shoot her. Might you be interested in taking her to train for a mascot? You could be famous or uh more famous."

The boxer was rubbing his chin and had his head tilted to the side. I said, "Just picture how the crowd will react when you bring Klandagi into the arena with you. She is scarier than any ole snake. I can just see a picture of you on the front page of the Tulsa Tribune."

The boxer asked, "Where's your daddy, I just might have a talk with him. I have been looking for a mascot. Right now, I couldn't pay much, but I could send you the rest in a few months."

I hadn't even thought of getting money for Klandagi, but I liked the idea. I asked the man for his name again since he didn't say when I asked before.

He replied by asking, "My fighting name or my real name?"

I said, "Both," and he grinned.

He said, "I bet you don't take no crap off anybody. I am Billy McQuiston, but, in the ring, I am "The Fighting Irishman.""

I said, "Glad to meet you Mr. Irishman."

The Irishman shook his head and said, "Just call me Billy."

Cheatie spent a few minutes visiting with Billy. "Sir, I mean Billy, my daddy drinks a lot, and if you give him the money, he will spend ever last penny on git'n drunk. Since I rescued the cub and did all the work, I figure you should give me the money. Please keep quiet about paying me for Klandagi. My Momma is having a hard time of it, and I will use most of the money to help my family."

Billy laughed and answered, "Ah, I see, okay, I agree, we have a deal." Right then and there Billy handed Cheatie a $10.00 gold piece. He said, "I'm ah purty good judge of people, and I can tell you're an honest kid, so I'm gonna pay down on the lion so you don't sell her to anybody else." Cheatie had never held a gold coin in her hand before and just stood looking at the coin wondering if it was a dream. She was speechless so long that Billy concluded the child was demanding more gold and added a second gold piece to her outstretched palm. Then Billy said, "I need you to keep this transaction under your hat if you know what I mean. Don't want to ruin the surprise. In a month I should be able to come up with two more $10.00 gold pieces to make

4 in total. Will that be enough, I sure hope so? Now how do I find where you live?"

Cheatie put her hands on her hips and said, "Make that five total and we have a deal."

"Okay Little Cheatiebo, $50.00 dollars in gold is the price I am willing to pay. How about we shake hands on the deal."

"Sure." We sealed the deal with a warm handshake. Then I said, "I'm home most all the time." Billy nodded and suggested, "How about I follow you home tonight? I will camp out at your place and get some lessons on handling the cub before I take her? She will need to get used to me."

Cheatie answered, "That's for sure, she is suspicious of strangers. Have your gear packed in your wagon, and I will have Daddy drive by when we leave. I just might ride along with you if you don't mind. I could be giving you some pointers along the way. I think Daddy will be playing for a square dance later tonight, and if you come by, I will introduce you to him and Momma. We can tell them you are taking the lion off our hands without tellin' the details." The two of them winked at each other.

Cheatie strolled the carnival grounds, taking in the sights and sounds around the booths of games and side shows. She spotted Ethel and Annie Mae and walked in their direction. They both did an about face pretending that they didn't know her. I thought, *fine with me, I'm having more fun by myself.* The grounds were thick with milling people. Over the background noise, I heard the sound of a megaphone announcing the next showing of the wild animal act only ten minutes away, so I got in line. Mario had mentioned Clyde Beatty's big cat show and how he was the greatest animal trainer in the world. The admission was a nickel, and that is just what I had left other than the gold coins.

Fear of losing the coins caused me to clutch them tightly in my hand deep in a pocket of my coveralls. Mario had told us about pock-pickets or was pick-pockets, folks that distract you and then put their hand in your pocket? In the back of my mind, I was already thinking how I would spend the money. I just might buy me a horse and saddle. And to help I could buy everyone a pair of shoes and a winter coat. After that we could stock in a nice supply of staples and some bolts of cloth. It will be like the best Christmas ever. Then I decided to take

Granny's wisdom on such things and secretly keep some back for a rainy day.

The Clyde Beatty Show literally took Cheatie's breath away. Beatty performed with three huge Siberian tigers and three African lions, just as big. He had them jumping through burning rings, walking on hind feet, and sitting atop stools all in a row. He got them to do the tricks armed with just a whip and a chair. It looked like he had a gun hidden under his belt, but it was hard to tell for sure. He handled the cats very carefully, obviously aware that the animals were dangerous and could get out of control at any moment. Of course, that made the show even more exciting.

Willie Joe offered the circus boss a cut of the hat money collected if he could hold a square dance in front of the boxing arena at closing time. The raised arena became the stage, and as usual he put on a spectacular show that started with square dancing. Then he borrowed a guitar from one of the circus employees and sang several ballads that got folks waltzing and two stepping in a big circle.

The donations came up light. It appeared that most folks had broken their budget on the circus attractions. Of course, there were some willing to dig a little deeper to buy the illegal home brew being sold by some enterprising bootlegger out behind a shed. As the evening progressed, the audience members that were partaking of the libation were a rowdy bunch without the slightest inclination to leave the merry making. Early on Mattie and the kids had joined in the dancing but soon retreated to a wooden bench fifty yards from the dancing. About midnight when some of the dancers were snokkered out of their minds, Willie Joe left the stage for a quick break. On the way to the privy, he scooped the meager number of coins from the hat and disappeared with the expensive guitar.

After more than an hour he still had not returned. Folks started leaving, and Mattie and the girls searched for Willie Joe for the next hour before giving up. Mattie didn't know where the wagon and horse was parked. Billy came over and asked when they would be leaving. When Mattie told him that Willie Joe had disappeared, and they would have to search for the wagon, Billy offered to help. He loaded the family into his wagon and drove his team around until the wagon was found.

The seemingly endless wagon ride home represented hours of vexation; poor Mattie was exhausted and downright angry. She worried that Willie Joe had gone and got his-self robbed or even killed. How dare he just take the hat money and leave his family, people he's supposed to love and care about, standing all alone late at night far from home, not knowing what to do.

The circus boss had witnessed how Willie Joe skipped out on sharing the take, ran off with the guitar, and left his family standing flat-footed and stranded. He couldn't bring himself to blame the man's wife when she was so obviously a victim and emotionally devastated. The earring wearing and bearded muscle man that owned the guitar was the typical carnie. When he realized he had been snookered, he threatened to call in the sheriff, but because of the illegal whiskey being sold and more than a few folks too drunk to walk, sprawling about, he vowed to hunt down the guitar thief without involving law enforcement, come hell or high-water.

Mattie was thinking that somewhere along life's pathway Willie Joe had been stripped of his humanity. He had violated his conscience for too long leaving him "busted, disgusted, and not to be trusted." A song writer named Harlan Howard penned the following words that fit Willie Joe like a glove. "—a lying, cheating, cold dead beating, two-timing, double dealing, mean and mistreating loving heart."

Both wagons arrived back at the Wainwright home well after daybreak. Cheatie took Billy to meet Klandagi and showed him how she fed the cub. Before turning in for some rest, she suggested a camping spot for his tent. "Billy, feel free to use the outhouse and draw all the water you need." The following day Billy confessed that he did have the money to pay the other thirty dollars and handed over three additional shiny coins.

Mattie gave Delia a brief explanation of Willie Joe's betrayal while she prepared toast and coffee for her exhausted and heart sick daughter. Delia, who had opted to stay home with Stella Ruth and Klondagi, sent Annie Mae and Ethel to do chores while she tucked Mattie into bed. The two girls had slept in the bed of the wagon on the trip home, so they were sent to do their chores away from the cabin so Mattie could rest.

Staying in touch with regional or national events was hard in those days, and Cheatie lost all track of Billy McQuiston and Klondagi. There would always be a special place in her heart for memories of Klondagi.

The trip to the circus was the beginning of a cavernous rift in the already precarious relationship between Mattie and Willie Joe. It was at least two months before Willie Joe was allowed to set foot in the house. Mattie Harriet was one mad Cherokee; Willie Joe had finally managed to exceed her tolerance. After years of abuse Mattie was fed up. He would have to earn his place back into the family, or he could just be on his way.

After the circus debacle Willie Joe was whereabouts unknown. Millerton and the surrounding area was hostile territory. He had a cadre of men ready to rough him up or worse, so he had to take a sabbatical from show biz. After months of not a word from him, Mattie found Willie Joe bedded down in the barn. He was suffering from a high fever and showing symptoms of influenza. Mattie and Delia both thought he was in danger of dying and took pity on him. He was so glad to be back home it looked like he might turn over a new leaf and correct his waywardness. He did not dare show his face in Millerton, so the temptations were few.

Eventually his baser urges took control, and Willie Joe went back to his old lifestyle of bingeing and carousing. The trouble with Willie Joe came to a climax when he showed up crazy drunk out of his mind after being gone for months. It was after midnight when he forced his way into the house and tried to crawl into bed with Mattie. She was having none of it. She barred him from the bed and told him to leave. That is when he slapped Mattie across the face so hard, she fell back on the bed. When he tried to lie down, Mattie drew up her feet and kicked him in the abdomen hard enough to wind him. He glared at Mattie and prepared to teach her a lesson. Annie Mae had sneaked up on him from behind and hit him over the head with the big iron skillet. He fell to the floor like a sack of potatoes. Annie Mae looked at him and concluded that he was dead. She started screaming, "I killed daddy, look, he's dead!" Mattie and Delia hovered over Willie Joe and began to sob in the most mournful and hopeless manner. Cheatie and Ethel clung to each other and wept. Delia come to herself and knelt to see if he was breathing.

Granny's examination took what seemed to be an eternity. She raised her head and yelled over the loud crying, "Quiet, I cain't hear." She put her head back to his chest and listened. Then she moved her ear to his nose to detect breathing. She looked up and said, "I thought he was a goner, but he is breathing, and his heart is beating regular.

That don't mean he is out of the woods. She looked at Annie Mae with a raised brow and said, "Iron skillets can do a lot of damage to a human skull." Willie Joe groaned and tried to sit up but fell back in a swoon, and they all just stood and stared at him.

No one knew what to do. They were all standing around him, looking at one and then the other, with terrified looks on their faces. Then something happened so bizarre it made them laugh for an instant, halting the tears flowing down their cheeks. Three-year-old Stella Ruth had awakened and was watching unnoticed. The toddler brazenly walked up to Willie Joe and kicked him on the thigh and screeched in her high little voice, "No more hittin' my Momma! You ain't my Poppa no more." And when she recoiled to land another kick, Granny stopped her.

The confusion of the scene created a dichotomy of emotional responses: weeping and laughing, fear and courage, guilt and innocence, and last of all passivity and aggression. Still smiling from Stella Ruth's antics, Mattie and Delia rolled Willie Joe onto a blanket and drug him to the other side of the room and covered him up. Granny said, "I think he will be okay unless he has a cracked skull. All we can do is wait and hope he gets better. There's not much bleeding, so let's leave him be. He can clean up when he's awake. Back to bed girls and be sure and thank the Good Lord that he is alive. Good night."

Mattie pulled Annie Mae into bed with her and put her arms around her in a most tender manner. When she went to kiss Annie Mae's forehead, she was reminded that she had a busted lip. Mattie whispered, "There now my little Annie Mae, it's gonna be okay, thank you for coming to my rescue; here's to stickin' up for each other. I'll never forget what you done. Now try to get some sleep, it will be daylight before long."

Cheatie got to thinking about how unpredictable her Poppa could be, and after a few minutes she got out of bed and took some clothesline and tied Willie Joes' hands together behind his back. Then she tied his feet together too. When she looked up Granny and Mattie were both watching and nodded their approval. By daybreak Willie Joe was awake and trying to get out of the bindings. Cheatie got Ethyl to help her, and they moved him to the porch before untying him. Cheatie whispered, "Ethyl bring Poppa a glass of water and a wet cloth for cleaning up." After helping Willie Joe wash the blood and crud off his face and hands, she said, "A bad thing happened here last night."

Willie Joe shook his head and asked, "What are you talkin' about? I have a turble headache, and I don't remember getting home. Tell me what happened?"

Cheatie said, "Poppa, you were drunk and started hitting Momma; for the last time, mind you! The last time, got that? Here, I packed you some food and the few things of yours that is here. I reckon you should go be with those friends you seem to like so much whoever they are. You can't live here no more. We all know you ain't ever gonna change. Goodbye Poppa and I will try to come and see you in town sometime if I can find you."

Willie Joe's by-line had just added a second line to *Busted, Disgusted and Not to be Trusted*:

"Defiled, Exiled, No Longer Domiciled"

Willie Joe is believed to have contracted a venereal disease during the roaring twenties though it was never officially documented. Thankfully, because of the separation, Mattie did not contract the disease. Willie Joe spent the rest of his life suffering the effects of a painful strain of what was at the time called "The French Disease." Since treatment with penicillin was not available until years later, he would necessarily have received instillations of poisonous heavy metals that hastened his decline into ill health. During Willie Joe's declining years, Mattie, motivated by compassion, allowed him to take shelter in the family home, but with the status of a boarder required to pay rent and contingent upon good behavior.

Christmas that year would be like none other. Cheatie found an opportunity to speak with Mario and swore him to secrecy. "Mario, what I am about to tell you must be our secret, okay? I had been caring for an orphan lion cub for almost a year."

Mario said wait, "What, did you say you been caring for a lion, a real mountain lion?"

"I have, but I should of knowed she would git too big and dangerous, so I decided to find her a home at the circus. I asked one of the boxer fellows if he would take her, and he thought I wanted to sell her. I figured we could use the money, so I went along with it all. He needs publicity and wants a mascot to take into the ring at the start of each fight. He paid me in cash, and I want to use most of the money to help our family. Can you help me? If I give you a list, will you deliver the goods on Christmas Eve and never reveal who paid for the things?"

Mario was suddenly smiling from ear to ear and said, "Good for you, of course I will help out any way I can."

Before handing Mario the list, I made sure no one was watching. "Add it all up so I don't spend more than I have to pay with. You must say the food and presents are all from St. Nickolas. Do you think you can get the things on the list by Christmas Eve? I sure hope so."

Mario was thinking about how happy the goods would make Cheatie's family while anticipating the profit he would make from such a large order. "My dear little Cheatie, even if I have to go all the way to Texarkana, I will do my best to fill your list."

Mario read the list aloud with Cheatie listening: a bushel of navel oranges, a box of chocolate bars, and mesh bag of Brazil nuts. Mario was instructed to drop off a new harmonica with a neck stand for Willie Joe at the Millerton post office. Momma and Granny both got a pair of shoes and a big jar of rose scented glycerin and lanolin skin cream. A pair of magnifying spectacles for Momma and for Granny a fancy varnished humidor with at least a year's supply of snuff. Annie Mae and Ethel each got matching water-repellant winter coats with quilted lining and galoshes and for Stella Ruth, a zippered snowsuit with a matching cap, high top shoes large enough to allow for growth and a big Raggedy Ann Doll.

Cheatie got herself the same coat and galoshes only in a different color from Annie Mae and Ethel's coats. The rest of the Christmas surprises were practical things like a box of shot-gun shells, three bolts of fine cotton cloth, a big box of yarn in several colors, a new frog gig, three bags of flour, two bags of sugar, a tin of coffee, and two dozen mature Rhode Island Red laying hens. She also bought two five-gallon cans of kerosene and a case of Mason canning jars with extra lids. There was a carton full of selected garden seeds. In the box with the small stuff were some giant spools of heavy-duty sewing thread, a paper of needles, and a nice pair of scissors. With Mario's help a neighbor was commissioned to deliver four cords of seasoned and split firewood, all neatly stacked in the shed the day after Christmas.

Finally, Christmas Eve arrived. Immediately upon arrival the bombastic Mario unloaded a huge turkey hen in a coop, a wrapped sugar-cured ham, several tins of canned cranberries, and a large bag each of potatoes and onions. Mattie and Delia ran out of the house to meet the tinker and stopped frozen with surprise. Mattie said, "Wait, Mario, we cain't afford all of this food. Put it back before the girls see it."

Mario threw back his head and roared with laughter and said, "Settle down Miz. Mattie, the things I am delivering to you is already paid for. I believe it is from someone named St. Nickolas. That is all I'm allowed to tell you, so just smile and be thankful! Ha, ha, ha!" Later out behind Mario's wagon Cheatie settled the bill that turned out to be more than she counted on. She would be foregoing the saddle horse, but she didn't mind that much. Cheatie still had two silver dollars to hide away for a rainy day. Cheatie put on an award-winning performance of being totally surprised, and no one suspected her of being the benefactor.

Forever after when Cheatie heard someone say that it was more blessed to give than receive she could testify to the truth of the statement, after all such wisdom came straight from the mind of God. Cheatie was so thrilled over providing for her family she had trouble sleeping at night for a few days. The same conversation was repeated over and over as to who St. Nicholas really was. Of course, Stella Ruth didn't have a problem with St. Nick being the source of the presents.

Mario even had a gift for the Wainwrights, a basket of three six-week-old kittens, white with black markings, from a family of superb mousers. Unbeknownst to Cheatie, Mario kept a smaller than normal profit from the grand total. He had never known people that deserved help more than Mattie and her brood.

Mattie called Mario aside and said, "Mario, you are staying for the night and dinner tomorrow and we ain't takin' no for an answer so put your stock in the corral and feel at home." Mario gladly accepted the invitation and made himself helpful by killing and dressing out the turkey and peeling a big pot of potatoes. He slept in his home on wheels but rose bright and early on Christmas morning ready to celebrate. It was turning out to be a very special occasion for him too. He would have been alone at the camp since Gypsies do not recognize December 25th as a holiday. Having come from Eastern Europe, Christmas day there was celebrated on January 7th, the date recognized by the Greek Orthodox Church.

On Christmas morning Mario stood by the Christmas tree and sang two Christmas songs. The first was, "God Rest Ye Merry Gentlemen" and then gave an operatic rendition of the ancient 17th

century French carol, "Bring a Candle Jeannette, Isabella" in English
and then in French.

God rest ye merry, gentlemen
Let nothing you dismay
Remember, Christ, our Savior
Was born on Christmas day
To save us all from Satan's power
When we were gone astray
O tidings of comfort and joy,
Comfort and joy
O tidings of comfort and joy.

Jeannette Isabella
"Bring a torch, Jeannette, Isabella!

Bring a torch to the cradle, run!
It is Jesus, good folk of the village
Christ is born and Mary's calling:
Ah! Ah! beautiful is the Mother
Ah! Ah! beautiful is her Son!"
Un flambeau, Jeannette, Isabelle
Un flambeau, courons au berceau.
C'est Jésus, bonnes gens du hameau,
Le Christ est né, Marie appelle
Ah! Ah! Que la mère est belle,
Ah! Ah! Que l'Enfant est beau.

Chapter 12

GOLD FEVER

The subject of the crowded living arrangement came up while Wathena and Patrick were sitting arm in arm by a fire. Living with Falls-From-Heaven and his extended family was stifling to Patrick. As newlyweds they needed privacy. Patrick spoke at length about his dream of establishing a farm nearby. He asked Wathena, "Are we required to ask permission before choosing a plot of land?"

Wathena said, "Yes, you must. I'll ask the council, but they will likely say no. Stands-Alone will do all in his power to prevent such a departure from tradition." Wathena was conflicted between honoring tradition and supporting Patrick.

Patrick had a frown on his normally happy face. He explained, "We white people prefer to have our own dwelling, especially as newlyweds."

Patrick convinced Wathena that their new dwelling would have the best of both worlds. They could combine European with the Tsalagii culture. "Patrick, I see your dream, and it sounds wonderful. We can ask but if the elders refuse us, we will be forced to move away from the Thunder Clan and live independently. Leaving the Clan is not a good choice for me; I feel an obligation to my people."

"My lovely Wathena, I want us to have the best of both worlds. Can we at least try?"

It was October when Wathena approached the tribal counsel and requested an audience to discuss what she and Patrick had planned for their future. Within a few days the council notified Patrick and Wathena that they should come to the council hut to plead their case for an independent dwelling away from the village. After tedious pauses for passing the pipe, and a slow introduction to the reason for the meeting, Wathena was asked to state her request. She answered with, "Patrick will tell you of his plan."

Patrick was not expecting to be the spokesman. He stood and called each of the elders by name in a tone that was mindful of their status. He felt unusually nervous with so much riding on this meeting. Patrick looked at Wathena and took heart from the confident smile she flashed him. "Please hear of my vision. I figure to provide for a wife and family by farming. That has always been my dream. I ask permission to choose some land and build a log cabin and barn. I will grow tobacco, maize, and vegetables to sell to travelers. The food will be shared with the clan. I will breed horses and cattle, chickens and pigs. The people of the Thunder Clan would always be welcome as guests. Then Patrick thanked the committee for hearing his request and sat down. Patrick and Wathena were asked to leave the hut and return when white smoke came from the vent.

After a very long hour white smoke appeared above the mud hut, and they reentered. They seated themselves on the floor, cross legged as before. They both kept their eyes lowered and waited for the pipe to make the rounds. Falls-From-Heaven stood and addressed Wathena and Patrick directly. His pronouncement was brief, "The vote was not unanimous, and your request is being granted on a temporary basis. My daughter, as your Father I have been appointed to help you select a site for your farm that will not disturb game migration or disrupt water ways. The Council has spoken." All in attendance rose and filed out of the structure without further comment. Patrick tried to thank the elders, but they ignored his overtures. He was feeling rebuffed, as though he had committed a breach of trust. Patrick took Wathena by the hand and walked to a secluded place on the stream to discuss what had just happened. Only Stands-Alone had voted no. He was standing in plain view and appeared to be in a trance. He was shaking a gourd and chanting in a loud and tormented voice, "Bad medicine, very bad medicine, evil is coming, bad medicine!"

Early the following morning Falls-From-Heaven went with Wathena and Patrick to choose a site for a farm. A few miles to the north-west of the Thunder Clan's village, Patrick found the perfect setting. The place had everything for a homestead: abundant timber, year around spring fed stream, rich loamy soil, a shallow water table, and flood fertilized meadows. Patrick was eager to start clearing the land, but initially constructed a temporary shelter so that the two of them would not lose time walking back to the village each night. Most nights, and in spite of his fatigue, Patrick's excitement made it hard for him to fall asleep. He would work so hard that Wathena had to use her feminine charms to entice him to take a break. It was obvious to Wathena that Patrick needed help. She would ask Uncle.

Soon after the request for workers was made, four of the young warriors that had graduated with Patrick appeared and camped out on the farm. They indicated they would be there as long as Patrick needed them. They helped Patrick fell the trees and notch and stack the logs for the log cabin. Patrick wanted a sturdy log cabin home, one that he could be proud to show Rory if he ever came for a visit. Patrick's youthfulness and his physical conditioning enabled him to work the long hours day after day necessary to establish a working farm in an amazingly short period of time.

Stands-Alone remained firm in his opposition to a European style farm house on tribal grounds. He pleaded with the elders to rescind the decision. He was certain that a farm would anger the gods and bring tragedy on the whole clan. The spirits had brought misfortunate for lesser violations. A few of the more traditional members of the Thunder People took the warnings seriously, but most discounted Stand Alone's prophecy as the murmurings of a foolish old man. Wathena did not dismiss the prophecies of Stands-Alone, but the bond she shared with Patrick muted her foreboding.

Patrick told Wathena, "There are no gods other than the one true God, Creator of the Universe, called Jehovah, Yahweh, or Elohim. This God that can be everywhere at once, knows the thoughts and intents of all men, and is able to control events as He chooses. The God of the Bible loves all mankind the same whether Indian, or European, or Negro."

Patrick's imaginings for a life of adventure had become reality. But the atmosphere had changed, permanently. He could not escape the feeling that everything had been going too well. Every aspect of his existence with the Thunder People had made him feel welcome until the split decision over the farm. A cooling, and distancing took place. During the first year after Patrick and Wathena moved to the farm, they gradually drew apart from the clan. Patrick had a feeling of approaching doom. Why was he waiting for something catastrophic to happen? He blamed "Old Spider." He surprised himself to dredge up the term of derision for the old man. With all of his silly carrying-on, the Shaman had infected the previously happy village. He sensed a sadness in Wathena, but he did not how to reassure her. He could only hope the moroseness would pass.

As soon as one project was finished, Patrick would immediately launch the next. He became a regular at Oscar Jackson's trading post. That was his source for tools, materials, and anything that could not be produced on site.

Once her routine chores of cooking, wood gathering, and tending to her garden were completed Wathena worked beside Patrick, shoulder to shoulder. The first 40 acres grew to 80. The two-room log cabin with a loft and front and back covered porches was just perfect, the home Patrick had always dreamt of. Once the house was habitable a barn and several sheds were constructed of logs. His corn and tobacco yields were exceptional. He planted a fruit orchard and helped Wathena with her vegetable garden. He had located the garden in a low place that could be irrigated. Some of the produce was sold at the Jackson Trading Post to pay for building supplies and staples. The constant stream of wagon trains was eager to purchase eggs, butter, and cheese as well as potatoes, onion, and carrots.

Patrick's farm had some failures but overall was producing a good harvest by the end of the second year. He and Wathena took great joy in providing a large portion of their bounty to the Thunder Clan people. Patrick bartered for farm animals. Within a few short months he had acquired a milk cow, a boar and sow, and two dozen laying hens with a rooster. He traded for a nice one-horse buggy and a fine saddle horse. He was soon able to bring in two Mules for plowing and half a dozen beef cattle. There were always tree stumps to be burned or cross fencing to stack. Patrick diverted a small spring fed tributary from the ridge top into a pipe for irrigating the orchard. Wathena noticed the signs of overwork in Patrick. It was as if he was driven to accomplish more than his human strength allowed. His health was suffering.

Patrick's thoughts went back to his childhood on the farm. How he would benefit from his father's agricultural knowledge. Thinking of growing up made him yearn for Rory that much more. Patrick was experiencing a form of separation anxiety unique to identical twins, but he chose to deal with his pain privately. If, and when Rory came for a visit, he would let Wathena be surprised. As young boys, even their parents found it difficult to tell them apart. Patrick had been scheming to convince Rory to come west and settle nearby.

Patrick spent hours making the case in a detailed letter. The letter was sent east by travelers passing by Jackson's Trading Post. As the new federal government of the United States matured, it would establish and oversee a postal service but that would take time. Patrick had no way of knowing if his letter reached Rory.

Patrick thanked God every day for Wathena. Their relationship grew deeper with each passing month. Wathena became increasingly curious about Patrick's practice of kneeling and praying. "Tell me more about your God. What does he look like, where does he live?"

It was the perfect opening for Patrick to teach Wathena about the God of the Bible. "I'm glad you are asking. I will begin a detailed study, but for now I will answer your question." A non-committal Wathena listened intently and drew parallels with her vision of the Creator. Patrick said, "This is difficult to understand at first, but the God Head is actually three separate beings named Father or Yahweh, second, the Son, also known as Immanuel or the Word, and the third divine person is the Spirit, or the Comforter. They are all three God, they dwell outside of time and space, are all knowing, and tolerate no other gods. They have always existed and will have no end. We are their creation, and they love each of us and want us to spend eternity with them after this life."

Patrick had taken the buckboard to the Trading Post with a list to fill. It was serendipitous when Patrick discovered a Robert Aitken Bible for sale. There, on a shelf with a few other books was one copy of the Bible. He quickly placed it among his other purchases on the counter. He could hardly contain his excitement at such a find, and at a good price. Patrick was told that the King's prohibition against printing Bibles was no longer in force.

The printing business sprang up in the newly established United States of America with only one or two printing presses at first. One of the first acts of the newly seated government under George Washington and the Continental Congress had been to commission Robert Aitken to begin printing Bibles. The printing presses of Robert Aitken's day were tedious and slow to operate but turned out very good books. It is believed that George Washington had planned to award a copy of the Aitken Bible to each member of the Continental Army upon demobilization, but sadly the printing process wasn't completed in time. Patrick's Aitken Bible made it possible for him to reestablish the family tradition of daily Bible reading.

On a subsequent trip to Jackson's Landing for supplies, Patrick saw a man trying to sell two Negro slave families. Patrick observed the spectacle for a few minutes and identified the slave owner as a brutal man. The slaves were shaking with fright. As he hawked the two families, he indicated that they could be purchased together or separately. Slave ownership had always been repugnant to Patrick. While he looked on, the master took a whip to one of the women for resisting his order to undress. Next, the owner ordered that the entire group of slaves remove their clothing. Forced to stand naked, he could see that they suffered from malnourishment and wore the marks of the whip, even the children. The Negroes were terrified almost to the point of dementia. A great feeling of indignation swept over Patrick. He shouted to the owner, "Sir, what is your best price for the six Negroes?" The man answered, "I'm about to hold an auction, and you're welcome to join in."

An auctioneer showed up and began the sale by showing the two families. Patrick was shocked at the opening price of $800.00 paseos, but upped bid to $850.00. The haggling went back and forth a couple of times. One by one the other bidders fell away. Patrick asked the auctioneer if the slaves spoke English and was assured that they did. Patrick shouted for the master to allow the shivering blacks to dress and in obvious disgust pretended to walk away. The owner responded by rushing to Patrick and asking what he would be willing to pay. Patrick halved the eight hundred to $400.00, and the tyrant said, "sold!" Patrick paid the slave owner and took the trembling people behind an outbuilding. He told them to sit on the ground. He asked if they understand English, and they nodded yes. Then he softly spoke to them so that others could not hear. He said, "Stay here while I fetch food and blankets at the store. Sorry for your mistreatment, with me you will be treated well, no whipping, do you understand?" Big eyed the poor people nodded in agreement. Patrick hurried to purchase a large bag of deer jerky, several loaves of sour-dough bread, a bushel of apples, and a keg of apple cider. He handed each person a blanket for their shoulders. He spread the food on a blanket before the people and offered a brief prayer. Patrick took a seat on the blanket near the Negro children, pointed at his chest and said, "Patrick." He started handing them jerky, bread, an apple. He stopped. The terrified children dodged and flinched with each gesture in their direction. Patrick picked up the youngest, a toddler, and hugged it. He kissed the child on top of its head and encouraged him to eat a thin slice of apple. The rest of the children smiled and held out their hands for some of the apple. During the meal Patrick noticed the many scars from past whippings, some not fully healed. Patrick could not escape the notion that God, through His providence, had arranged this opportunity to rescue these unfortunate people.

Patrick noticed that he was being watched and decided to depart without completing his trading mission. Since Patrick had ridden astride bringing only one pack animal, he loaded the two women and their smallest child on the two horses and walked alongside the men. Patrick was gratified that half of the bushel of apples had been eaten and very little of the other food remained. As they left the trading post, Patrick saw Oscar Jackson watching his departure. He waved to Oscar and shouted that he would be back in a few days. Patrick admitted to himself that he had acted impulsively but was convinced that it was the right thing to do.

Right away the two Negro families healed both physically and emotionally. Patrick earned their trust, loyalty, and eventually their true brotherly love. Patrick was pleasantly surprised when he realized that the two black men were knowledgeable farmers and would provide more than mere manual labor.

During their second year of marriage, a daughter was born to Wathena and Patrick. Parenthood transformed the young honeymooners just as it has millions of parents through times eternal. As soon as they held the child in their arms, their world drastically changed. A daunting sense of responsibility came over them and rearranged their priorities. They named the girl Little Doe and found indescribable delight in the nurturing process.

Patrick had experienced the death of his parents, poverty, and some close calls on his life. He was conditioned to expect life's ups and downs. After his adoption into the Thunder Clan, Patrick's existence exceeded his most fanciful dreams. When he and Wathena asked permission to create a European style farm on tribal grounds, Patrick's relationship with the Thunder Clan suddenly changed. He intuitively sensed that he had disappointed the elders by rejecting their culture. His perceived lack of gratitude for being adopted insulted them. He had taken from them their pride, Wathena the Ye Ho-Nawa. As a result, both he and Wathena were suppressing a sense of foreboding about the future.

Wathena and the two African women, Sara and Lottie took great pride in their garden plot and orchard. They were teaching gardening skills to the four children. Patrick was schooling them in reading, writing, and arithmetic. Wathena was planning to teach the children the skill of wilderness survival and foraging for wild food in the future. That could come when they were a little older.

Fair minded, Patrick educated the black children alongside Little Doe. He had unknowingly violated statutory law that forbade educating slaves, not that it would have made a difference to him if he had known.

For the next five years the Larson family prospered. Little Doe was thriving, and with each passing day increasingly reflected the genetic stamp of both parents. She had her Father's fair skin and curly hair, but her hazel eyes, brunette hair, and delicate facial features were a miniature copy of Wathena.

True to his promise Patrick helped Wathena blend Indian household items with European style furnishings. There were shelves of books, comfortable upholstered furniture, and a spinning wheel. Cast Iron cooking vessels hung over the hearth, and pewter kitchen ware and porcelain dishes stored in a sideboard for setting the table in fine style. The cabin was decorated with beautiful Cherokee art. The interior was replete with shelving that held a collection of brightly colored clay pottery, various sizes and shapes of wooden drums, intricately woven wool blankets hung upon the walls, covered furniture and carpeted the wood flooring. Patrick's prized bear skin rug and rack of deer antlers hung over the fireplace, all symbols of the new life he had established with the Tsalagii.

Wathena, busy preparing a stew for the evening meal heard Patrick's excited calls coming from the field. She rushed to the porch and tried to prevent him from waking Little Doe from her nap, to no avail. As he sprang to the porch, he held out his broad, meaty hand

and placed a rock in her hand. It was heavy for its size, and as she looked closer, she saw that it was a shiny yellow color. "What is this?" she asked.

Bubbling with excitement, he said, "Don't you know, it's gold, real gold! I found it at the creek. It was just lying there among the pebbles. Look, isn't that a strange shape for a gold nugget, it looks like a crouching cat."

"Patrick, it does look like a cat, it's beautiful!"

Patrick grabbed Wathena around the waist, lifted her off her feet and spun her around yelling "Yahoo."

A squinty eyed Little Doe was holding out her arms to Patrick and said, "Daddy, me too, go round and round, me too?"

Patrick spun Little Doe around several times until she squealed with excitement. The child had an angelic laugh. Patrick said, "Wathena, wouldn't it make a pretty necklace? On the next trip to Jackson's Trading Outpost, I will order a gold chain so that you can wear it around your neck. I'm going back and look for more gold in the creek, come on, go with me." He yelled to the heavens, "We have gold in our creek!" Wathena had no appreciation for things like gold but managed to show excitement. The three of them headed for the creek.

Wathena's quick and curious mind helped her to adapt to Patrick's lifestyle. Her talent for imitating sounds helped her to mimic the intonation and cadence of the English language. By the time Little Doe could walk, Wathena had become fluent in English with hardly an accent. Patrick encouraged Wathena to read the books he had accumulated. Her vocabulary of English words grew at an astounding rate with each book. What had begun as an assignment and a chore became a self-motivated quest for knowledge.

Wathena learned to appreciate the household conveniences and comfortable furnishings. She accepted the changes her marriage brought, but underneath she was still a Tsalagii warrior with the mind-set and wilderness skills held at the ready.

Wathena, like many other indigenous women in Appalachia mastered cloth making. Yet others of her tribe, who were more traditional, followed the Shaman, preferring to live in the ancient ways. These differences caused a division of the Thunder People. The traditionalists decided to relocate to a more remote area. Taking great care to cover their tracks, Stands-Alone led the more shy and suspicious members of the Thunder People to a new location high into the Great Smoky Mountains. They were determined to forever conceal their location and live in isolation. The remaining Thunder Clan led by Falls-From-Heaven was reduced to a third of its original number.

The 1783 Treaty of Paris that ended hostilities with Britain was tentative and on-going friction that led to the War of 1812. Spain was contending for the Florida peninsula, and France was seeking to expand its imperial reach. Some of the southeastern tribes sided with the British, some with the Spanish, while the Tsalagii chose to be friendly with the American Colonies. Though both Presidents Washington and Jefferson initially sought to deal with the Tsalagii Nation fairly, the influx of land-hungry settlers, who flooded government offices, soon over-ran any support for protecting the land rights of the indigenous people. Hordes of white settlers flooded onto tribal grounds following the War of 1812, many of whom were cast-offs of eastern society. The treachery and violence of the opportunists devastated the Indian Nations and in an especially brutal way impacted the Cherokee Nation.

Patrick and Wathena were caught up in the whirlwind of events. A superstitious person might conclude that Patrick's farm and the cat shaped gold nugget had pronounced a curse upon the Larson family as well as the entire Thunder Clan. The waves of white immigrants were invincible and started forcibly homesteading Indian Ancestral Grounds that were presumably protected by treaty with Government Authorities. Patrick mistakenly assumed that being a White Man would protect his farm from encroachment. A second factor increased the jeopardy he fell under. Marriage to an Indian branded him as a "sqaw-man," a term of derision that described his diminished social status.

***

During the years between 1803 to 1811, Wathena, Patrick, and later Little Doe lived a happy and prosperous life. Still, both Patrick and Wathena had the sense that something was wrong, they were waiting for something to happen, but there was no reason for such anxiety. They were young, healthy, and enjoying blessings too numerous to name. With the help of the two Negro families, the farm's bounty was awesome. The revenue from the produce provided adequate funds to purchase building materials and some of the finer things in furnishings and implements. Because Patrick found the two black men dependable, he was comfortable with leaving the farm to take short trips to purchase supplies and barter goods. Little Doe had just turned seven when the little family went to visit the Thunder Clan. They were there for a wedding and ceremonial dance.

The timing of the visit was uncanny. Thanks to Patrick the wedding was a playful event that featured the now customary Goose Stepping and a dance introduced by Patrick Bear Wrestler. The evening following the wedding is when the great earthquake struck. Just as Tecumseh had predicted the gods gave witness to the words he had spoken. The last stick had been burned.

In December of 1811 the first of the New Madrid earthquakes rearranged North American and took the Mississippi River watershed along. An area encompassing thousands of square miles was broken and rearranged. The 1811 earthquake would go down in recorded history as one of the most significant events of the century.

The earth began quivering and rolling from side to side. The ground beneath the hut began undulating followed by terrible jolts and shaking; the movement turned the village into a pile of rubbish. The People awoke to a dark world of horror. Terrible eerie sounds rose out of the depths of earth. Patrick noticed the people murmuring, but he only caught snippets of what they were saying. Did he hear correctly, "—Tecumseh—last stick— last night—prophet— stamping his foot." The crowds huddled together and started to chant. "The spirits have spoken, listen, listen, listen!" were the words of the repetitive drone. The People scurried about in the darkness, running pell-mell and bumping into each other. Stands-Alone began gathering everyone in the ceremonial arena. The assembly picked up the chant, "—listen, listen, listen" started by the boys. "The spirits have spoken, listen, listen!"

The scent of human fear was detectable. The people were gazing toward the sky. Earlier in the evening there had been a bright meteor light up the sky and crash into earth. It was being hailed as a repeat of the meteor that had marked Tecumseh's birth. The astrological event was referred to as a "Panther Across the Sky" or in the Shawnee language, "Tecumseh." The re-appearance of the meteor had just fulfilled Tecumseh's prophecy signifying a stomping of the creator's foot. The paranormal event had sanctioned Tecumseh's mission to cleanse the land of white people.

With each tremor Patrick and Wathena's hut crumbled, and they barely escaped before it collapsed. A sudden gush of flood water came from an unknown source and surged through the rubble that had housed them. Patrick lifted Wathena and Little Doe into his arms and ran into the darkness. He was able to gather up three blankets and a buffalo robe before the water saturated them. A state of panic prevailed. Patrick had to guard against collision with other frightened villagers while he searched for higher ground. There had been no rain for days, hardly any clouds, so rain did not explain the source of the flash flood. Patrick decided the water was coming from the earthquake's motion that sloshed the rivers and lakes over their banks.

The night was unusually cold, and the water that engulfed Patrick's legs and feet was numbing. Each time the earth shook, the water would change directions and sweep across the village carrying along the rubbish of the broken village. Horrible sounds were coming from rockslides, falling trees, and groaning sounds from beneath the earth's surface. Patrick and several others remembered a certain rocky outcropping with a few low shrubs and two small trees. The raised area was about 10 feet higher than the surrounding ground, so far, high enough to stay dry. Patrick seated Wathena and Little Doe on a rock near the center of the island and wrapped them in the covers. One of the aunts took two of the blankets from Wathena and spread them on the ground. She invited the most vulnerable to crowd onto the blankets' meager insulation from the cold ground. Wathena kept one of the blankets about her shoulders and willingly shared the buffalo robe with others. Patrick returned to the gravel strewn incline where he was needed to help the most fragile people scale the steep perimeter of the outcropping. Patrick recognized the deadly exposure that threatened so many and recruited the strong and healthy to help him build up fires and carry the injured to the pallets.

Patrick yelled to his companions, "We need fire, can you help?" A couple of boys led Patrick to the raised fire pit that had been burning earlier in the evening. The boy dug into the ashes, and there about six inches beneath the surface they found a few hot coals not yet drowned by the ebbing flood waters. Patrick quickly removed the coals by scooping them up with two flat rocks and slogged his way to the island's dry ground. The boy started collecting dry kindling and enlisted others to help find firewood.

Once a fire was going the old people, babies, small children were arranged in a circle to best be warmed. Patrick began building more fires and sent the able bodied to bring more wood. Without Patrick's critical thinking, the death toll would have been much higher; as it was, they lost only five Clan members who were killed by falling trees and collapsing huts.

Still more fires were started, and the high place was covered with people seeking the warmth and light. The aftershocks continued, and after one especially violent one the water that had transformed the mound into an island drained away never to return.

Tecumseh's prediction had come about in a monumental fashion, a fact that skeptics were now forced to acknowledge. Tecumseh had stamped his metaphorical foot, implying divine approval from the Great Kanati. His mission to consolidate the Nations into a confederation with the purpose of ridding the continent of white people had been providentially endorsed.

Patrick's thoughts went back to the night with Strider at the Shawnee village. He noticed that the people were repeating Tecumseh's name over and over? Strider's sudden change in attitude now made sense.

It took the Thunder People weeks to rebuild the village and much longer to replace the spoiled stores of food. As an industrious people, they commenced the recovery, grateful that there had been so few killed. Something had changed, and it set Patrick on edge. He could sense a certain dread in the people. Stands-Alone became more disconnected to everyday life and retreated into the darkness of his hut. The old Medicine Woman, Dancing Spirit took on an exaggerated strangeness and seemed to exist in a constant state of fear. Soon afterward Stands-Alone caused a schism in the Thunder Clan. He led the more traditional members high into the Shacomage to meld into wilderness seclusion.

One winter day Patrick returned from a trip to the trading post with the news that a large number of the Creek Nation of Southern Alabama known as The Red Stick had formed an alliance with the British and was being supplied with weapons purchased from the Spanish in Florida. The Red Sticks were brutalizing settlers all over the south-east territory. Andrew Jackson, (a distant cousin of Oscar Jackson, owner of the trading post), and his sidekick, Sam Houston, were recruiting volunteers for the Tennessee Militia. The plan was to march to Alabama for a show down. About a month later, in early February 1814 the militia with Jackson at the head arrived at the Larson farm. Patrick invited them to camp for the night, and by bedtime Jackson had convinced Patrick to join the force. Wathena privately asked Patrick to reconsider, but Patrick's ire was up over the treachery of the British, and he figured it was time to put a stop to their tyranny once and for all. Patrick felt assured that Jasper and George would be able to handle the spring planting without him, and he would certainly be home before the harvest began.

Wathena glanced out her kitchen window and took a few minutes to observe the two militia officers as they gathered around a bonfire with the recruits. The fire was only a hundred feet from the cabin, and her eye kept going back to Andrew Jackson. She felt an instinctive loathing for the man. Wathena's immediate perception of Jackson alarmed her. His posture and interaction with the men revealed conceit, self-absorption, and ruthlessness. Once Wathena met the man, she glimpsed thinly disguised avarice. Well into the evening, Patrick, flushed with excitement, took Wathena to meet Jackson. The dark side to Jackson's personality had escaped Patrick's notice but was glaringly apparent to Wathena. The Colonel's manner lacked sincerity, or warmness. Only partly hidden below the surface was a deep-seated narcissism. He hardly acknowledged Wathena's presence and abruptly dismissed her with a curt nod. But as soon as Patrick was distracted by others, Jackson did a very curious thing. He walked over to where Wathena sat visiting with Sam Houston and interrupted the conversation. Jackson avoided eye contact and spoke to Wathena without using her name. He asked to see the gold nugget he had heard about. Wathena hesitated but then pulled it from under her tunic. The sight of the gold broke through Jackson's subterfuge to reveal an avaricious expression. When he realized his lapse, he made eye contact long enough to verify that he was found out. He immediately turned and walked away. The incident spoke volumes, justifying Wathena's dislike and suspicion of the man. Wathena felt the hair upon her scalp and arms prickle. Poor Patrick was oblivious to the true Jackson.

Throughout the evening of sabre rattling around the campfire, Wathena observed Jackson's same superior attitude toward the Indians who had joined the Tennessee militia. As for Jackson's companion, Sam Houston, she felt an instant connection. When Patrick introduced Wathena to the large and somewhat inebriated Houston, he tipped his hat and began a lively conversation in the Tsalagii language. Wathena was struck by his genuineness. He was a good listener and asked pertinent questions about her past.

As they spoke, Houston continued drawing swigs from a jug hefted upon his arm. He began slurring his words. What had begun as stimulating repartee devolved into sexual innuendo. Wathena was interested in relating her own strategy for defeating the Red Stick Creeks. Houston was breathing heavily as he complimented Wathena's knowledge of warfare. "My cdear, I'm slo-honored to meet such a blootiflu woman. I have heard of Cherokee Warrior Women ah, like chu, but, but ain't met, ah the name for it is ah, 'Ye Ho-Nawa.' I'm interested in hearing your, ah more bowt-chur storlee."

Wathena offered a condensed version of her parents' death and the childlessness of her adopting uncle. Houston edged closer on the log until their elbows touched. As his infatuation with Wathena grew, he found excuses to touch her. The intensity of his gaze became inappropriate. As he removed a crawling bug from Wathena's hair, he had a large portion of his body touching hers. Wathena said, "Please stop," and moved away from him. Houston chose to ignore Wathena's rejection and advanced toward her. Wathena glanced around to see if Patrick was watching them, and Houston misinterpreted that as encouragement. Then he brazenly took hold of her hand and raised it to his mouth and kissed it, mumbling that she possessed great beauty. Wathena was thankful that Patrick was otherwise occupied, and that Sam Houston's flirtatiousness went unnoticed. Wathena decided it was time to go back to her cabin before Houston made a scene. Wathena made a show of standing and covering her mouth, faking a yawn. She said, "Good evening Mr. Houston. I have an early morning, so I'm going in for the night." When Houston stood to follow, she whirled around to squarely face him and stretched her palm in his direction in such a manner that stopped him mid-step. He could not mistake the message on her face. The tipsy Houston quickly turned away and almost lost his footing. He stumbled his way back to the log by the fire and resumed his drinking binge.

From inside the cabin Wathena could hear Houston's booming voice. The subject of conversation around the fire changed to the Lewis and Clark expedition, and Houston had a lot to add to the conversation. According to Houston the exploratory expedition had been a monumental success! Thomas Jefferson had welcomed the party of adventurers to their home in the year of 1806, and with great fanfare. The great body of intelligence gained from the trek introduced the prospect of expanding the nation all the way to the Pacific Ocean. The vision for expansion was supported by both Andrew Jackson and Sam Houston. Both men would eventually have a hand in the imperialism of the United States. The call for expansion became known as "Manifest Destiny."

Wathena had gained insight into the character of the man who would one day be president of the Republic of Texas. Though dynamic and personable, his reputation as a womanizer fit. During Wathena's conversation with Houston, Andrew Jackson became silent and withdrew from the camp fire to sit upon the cot in his tent intently cleaning his weapons.

The uneasy feeling in Wathena's stomach grew stronger. Stands-Alone's cryptic warnings were repeating over and over in her mind; the dire warning concerning contact with White Men was more troubling than ever. Wathena knew it was too late, the course was unalterable. As soon as Wathena was alone with Patrick, she asked how Jackson knew of the gold necklace. Patrick got a surprised look on his face and said, "I really don't know. He didn't hear it from me. The hour was late when she finished packing Patrick's saddlebags. As she fingered her gold necklace, her sense of foreboding felt like a great weight. Alone in bed, Patrick and Wathena's passion was kindled. Facing a prolonged separation, their love making was exceptionally ardent but sublimely tender.

At daybreak tears welled up in Wathena's' eyes as the army rode south from the Larson farm. Patrick rode beside Large Shadow, a frequent companion. The two men had become close friends over the past 2 years. As Patrick and Large Shadow prepared to mount their horse, Wathena had a private moment with her cousin. Wathena said, "Come back safe and please watch out for Patrick. Large Shadow assured Wathena he would guard his with his life. Patrick gave Wathena a quick kiss and hug and sprang into the saddle glowing with excitement. She stood in front of the cabin until they were out of sight. She dried her eyes and busied herself with her chores. There was always work to be done, and she was grateful for the distraction.

Little Doe, Tessie, and Jake would have to miss their formal schooling until Patrick returned. It was the perfect time for Wathena to teach the three children wilderness survival, foraging for wild food, and hunting with a bow. Wathena's planned to teach the children how to start fires, stalk game, and self-defense. She would also teach them about medicinal herbs and how to tan hides. Due to the isolation of the farm, it was only prudent for the children to be proficient in wilderness ways. Wathena was a preeminently qualified instructor.

The days sped by for Wathena. To free up time she re-arranged her schedule and shifted some of the work to Lottie and Sara. Wathena's deep forest sessions were demanding and intense. She included breaks for being playful. She delighted in their musical laughter. Fatigue from the long days helped Wathena cope with the loneliness of her bed.

As the weather grew warmer, Wathena planned a trip to Jackson's Store to sell farm produce and trade for needed supplies. She decided to use the occasion as part of the children's survival curriculum. Each child prepared a hand written shopping list. Wathena wanted to teach the children the art of bartering. Little Doe had her heart set on a China doll and a bag of hard candy, and Tessie and Jake also wanted candy and toys. "Little Doe, do you have your basket of barter items packed?" "Tes, Jake Boy, have your baskets ready to go? We leave in five minutes." Are your lists finished? All three of you make me so proud! What hard workers you are."

The hand-woven willow baskets full of trade items were stacked in the bed of the Larson's one-horse buggy. For trade items they loaded up root crops, baskets of early maturing vegetables, beeswax candles, and hen eggs. Due to the heavy flow of westward bound wagons, the produce was certain to be in great demand at Jackson's Trading Post.

On the buggy ride to the outpost, Wathena started feeling dizzy and nauseous and was forced to stop and vomit. When they arrived at Jackson's Landing, she was still feeling nauseous. At first, she attributed her condition to something she had eaten but then realized that she might be pregnant. Patrick had been gone well over a month, and yet her period of bleeding had not happened. She and Patrick would welcome a second child. The thought of a new baby brought a smile to Wathena's face. Perhaps it would be a boy.

Jackson's Trading Post was bustling, and the compound had groups of campers, and a few wagons were selling food from their tailgate. Wathena walked with the children to the food concessions. They were selling little cakes of sweet bread, boiled eggs, whiskey, and wild-west magazines. Wathena purchased four of the cakes, and they ate them on the way to the store. When Wathena walked through the door of the store, all eyes were on her. Conversation had stopped abruptly. At the counter she announced that the children had some purchases to make. Little Doe read her list and handed it over to the clerk.

The children had written the lists on slabs of bark using charcoal. Oscar Jackson complemented Little Doe's efforts at writing and wanted to talk. He said, "Good morning Ms. Larson. I heard that your husband joined up with the Colonel. Ya know, I been wondering if he found any more gold in yer crick? Just curious, that's all. Well, no never mind, that box of iron nails never did come in. Since I am feelin' bad that it's taking' so long I just might ride out and deliver them myself."

Wathena replied, "Oh no need in going to all that trouble. Thanks for the offer." Wathena didn't like the questions and changed the subject. Her mind went back to that last night around the campfire. Wathena had noticed a lot of interest in her golden cat necklace. Why would rough and tumble men be interested in a necklace? She placed it inside the neck of her tunic out of sight. Wathena mentioned that Tessie and Jake brought a list too. "Go ahead and show Mr. Jackson," but when the black children stepped forward to present their list, Jackson stood back and said, "Who's been schooling these piccaninnies?" He turned his back to the children and refused to look at Tessie and Jake's writing. Wathena shrugged and innocently replied, "Patrick has been teaching them, why; is that a problem?" She was puzzled by the sudden hostile atmosphere. The normally cheerful Jackson was visibly irate. Jackson abruptly told Wathena, "Get these piccaninnies out of my store and take your business elsewhere in the future." Why was Oscar Jackson so angry? An incredulous Wathena would never understand the strange ways of white people. This was a matter for Patrick to resolve when he returned.

Wathena gathered the children and walked toward the buggy, telling them that the shopping had been postponed. Little Doe said, "Mommy, I didn't like that man, he's mean." Wathena worked up a sweat repacking the buggy. On the trip back to the farm, the disappointed children were able to sell some of their trade items to a string of moving wagons. The few coins they earned were some consolation to the children. The bartering lessons would have to wait.

The children were bright and able students who quickly grasped Wathena's wilderness training. Some of the schooling went beyond survival and delved into the cultural aspects of being Tsalagii, including dressing in traditional buckskin garments. Wathena took them through the tanning process beginning with felling the animal to sewing the finished garment. The children were quickly learning the native language. The three of them found tales of Tsalagii folk lore entertaining. The trio would have the opportunity to preserve and pass along the oral history of the Thunder Clan to future generations. It was important that Little Doe be prepared to join the ranks of Grandmother family historian in her old age.

Since Patrick's departure Wathena's struggle with anxiety was worsening. During the daytime she managed to maintain the appearance of normalcy, but her nights were filled with troubled dreaming. Sara and Lottie were commenting on how tired she looked. She was hearing Stands-Alone repeating his warning over and over and a recurring nightmare of the repugnant Andrew Jackson transforming into a blood thirsty demon and chasing her through the forest. Wathena became more and more impulsive and moody. She felt a constant, irresistible urge to watch for Patrick's return by watching the road to the south. Of late she was compelled to leave a candle burning at night and insisted on stocking Patrick's favorite food. She was having trouble concentrating.

Chapter 13

PURSUED BY
THE DEVIL

On a clear day in late April, Wathena saw a distant rider coming up the road. It had been almost three months since Patrick had gone to fight with the Militia. The rider was coming at a slow pace, and it took time to recognize the horseman as her cousin, Large Shadow. Patrick had convinced Large Shadow to join the Tennessee fighters. The glare of the sun caused Wathena to shade her brow with her hand, and what she saw was not a welcome sight. Wathena noticed that Large Shadow's horse was staggering and heavily lathered. Wathena began to walk toward Large Shadow. The condition of the horse was confirming her worst fears. She froze in place as Large Shadow tried to dismount but instead fell to the ground. He had a bloody wound to his right shoulder. Wathena moved to assist him but was too late to prevent his fall. Then she spied Patrick's saddlebags draped over the rump of Large Shadow's mount.

The spent horse snorted and staggered before crumpling to its knees. The animal's pain filled eyes were staring at Large Shadow. The weary horse rested his head, now too heavy to support, upon the ground and breathed a few tortured breaths before dying. Large Shadow crawled to where the horse lay. He tenderly stroked the muzzle and bent to speak a final farewell into the lifeless ears. The stoic and noble Large Shadow became faint and was forced to lie back upon the ground

Wathena knelt beside Large Shadow and searched her cousin's eyes. The obvious message his expression revealed was too horrible: shaking her head in denial she thought there must be a mistake, not Patrick; then Large Shadow whispered, "Bear Wrestler is gone, die in battle at Horse Shoe Bend. We were both hit crossing the river on a raft. I want to protect him but no cover on raft. Forgive me Wathena." Wathena collapsed to the ground, and her stricken expression was so horrific it forced Large Shadow to look away.

A devastated Wathena shrieked, "No, No, I can't—no!" Then tradition took over. Wathena removed the saddle bag from the dead horse and collapsed upon the ground near Large Shadow. While clutching the bag to her breast, she began singing the ancient death dirge that would prepare her for acceptance. Wathena's vocalizations began as a whimper that intensified into an ear-piercing wail. Little Doe heard the sound from where she was gathering eggs in the hen house. She briefly stood still to listen and then ran to her mother's side. Wathena merely pointed to Patrick's saddle-bag, and Little Doe knelt beside her mother and began her own death song.

The high quavering sounds carried to the field where Jasper and George were tending the tobacco field. When the breathless men arrived, a very weak Large Shadow whispered enough details that they were able to understand what had happened. "Patrick, shot in back, killed, on raft in battle. I hear bullets, come from behind, I know. Jackson's Sargent ordered Patrick buried in pit with enemy soldiers. They made me stay back but I know, I know."

Jackson claimed victory but with massive loss of life. Next Large Shadow said that the militia was only a few hours behind him, and he warned that they were confiscating Indian property along the river and near ponds. Resistors were being shot. Large Shadow gasped out enough information to reveal that the naïve Patrick had confided in Andy Jackson, and his thieving cohorts about the gold nugget discovered in the stream.

During casual conversation Patrick had revealed that he was schooling the slave children alongside his own daughter. Large Shadow warned Wathena, "Patrick talk too much." Not even Large Shadow knew that Andrew Jackson already knew of the gold discovery from his cousin Oscar before he recruited Patrick.

The corrupting madness that comes with "GOLD FEVER" would sweep across the native lands of Georgia, North Carolina, Virginia and Tennessee: the disputed territory including a gigantic swath of land claimed by the Cherokee. Legislation was passed outlawing land ownership for all Indians. The same Georgia Legislature outlawed Indians suing white people. Suddenly the indigenous citizens were deemed unsuited for land management, were denigrated for disgusting cultural habits, and ridiculed for their low intelligence. The official position of the government regarding American Indians was to deny them rights and declare them to be sub-human.

Sara and Lottie helped Wathena to a standing position and partly carried her to her bed. They took turns sitting with Wathena. At first Little Doe stayed beside her mother and accompanied the mourning song. Wathena had positioned herself in the middle of the bed with her legs crossed in front of her and her hands on her knees. After more than an hour of singing the dirge, Wathena faced Lottie and asked her to take Little Doe to the kitchen for food, "Please close the door behind you." Lottie hesitated, and Wathena gave her a cold look and said "now"! The black woman said, "Yessum" and took Little Doe by the hand. As soon as the door closed, Wathena drew her knife and sliced off her braids level with her ear lobes. Next, she slit her sleeves to expose her lower arms. Sara opened the door a crack and peaked into the room just in time to see Wathena preparing to mutilate her arms with the knife.

Sara screamed, "No, everbody come quick!" It took the combined effort of Lottie, George, Jasper, and Sara to restrain Wathena from disfiguring her arms. Wathena fought like a lioness to keep control of the knife but was overcome by the strength of the four adults. George and Jasper tied Wathena to a chair where she continued to struggle. So vicious was her struggle to free herself even the adults were frightened. Little Doe ran to hide in a closet, covering her ears. After a few minutes to think, Little Doe returned to Wathena's bedside with a calm exterior. The threshing and straining stopped the moment Little Doe walked into the room.

Little Doe quietly sat upon the bed next to Wathena's chair and said in a matter-of-fact voice, "Momma, I think Papa would be glad about the baby, don't you think?" Little Doe, with maturity beyond her years, continued the one-way conversation with her mother. And think how proud Papa would be if he could see the garden and fields. I will never forget him teaching me reading and writing. Momma do you think he can see us right now?"

The presence of Little Doe took the fight out of Wathena. A calmer Wathena was able to convince her friends to untie her. She lifted Little Doe to her lap and began to rock the child. "My precious child, your Papa is in the world of the spirits, and yes I believe that he hovers above us and is able to see us. He may even protect and guide our movements at times." Mother and daughter began a softer and more mournful version of the death trill.

Wathena had suddenly realized that she must be strong and provide support for her suffering child. Little Doe needed to experience a reasonable and measured grieving process to heal properly. During the seemingly endless night, with Little Doe sleeping on the bed beside her, Wathena prayed to Kanati for the strength to exact the required revenge on the evil and arrogant Andrew Jackson and Oscar Jackson. Wathena was a strong believer in the ancient tradition of the Thunder People that required revenge upon murderers and the words of the death dirge heralded her resolve to the spirits. Wathena took an oath to kill the persons responsible for Patrick's death. Exacting retribution for Patrick would assure him a peaceful existence in the afterworld. Exhaustion allowed Wathena a brief period of sleep just before daybreak. Crowing from the henhouse woke Wathena, and she rose from the bed that would never again be the place of her nightly slumber. In this instance Wathena's usual clairvoyance had failed her, perhaps because the gist of the truth would be too painful.

Wathena rose and prepared a nap sack with food and water. She went to Large Shadow and dressed his wound. She refreshed his drinking gourd and left some bean bread in a clay pot. Wathena knew that Sara and Lottie would look after his needs during her absence. As she went about her preparation, she found herself blinded by her bobbed hair. Wathena searched through a drawer and pulled out a strip of leather lacing. She parted her thick, dark brown hair in the middle to expose her red part and tied the strip of hide around her head just above her eyebrows.

The part in her hair was kept permanently dyed with a red ochre pigment. The color was used by clan females to enhance beauty. Cutting her long hair reflected Wathena's metamorphic transition to a vengeful warrior. Gone was the comely and happy Tsalagii maiden known as Wathena; her appearance now reflected a ferocious Ye Ho-Nawa.

It disturbed Little Doe to look upon her mother's changed appearance. Little Doe's loyalty and support for her mother was deeply ingrained, and she wanted to participate in the grieving process. Some force was compelling the Warrior Woman to return to the scene of the bear fight where she had saved Patrick's life. There she would gain insight and know how to prepare for what lay ahead. Because Wathena's destination was not a personal decision, she packed her satchel for the unknown. The gear bag was packed with two oil cloth ponchos, a honing stone, a flint, jerky, dried raisins and plumbs and a gourd filled with water. Wathena wore her everyday doeskin garment, a mid-calf length tunic, and moccasins. She carried her usual hiking gear of bow and quiver, a sheathed knife about her waist. Encircling Wathena's neck was the cat-shaped necklace and her sacred medicine bag.

As she and Little Doe walked along the creek bed, Wathena felt as if she was viewing her actions remotely. An image of Andrew Jackson's arrogant countenance kept appearing in her mind's eye. The day that Oscar Jackson had refused to trade with her because of the black children was speeding through her thoughts. Large Shadow had cleared up the mystery about the hateful law that forbade schooling black children. The matter arose about the source of the bullet that killed Patrick. Large Shadow had insisted that it come from behind, and that explained the call for his quick burial in a mass grave.

Wathena now realized that Andrew Jackson was a criminal opportunist disguised as an officer and a gentleman, perfectly willing to rise above his fellow men even if it meant over their dead bodies. Oscar Jackson was cut from the same pattern. Patrick and Large Shadow were mere pawns in an expansive chess game. Andrew Jackson's father had died when he was young, and he and his mother went to live with relatives. Jackson was left an orphan at the age of fifteen when he lost his mother. Jackson had grown up poor and was forced to deal with a scrappy, loveless home life. Against the odds he managed to achieve success using basic backwoods intelligence and a belligerent personality. Once offended, Andy Jackson would often challenge any offender to a duel with pistols. Jackson narrowly escaped death several times while facing down an adversary. Jackson was known for his hard heart and hot temper and after the great victory at the Battle of New Orleans would be aptly called "Old Hickory."

The path that Wathena and Little Doe followed was beautifully decorated for spring. Under normal circumstances Wathena and Little Doe would have been celebrating nature. Wathena used a hushed voice to explain that their life had changed. From this day forward, she and Little Doe would lead a very different existence. Wathena no longer trusted whites. Large Shadow had been right about them except for Patrick. Patrick Larson was a unique individual, a tender-hearted and well-meaning man. Wathena's Thunder People had been warned repeatedly and reminded of the sicknesses the Whites often spread. Since learning of Patrick's senseless death, Stand-Alone's plea was tormenting Wathena. Wathena realized that exacting revenge was the only possible way to give peace to Patrick in the afterlife and therefore provide closure to her own torment.

They stopped to drink from a spring. Why wasn't the spiritual world grieving? How could the birds sing and the animals play? The answer was obvious; she had brought the trouble on herself when she ignored the warnings of Stands-Alone.

During the journey, Wathena felt the sickness sweep over her and paused to retch. The sickness served as a reminder of the new life growing within her. Other than the memories, all that remained of Patrick was Little Doe and the unborn child. From this point forward Wathena's first priority would be protection of Patrick's two offspring.

The creek bank was largely unchanged, even the fallen limb rested where high water had washed it about 20 feet down stream. Wathena seated Little Doe on the bolder where Patrick had left his gear on that landmark date more than eight years before. Wathena looked toward the heavens and then prostrated herself on the ground the exact area that had absorbed Patrick's blood. An ancient prayer song poured like a torrent from Wathena's tortured spirit. The death trill raised gooseflesh on Little Doe, who then slipped to the ground beside her mother. The child began her own high-pitched warble. The mingled sound of the two voices resulted in a sonorous timbre so filled with pain it drove the more timid forest spirits to seek shelter. The mother and daughter were not yet aware of a third supernatural presence, silent and hidden, waiting to deliver a message. The sun had sunk well below the tree line, and mental exhaustion was forcing an end to the dirge when a startling scream broke the silence. Wathena froze, and then quickly looked around as she drew an arrow from her quiver. Looking in the direction of the scream, her eyes locked onto a magnificent puma's amber eyes. After a few seconds of eye contact, the puma turned away, took a few steps, paused and peering over its shoulder, re-establishing eye contact. Wathena realized that the lion wanted her to follow; the animal must be delivering a warning or perhaps a summons. She knew she was being called back to the farm. The puma disappeared into the undergrowth. Strangely, the big cat was not threatening. Wathena sensed a spiritual connection with the puma. The panther had departed in a northerly direction. Wathena struck out toward the farm with Little Doe calling, "Wait for me, I am frightened of lions, remember?"

"Come, child, we must hurry." It was totally dark when they approached the outer border of the farm. A very faint sound caught her attention. Wathena detected a rustling of the leaves and then a groan. The sounds were coming from Large Shadow. She had almost tripped over him. She knelt and ran her hands over his face but drew back when he groaned with pain. The beloved uncle had been scalped, and his legs were mangled. "Oh no, my dear Large Shadow, who did this to you?" He just waved his head from side to side. He was bleeding out and going into shock. Wathena realized he needed to speak with her. She placed her ear to his mouth. Wathena assumed correctly that he had crawled from the farm house. Large Shadow spit forth and panted out his final words, "Jackson's men—wait for—you—at farm, they kill you,—run—hide—. Negroes all dead. They want your land–the gold! Run—hide. Never come back." Large Shadow's voice trailed off as his spirit departed. I must go where, thought Wathena? She was gripped with terror. And then she heard men approaching. Wathena closed Large Shadow's eyes and pulled his body under a bush. Through the trees and brush Wathena could see lighted torches approaching. After crossing to the opposite side of the little river, she could see that the searchers had fanned out and were walking in her direction.

Wathena's first thought was to run toward her family's village. This is the direction Jackson would expect her to take. Her thoughts were fast tracking, fueled by a burst of adrenaline. She was analyzing all possible escape routes. Within a matter of seconds, she settled on a plan. Without a moment to waste, took Little Doe by the hand and turned in a southward direction. Wathena realized that the child could not keep up and took Little Doe on to her back piggy back. She tripped twice and sensed that the search party was gaining on them.

She realized that she could not out run the mob with the added weight of Little Doe. Then she thought of the most recent lesson she had been teaching the children.

Wathena knelt in front of the shivering child and said, "Remember the lesson on breathing through a reed while submerged in water. Are you ready?" Little Doe said, "Yes mother." Wathena and Little Doe removed their clothing and hid them along with her bow and quiver.

Wathena strapped her hunting knife to her waist and helped Little Doe wade into the icy water. As soon as Little Doe contacted the water, she tried to jump into Wathena's arms. Wathena held her down and whispered, "Wait, your body will adjust to the water. Look at how close those men are, this is our only escape; you are Tsalagii, you can do this." Wathena sliced off two long cattail reeds and handed one to Little Doe. Wathena noticed that Little Doe's shivering was worse. Her state of fright and the icy water was almost too much for such a small body mass. A look of resolve from Wathena fortified her. "We are children of the forest, and we can do this, say it after me, we can do this."

Little Doe inhaled and said, "I can do this, I am doing this!" And she smiled at her mother. With survival at stake Wathena and Little Doe found the necessary toughness. As they wadded deeper into the numbing creek, a deadly cottonmouth water moccasin hissed a deadly warning, but then swam away. Little Doe opened her mouth to scream, but Wathena was able to muffle her with a palm.

Mother and child waded to the center of a stand of cattails where the water depth reached mid chest on Wathena. Next, she dislodged a large stone from the creek bottom to anchor them below the surface. Wathena sank to a squatting position and held the rock on top of her thighs. Then she seated Little Doe atop the rock. To hold Little Doe beneath the surface, Wathena's right arm encircled the child's neck. She used the fingers of that hand to pinch off her own nostrils. Her left hand held the cattail reed in a vertical position with the end several inches above the water's surface. Little Doe pinched off her own nose with one hand and held the reed with the other. The difficult maneuver was successful only because Little Doe had been practicing the maneuver.

Wathena was able to see the light of the torches submerged when she opened her eyes and would know when it was safe to come out of the water. The bank was crawling with the men. Their garbled voices penetrated the water. Wathena's fear was spiked with anger. A cramp caused her to slightly shift her position, and the rock slipped between her legs. Suddenly Wathena became buoyant and was only able to stay submerged by digging her feet into the substantial tangle of cattail roots. Thankfully, the roots were mature and well anchored. Eventually, the light from the torches faded, and Wathena lifted her face above the surface of the water very slowly, in total silence.

The darkness of the creek bank was an invaluable ally and helped to obscure any sign. How did the men know where to search? And then, Wathena remembered that her knap sack had not been hidden.

The men had rounded a bend of the river and were well out of sight, but their calls to each other were audible. The tone they used was angry and full of frustration. Cautiously she carried Little Doe out on the bank. The two of them picked their way into a dense thicket of brush. Amazingly, Little Doe did not cry out when thorns tore at her bare skin. She was truly a child of "The People." Wathena whispered that they must lie silently until the sounds of the men were far away. They clung to each other for warmth. Wathena placed Little Doe's feet between her thighs and her small hands in the pockets of her arm pits. Wathena kept the cattail reeds near in case they were forced to go back into the water. The cold damp night air was brutal and after a half hour Wathena decided that it was safe to get dressed.

Wathena mentally mapped the best route to the camp of the break-away group that split off from the Thunder People. Wathena knew the general area, but locating them would be a challenge. The route would require a dangerous climb up the riverside cliff to the top of a rocky ridge. There they would leave no footprints. When they reached the ridge top, Wathena remembered a hidden riverside cave a few miles ahead that had been used by her people for generations. The hiding place was about 30 feet above the river in the side of a sandstone cliff. The only access from above or below was an ancient cottonwood tree. The west-facing cave would be hard to find in the dark, but if she could locate it, it would provide the perfect resting place.

The darkness made travel treacherous, and Wathena stubbed her toe and then fell head long onto the gravel, suffering a minor gash to her forehead. Fear pushed her onward and blunted the pain. Her fleeting thoughts recalled childhood visits to the cave with Falls-From-Heaven. She remembered the cottonwood tree that grew beside a clump of cedar trees that hid the mouth of the cave and acted as a ladder. A tangle of grapevines hid the opening to the cave. After trudging the ridge top for more than five hours, the exhausted pair collapsed on a flat stone. From the outline of the surrounding rock formations against the sky, Wathena thought the cave was located just below. She left Little Doe seated against a rock and climbed down a cottonwood tree that seemed right. A half-moon was just clearing the trees above the eastern bank and partly illuminated the cliff face.

Wathena knew how brittle cottonwood branches could be and carefully chose only the sturdiest limbs to bear her weight. She broke off a limb to probe for the opening. Was this the right place? It looked so different in the moonlight. Finally, the limb found an opening behind the matt of vines. Holding to a higher limb, she walked on a sturdy lower one that extended to within a few inches of the opening. The scent of a cat, most likely a puma caused Wathena to draw her dagger. She was faced with a choice; chancing an animal attack or finding a different resting place. Puma reasoned, *since pumas are nocturnal, it was likely to be out hunting and upon return will detect our human scent and go away without bothering us.*

She shook the branch to make some noise, and at that moment a growling puma dashed from the cave and sprang onto a limb just above Wathena's head. Wathena almost lost her grip on the branch that supported her. She heard the lion scrambling up the tree above her, raining down sticks and bark onto her head. Then Wathena realized that the puma was headed toward where she had left Little Doe. Wathena dropped the stick and started up the tree after the puma. Her muscles propelled her upward with super human strength. While climbing, she held the knife in her teeth. When she jumped from the tree to the rocky summit, there was Little Doe, unharmed and sound asleep. Wathena wondered if this was the same animal she had encountered earlier in the day. Wathena sat silently, listening for any sound that would indicate that the lion was still nearby. With hardly more than a snarl, it had quickly disappeared into the night. Wathena whispered, "Go in peace, sleek hunter." Later, as she rested, Wathena contemplated the presence of the great cat. Was the lion sent to protect her? As soon as possible she vowed to thank Kanati and burn a pinch of tobacco. The act of communing with the Great Spirit would give her insight; perhaps Kanati had chosen the great cat as her medicine animal? What knowledge could she glean from the way of the puma?

Wathena said, "Little Doe, wake up, we must climb down the tree to enter the hiding place." Wathena helped the drowsy Little Doe to climb onto her back for the descent to the cave's entrance. Parting the tangled vines, Wathena crept into the cave. The darkness inside was almost total, but all was quiet, so she removed Little Doe from her back and placed her upon the sandy floor. Stepping from the tree limb to the cave entrance in almost total darkness required extreme caution. Once inside Wathena felt safe from the trackers. Her first act was to urinate at the opening of the cave to ward off the puma. Then she went back out to the tree and cut a strong limb and sharpened it to use as a spear. The animal scent reminded Wathena to be alert. Seated against the back wall of the cave, with the sharpened spear in hand, and hunting knife loose in its scabbard, Wathena napped beside Little Doe until daylight.

After some dreadfully long hours daylight illuminated the interior of the cave. Wathena quietly explored the familiar enclosure. She wanted Little Doe to continue sleeping. Near the back of the cave, resting on a natural shelf were several ceramic pots. She removed one pot and kneeled at the fire pit. Directly above was a natural vent in the ceiling of the cave that surfaced over a hundred feet from the actual cave. The cave was just as she remembered. At the entrance of the cave were two large limbs extending from the trunk of the giant tree to within a few inches of the cave opening. The cave was small, only seven feet at the highest point. The entrance was a hole about five feet circumference. The room broadened into a circular area about ten feet across with a mostly flat sandy floor.

Food would be the priority of the day. The loss of the knap sack was unfortunate, but not critical. Careful not to wake Little Doe, Wathena searched the pots on the shelf and found flints for starting a fire and she set about collecting a tinder bundle and dead wood from the cottonwood. Once the tender bundle was burning, she placed it under the little pyramid of sticks. Striking a spark with a flint and steel was another skill she had been teaching the children, and had Little Doe been up from her slumber Wathena would have turned the task over to her. That was one survival skill that required practice.

Soon a small cooking fire was going. Then Wathena felt Little Doe's hand on her shoulder. Hand in hand, mother and daughter stood at the mouth of the cave and in unison sang the morning song to thank the Great Spirit for leading them to safety.

We n' de ya ho, We n' de ya ho,
We n' de ya, We n' de ya Ho ho ho ho,
He ya ho, He ya ho, Ya ya ya

Little Doe eagerly helped braid a grapevine rope. They lowered a clay pot to the stream below for water. After drinking their fill, the pot was propped over the small fire supported by flat rocks. Next Wathena climbed to the top of the cliff and collected more firewood. She used the vine rope to lower the bundle of firewood to the cave opening, and Little Doe snagged the rope with the sharpened limb and pulled the firewood into the cave.

Wathena told Little Doe to keep the fire going and she would descend to the river below to forage for food. Cattail shoots were plentiful, and several mallards were paddling on the river. Wathena said, "The Provider hears our hunger pangs," and Little Doe rubbed her tummy and grinned. Wathena removed her buckskins and draped them over a branch. After dropping silently into the water feet first, she tied cattail reeds and brush around her head. Then she allowed her makeshift blind to float toward the waterfowl. An unsuspecting drake came near to peck at the floating debris and was quickly yanked under by the feet. Wathena snapped the neck of the submerged mallard and secured it to a cord around her waist. As Wathena stalked a second mallard, her effort was foiled by a playful otter. Wathena decided that one duck would suffice for breakfast, along with a large bundle of cattail shoots. Wet and naked, Wathena hefted her body back up to the cave and warmed herself by the fire before dressing. Now they had the making of a meal. Wathena saved the innards of the duck to be used for fish bait. The feathers would be useful for stuffing their moccasins. The duck meat was cut into strips and skewered on sharpened sticks. While the meat roasted, the cattail shoots boiled in the pot. By the time the meat was brown and dripping their hunger was more than ravenous.

Wathena felt safe in the cave. She didn't want to push too hard and asked Little Doe, "Why don't we stay here one more night?" Little Doe hugged her mother happily agreeing. They added padding to their bed. The heap of duck feathers was stuffed into their moccasins. Wathena carved a barb of cedar in the shape of a fish hook. She carved a hole in the top of the barb so that it could be tied to a vine. After a mid-day nap, Wathena planned to go below to try for a catfish. Little Doe begged to fish, so a second barb was whittled. With the knife dulled, Wathena found just the right stone to restore the edge.

At an early age Little Doe, like all Tsalagii children had learned to swim. By late in the afternoon, Wathena and Little Doe were perched on a large limb just above a deep pool of the stream. Wathena dropped some pieces of the duck intestines into the water to attract the attention of the bottom dwellers. It worked, and Little Doe was soon hauling in a flailing catfish. It weighed about a pound, and within a few minutes a second catfish had latched onto Wathena's hook. Their success almost made them forget the dire circumstances that had brought them to this moment.

There would be no time to dry the fish, so they would cook all of it, and what they could not consume, they would carry along wrapped in leaves. Still fearful that the lion might return, Wathena decided to keep the fire burning through the night. She kept a pot of water handy to quickly extinguish the fire, in case the white men might double back along their path. As evening fell, a well-fed Little Doe was tucked into the cedar-lined bed. Wathena felt that she should reconnoiter the area and crept to the ridge above the cave. She heard nothing and concluded that the pursuers had abandoned the search. Now she could concentrate on locating her kin.

Snuggled next to Little Doe, Wathena tried to sleep, but her mind struggled with the reality of their situation. Patrick, Large Shadow, George and Sara and little Tessie, and Jasper and Lottie, Jake Boy, all gone, brutally murdered. She snapped back to the present and vowed to press on for the sake of Little Doe and the babe. Her future would be filled with sadness, something she must adjust to. It was late into the night before a troubled sleep consumed her.

The sound of twittering birds awoke Wathena. The faintest of light was seeping into the cavern through the vine covering. Wathena yawned and did a lazy stretch before adding wood to the gray coals of the fire pit. She set a pot of cattail shoots over the flames. Why not finish off the leftover catfish. A wave of affection swept over Wathena when she saw the bright eyes of her daughter pop open. The child quickly scurried to her mother with a bear hug. That day the morning-prayer was celebrated with a special reverence. They expressed thankfulness for their escape and the bounty of the duck and catfish.

The two of them worked together weaving a vine bag to carry the large pot with the quartz stone, the fishing hooks with attached cords. Little Doe's expression indicated that she was sad to leave the cave. She would gladly have stayed longer, but Wathena knew that they must press on. The journey would be hard on Little Doe, but Wathena would choose a pace that challenged her without exhausting her.

The first day of travel they made good time. The best shelter they could find for the evening was a hollow fallen log. It would be better than lying on the open ground. Crawling insects were sent scurrying by holding a burning cedar torch into the hollow. Next Wathena swept away the layer of debris that had collected in the log. Some of the insects returned during the night, but the exhausted pair managed to get some rest on a bed of soft cedar branches.

The second day a thundershower developed into a violent hailstorm. Wathena and Little Doe sought shelter from the hail in an overhang at the side of a creek. Burrowed into the moist creek-bank, they were protected from the pummeling hail, but were almost trapped by the swirling torrent of a flash flood. Just as the water level reached their burrow, Wathena pushed Little Doe up the slippery bank where she could grasp a shrub. The rising water started pulling at Wathena, and at the last moment she was able to wrap her arms around a small tree a few yards downstream. As they frantically climbed higher to distance themselves from the brown floodwater, the hail had grown larger and was battering them. Wathena would have to wait for the angry water to retreat before recovering their weapons and gear. An ear shattering bolt of lightning struck a tree only a hundred yards away. At least Wathena did not lose the hunting knife that she wore at her waist. As they sought new shelter, Wathena tried to place her body over Little Doe to shield her from the punishing hailstones.

Then, as suddenly as it had started, the storm was over, and a rainbow arch appeared in the eastern sky. Wathena sat Little Doe next to a tree to rest while she took a digging stick and searched for their gear. She found her bow and quiver still bound together, caught on some brush a hundred yards downstream.

By late afternoon, Wathena was forced to abandon the search for the pot that contained the flint stone. She was about to fashion a spindle and fireboard to start a fire when she smelled smoke. Then she recalled the lightning strikes. They followed the trail of smoke to a still burning tree. Never had a campfire been so appreciated. Wathena and Little Doe performed a silent prayer with their hands, communicating with the Fire Giver. It was now too dark to search for food. That would have to wait for daylight.

That evening, as the naked girls dried their clothes by the fire, they examined each other's bruises, and they were many. Little Doe ended up with a black eye when one of the bouncing spheres of ice bounced off a tree and struck with enough force to bruise but not seriously injure the child's eye. Wathena's back had the most bruises, but neither was seriously injured. Little Doe smiled and curled up on her mother's lap, soaking up the warmth of the fire. That night they slept by the fire and awoke in the morning cold and damp with dew, but when the coals of the fire were revived, they were able to get warm and somewhat dry.

There was more rain, and Wathena was driven by hunger to delay the journey long enough to hunt. She was hoping for a cottontail rabbit or even a deer. As a child of the forest, Wathena quickly located a deer trail. Wathena, trailed by a silent Little Doe, patiently tracked a small doe to the river. Downwind and undetected by the doe, they were able to climb to a stony ridge for a clear shot. Just as she released the arrow, the doe moved, and the arrow missed the heart and tore through its abdomen. Muscular reflex caused the doe to spring into the river. Wathena kicked off her moccasins and dove into the river from the rocky vantage point. She swam with strong overhand strokes to overtake the injured doe. After about three hundred feet, the doe became entangled in the branches of a dead tree that had fallen into the river. Wathena quickly closed the distance. Due to the thrashing hoofs of the crazed animal, Wathena decided to submerge and approach from the doe's blind side. Wathena was able to hold to the tree with one hand and grasp the deer with her legs as she slashed the deer's throat with her other hand. She had to apply more than usual force to cut through the neck muscle because the knife had lost a lot of its edge. Now Wathena had to devise a way to bring the dead doe to the bank. At first, she tried swimming holding on to one hoof. The swift rain swollen current was overwhelming, and she almost lost the deer. Wathena floated downstream with the deer in her grasp until she was washed against another fallen tree. She straddled the trunk. She tugged until she pulled the animal out of the current and secured it between tree branches. Then Wathena swam to the bank and found a growth of vines. She cut several long sections of vine that could be braided into a cord.

All the while Little Doe had been running down the riverbank, trying to keep pace with her mother. Before going back into the river, Wathena removed her tunic and refastened the knife and sheath around her waist. She waded back into the current and swam back to where the doe was caught in the tree. She tied one end of the vine rope securely around the deer's chest and the other around her own chest. Then she shoved the animal into the water and started swimming for the bank. The carcass of the dead animal floated down stream, taking Wathena along with it. The torrent was too strong. She would have to look for other food.

Wathena was near exhaustion, when she heard, "Mother, the limb." The child was holding a long branch over the water. Wathena smiled with relief but wondered how Little Doe had been able to keep up on the rugged bank. Little Doe used a small tree as a brace and extended the long sapling with both hands. When Wathena grasped the limb, she realized that the place Little Doe had chosen was shallow, only chest deep and she was able to stand. Then she carefully drew on the vine, hand over hand, until she hauled the doe near to the bank. As the doe neared where Wathena stood, she could see that the vine was unraveling. Just as the vine released the doe, Wathena was able to lunge and catch a hoof. Little Doe dropped the limb and jumped to the aid of her mother. The child realized that the water was over her head and started to tread water. Wathena held on to one hoof and lifted Little Doe on to her hip. As the two walked onto the muddy bank, they exhaled a giant sigh of relief.

The frenzied quest for sustenance by the two famished females had ended in a notable victory. By the fall of darkness, several thin steaks were roasting over a roaring fire, made possible by a flint stone discovered by Little Doe as they gathered wood. As soon as their buckskin garments were mostly dry, they pulled them over their heads and huddled by the fire, anticipating the coming meal. As mother and daughter stood rotating before the fire, fat began to drip onto the flames and give off a delicious aroma. Warmth relaxed the tension in Wathena's knotted muscles, and Little Doe had stopped shivering. Suddenly Wathena intuitively sensed danger. She whispered to Little Doe, "listen." After a moment Little Doe said, "I don't hear anything." Wathena dropped Little Doe's hand and walked to the tree where her bow and quiver stood. She surveyed the surrounding area, and whispered, "Something is out there in the dark. It may be a pack of — oh I see them, yes, we have attracted wolves. Stay calm."

The Spirits of the Forest had one more cruel challenge for the travelers before the day ended. Wathena and Little Doe's cooking had attracted a pack of timber wolfs. "We must walk very slowly to that big cedar tree. We must scale the tree without turning our backs on them. Keep staring at them, shout and wave, throw rocks, be brave my daughter!" Wathena's fake bravado worked, and Little Doe stayed calm. As the pack approached, Wathena drew a sturdy branch with a burning tip from the fire pit. The crouching animals would alternate between pausing and creeping toward the campsite.

The villainous carnivores' ears were laid back and they approached in a crouch. Their evil, orange slatted eyes reflected the firelight. Wathena placed her bow and quiver over her shoulder and surveyed the nearby trees. "Little Doe bring some of the cooking deer meat." Little Doe quickly removed the meat from the skewers and wrapped them in a square of deer hide and stuffed it into the neck of her belted tunic. Both Mother and child stood back-to-back and slowly walked sideways to the base of the grand old cedar tree. Wathena's shouts and threatening swipes with the burning branch slowed the wolf pack's advance. She and Little Doe covered the distance to the tree while maintaining eye contact. She knew that the bow was useless, so she dropped the weapon at the bottom of the cedar. Wathena lifted Little Doe onto her shoulders with one arm. This put the child within reach of the lowest limb. While Little Doe struggled to heft her leg over the branch her mother kept up the barrage of charges and jabs, swinging the burning limb with such force it made a swishing noise.

Incredibly Little Doe was able to pull her weight high enough to slip one foot over the limb and then raise her body to the limb. The cooked deer meat almost fell from her tunic, but she was able to catch it just in time as she righted herself on the limb. She scrambled to the next higher limb and waited. Below Wathena continued her ferocious threats with the burning branch, jabbing and striking at the emboldened beasts. She charged a small female and clubbed her on the head, burning the animal. The injured wolf temporarily retreated to the cover of the bushes, shrieking in pain. When the pack retreated, Wathena was able to spring high enough to grasp the lowest branch and then pull her weight up to the limb. Little Doe was frozen with fear as her mother dangled from the limb and kicked at the lunging attackers. Wathena started swinging her body and then brought her feet up to the limb. The maddened pack leapt off the ground in a last-ditch effort to pull the woman from the tree. Wathena's narrow escape left Little Doe so terrified she was shaking. "Mother, you are hurt?" Only a couple of feet above the highest leaps, Wathena looked up at Little Doe and said, "We are safe! We are really safe, at least for now."

Shaken by the near catastrophe, mother and child clung to each other for a few minutes. The activity on the ground got interesting. They were irresistibly drawn to watch the spectacle taking place where the remains of the doe lay. The pack had quickly turned to what remained of the deer. The pile of entrails, head, and all the rest was being rapidly consumed. Wathena and Little Doe had ring side seats to the macabre feeding frenzy.

Perched high in the branches of the magnificent cedar tree, Wathena and Little Doe were mesmerized by the spectacle. Wathena had studied wolf behavior as a child at the feet of her great-grandmother. Wathena began by explaining that social status determined the order of feeding. The alpha male and alpha female would go first, fending off any challengers. The ordered chaos was characterized by ritualized bluffing, posturing and sparring. The male pack leader ate his fill, and then the ranking female, who then invited her adolescent cubs to partake. Finally, the others fought over any meat that was left. Younger kits would be fed regurgitated meat from both male and female members of the pack.

As they watched from above Wathena removed the bundle of meat from Little Doe's tunic and wedged it into a fork of the tree. After finding a secure place to sit, they each fished out a hunk of rare, still warm venison. A ravenous Little Doe tore into her morsel of meat, and then gave Wathena a mischievous glance, bared her teeth and growled. Then Wathena glared back with a menacing curled lip and ripped at her hand sized slice of venison. The humor of the moment helped dissipate their adrenalin overload and slow respiration and heart rate. Wathena noticed that Little Doe grew silent and drowsy.

A crude sleeping rack made from branches across two large limbs and padded with cedar boughs allowed brief snippets of slumber during the miserable night.

Daylight was slow to come and found the duo exhausted and stiff from bone-chilling dew. They cautiously left the safety of the tree and retrieved their gear.

As the two continued their journey, Wathena complimented Little Doe on her bravery and performance. "Oh, this one, this Little Doe is truly a child of the forest!" Wathena admitted that the village might be hard to locate. They kept a sharp vigil for the wolf pack as they traveled. There would be no more open cooking fires. The fog burned off early and by mid-day the sky was clear with only an occasional cloud. Around mid-afternoon, as they made their way through a heavily wooded area, a terrifying sound met their ears. It was the whinny of a horse. Wathena and Little Doe immediately dropped to the ground and crawled into some underbrush. The sound was enough to cause panic. The memory of Large Shadow's mutilated body was too fresh. Wathena strained to see the source of the sounds. The scrapping sound they heard must come from a litter being pulled behind a horse. That was encouraging, so Wathena raised her head enough to see that the approaching party was dressed in the garb of "The People." What a wonderful sight! Three men were astride ponies, and a fourth was riding the pony that pulled the litter. She insisted that Little Doe stay hidden until she was satisfied that the travelers were friendly. As she approached them, they each fitted their bow with an arrow, but then realized from her dress that she was Tsalagii. The men dismounted and walked to greet Wathena. Then she called Little Doe from her hiding place. The men showed Wathena and Little Doe every possible kindness. The men moved to a place hidden from the road and made camp. Standing with her back to the fire, Wathena summarized the events that forced her to escape her home. After a meal of dried venison and bean bread, Little Doe was bedded down on the litter for a bouncy trip back to the Men's Village. Wathena rode astride, behind one of the men.

The rescuers belonged to a sister clan to the Thunder People and bore the name "Otter Clan." Wathena was pleasantly surprised when she realized that her cousin Trotter had married into the Otter Clan. Watching the two women greeting each other brought smiles to all who watched. The sweet reunion brought back a torrent of childhood memories. It had been almost ten years since they had seen each other. As soon as they had time to visit, they realized how much in common they had as adults. Both were recently widowed and expecting a child. Trotter immediately bonded with Little Doe and showered the child with attention.

Trotter moved Wathena and Little Doe into her lodge and provided them with fresh buckskin garments. Trotter told of her husband and that he had failed to return from a raid and was assumed to be dead. For the present, members of her husband's family were providing Trotter with food, shelter and protection until she could find a new mate.

Trotter patiently waited until Wathena was ready to speak of the tragic events that had brought her to the Otter Clan. A few days later, as Wathena and Little Doe were adjusting to the new surroundings, Trotter opened the subject by asking how Patrick had died. Wathena answered, "In battle fighting the British in Alabama." Following the daily bath, as the two women reclined on the creek bank watching the children play, Wathena and Trotter spoke about the circumstances that brought them together. Wathena spoke in a low and sad tone. She began by saying, "You would have liked Patrick. We had a great love! Without him the joy of life is lost to me. Have you ever seen a white man with red hair? Patrick had red hair and freckles. He was big and muscular, and very handsome. I was so proud when he qualified as a warrior. He won the winning point in his first ever ball game and fought bravely with his war party. Trotter, how I wish we had grown up together. I missed you terribly when you left our village."

Wathena continued, "Patrick felt that he could combine the best of white culture with that of our people. It seemed to work so well at first. To please him, I learned to spin yarn and weave cloth, I learned to read books and write with the letters: all to please Patrick. Now I struggle to want life. All I have left are the memories and his two little ones. Trotter, will you take care of Little Doe while I go to avenge Patrick? I am required to give him the tranquil afterlife he deserves." Wathena spent the next hour with the details pouring out of her soul in a torrent. She spoke of the Jacksons, the gold discovery, and the silly law about educating slaves. She described the arrogance of Andrew Jackson and included the likable but lecherous Sam Houston in her narrative.

Trotter was slow to answer but finally nodded her agreement. "As you wish. I will care for Little Doe."

"Trotter, I have decided to ask the elders to hold a renaming ceremony for me. I want to be called Puma-Woman. The great Puma will give me the medicine I need to avenge my family. I can't stop thinking about the hateful whites at Jackson's Landing. They are going about their lives with no sense of guilt for their evil deeds. Do they think that there will be no consequences for their actions? Trotter reacted with reservation to Wathena's unexpected plan for revenge. Trotter said, "You must remember that you are expecting a child, and that will hinder you in a fight and could endanger the child. Wathena kept her silence but put her arm around Trotter's shoulders and caressed her with a show of tenderness. Then after a few minutes of silence, Trotter lowered her eyes and muttered, prayer like, "May Kanati grant you strength to carry out your justice."

Wathena spent a few weeks with the Otter Clan. She did not want to leave Little Doe before she was comfortable living in Trotter's family. When Wathena was satisfied that she was fitting in with the other children, and had a healthy appetite, Wathena thought it safe to leave her for a few weeks. It felt good to be back among The People, but at the same time Wathena's grief was seething. Exacting vengeance was an obligation to assure Patrick a pleasant life in the unseen place. Wathena must stay focused and active.

Trotter proved to be very attentive to Little Doe, and the affection was mutual. Wathena was confident that Little Doe would be safe and well cared for in Trotter's care. It was during this period of time that Wathena first felt the movement of the baby she carried. The sickness of nausea had left her, and she felt strong and energetic.

It was a bright summer day, and Wathena took Little Doe to the river for a swim and used the occasion to tell her that she would be leaving on a journey after the naming ceremony scheduled for the following evening. Little Doe had overheard enough to piece together the reason for the journey. The child lowered her gaze in acceptance. "It is the way of the Thunder People's Warrior Woman, my mother."

Wathena had been developing a detailed plan of action. She would take what she needed to hole up in the lion's cave. The gear Wathena would need for the trip would of necessity be minimal. When an Otter Clan Elder offered Wathena a pack mule for the journey, she declined the offer at first and then changed her mind. Only the month before a raiding party had captured six mules from a white man. Wathena decided a mule would be helpful for transporting her gear and weapons. She could better concentrate on her mission. Wathena knew that the best plans sometimes fall apart and the unexpected should be expected. What awaited Wathena would be so bizarre and unthinkable she would not be able to bear the knowledge in her present state of sadness.

The renaming ceremony was practiced in the Otter Clan much as it was by Wathena's Thunder People. There would be a feast and the usual all-night dance. Early in the afternoon the village medicine woman, Noisy Bird, took Wathena to the stream to bathe. Next Noisy Bird ceremoniously anointed Wathena with purified bear fat as she sang a spiritual chant. Wathena donned new garments, and the two women returned to the large gathering place near the center of the village. The next part of the ceremony was to ask for the sanction of the Great Spirit. Noisy Bird, a sage and clairvoyant healer would seek approval for the name change and implore the spirits to aid Puma-Woman's mission of justice.

Noisy Bird officiated over the grand naming ceremony. The result of the tobacco smoke test was indecisive. The Great Spirit may have been otherwise occupied or perhaps skeptical of the new identity or perhaps unwilling that the revenge be wrought as planned. The smoke swirled and rose straight up, which was an ominous sign, but then a slight breeze swept the aromatic smoke to the north west, indicating a less that wholehearted approval by the unseen forces. The muted ah, ah, ahs from the crowd reflected concern for the sanctioned renaming. In cases of uncertainty the decision was up to Noisy Bird, and she chose to allow the ceremony to proceed. The opening portion of the ceremony began with a single drummer beating a slow rhythm on a large water filled drum. Additional drummers joined the lone man around the large round drum. The drama of the occasion grew with the increasing tempo and loudness. The intensity of the rhythmic drumming built to a feverish crescendo and then stopped abruptly.

At this point, the atmosphere became relaxed, and platters of food were carried from the cooking area and passed among the crowd. Laughter and friendly conversations filled the air. It was summer and a good time for holding a feast. The plentiful meal consisted of dried fish, roasted venison, boiled squash, a mixture of dried fruit and nuts, bowls of fresh grapes and berries, and finally the staple of the Tsalagii, huge bark platters piled high with cakes of bean bread.

Wathena and Little Doe were seated in the place of honor between the Chief Matriarch, Moon Woman, and Noisy Bird. Following the meal, Noisy Bird rose and stood directly behind Wathena and raised her hands to quiet the gathering. With the crowd silenced Noisy Bird sang a brief one verse chant. Next, she held up for all to see a doeskin pouch attached to a throng. The pouch was decorated with some colorful beading, and a fringe was sewn across the bottom. Medicine bags are of great importance to "The People" and impart life changing powers. Noisy Bird had chosen the contents of the small bag to aid Wathena in her quest for justice. Wathena was deeply moved by the thoughtfulness of Noisy Bird and grasped the moment to acknowledge her assistance, and it was the perfect occasion to express affection and gratitude to the Otter Clan for their hospitality. Wathena stood and made a brief statement to the large smiling crowd. She used her full voice and most dignified tone to address the audience. Her declaration was in the form of a solemn vow of loyalty and support for the people of the Otter Clan for as long as it was within her power.

Everyone waited in silence for Noisy Bird to place the amulet around Wathena's neck. First Noisy Bird untied the lacing at the neck of Wathena's tunic. There glistening in the firelight was the gold chain necklace that secured the strangely shaped gold nugget. The aging medicine woman had to move her head back and allow her eyes to focus upon the object for a brief moment. She had never seen the necklace. Then she touched the cat like shape and instantly removed her hand as though a bolt of lightning had given her a painful shock. Noisy Bird jumped back and refused to touch Wathena again. Wathena quickly replaced the gold nugget and closed her tunic. Noisy Bird was pale, and her countenance indicated she had seen a vision or received a message from the unseen world. Then the old medicine woman handed the amulet to Moon Woman. Moon Woman held the bag and expressed confusion about the deviation in the ceremony. Noisy Bird whispered for Moon Woman to place the medicine bag around Wathena's neck. Moon Woman agreed and rather unceremoniously hung the bag on the outside of Wathena's tunic. Noisy Bird was obviously unnerved but chose to cover over her strange experience and continue with the ceremony.

It was customary for a medicine bag to contain a collection of sacred items that would ward off evil and sickness. Puma publicly expressed her gratitude to both Moon Woman and Noisy Bird for the gift. She would inspect the contents at a later time in private. Noisy Bird stood and asked the crowd to sit. Whispered comments and murmuring from the crowd angered Noisy Bird and she shouted, "Silence." She moved to once again stand behind Wathena and without making bodily contact lifted her arms announced, "Behold, The Puma-Woman." This was the signal for the lead drummer to begin beating a slow rhythm on the drum.

Following Noisy Bird's proclamation members of the Otter Clan filed by Wathena to acknowledge her as the Puma-Woman and wish her much success in her quest to avenge her loss. An emotional Puma-Woman attempted to eat but her appetite failed her. She was troubled over Noisy Bird's reaction to her, and even though the ceremony was continuing as planned it did not feel right, as though the gods were communicating their disapproved. During the meal Puma-Woman noticed that Little Doe kept edging closer, until Puma-Woman tenderly lifted the child onto her lap. Puma-Woman was well aware of Little Doe's anxiety over the coming separation, and the strange reaction of Noisy Bird had not escaped the unusually intuitive child.

When all had eaten their fill, the next phase of the event began. Darkness had chased the remaining light from the place, and the fires were being built into huge bonfires. It was customary at this point in the ceremony for Puma-Woman to illustrate the circumstances that prompted her request for the name change. When the Puma-Woman arose from her position on the ground, a hush fell over the gathering. All eyes were on the elegant figure of the Puma-Woman. The atmosphere was laden with breathless anticipation. The drummers commenced the performance with a distinctive staccato.

Puma-Woman took up a position before Moon Woman and Noisy Bird and then began to sway from side to side, lifting her hands as though in prayer to Kanati. Measured and purposefully, her feet started to scoot and stamp, accompanied by gyrating, swooping motions with her arms as she spun around and around causing her tunic's wide layer of tin tipped fringe to splay out in a circle. While circling the fire pit Puma-Woman incorporated into her dance steps a series of pantomimes. The first act was the killing of the bear that had attacked Patrick.

With grace and athleticism, she took aim, and drew the bow to its fullest extent before releasing the arrow. After a couple of turns around the ceremonial circle, she gestured her wedding event by signing the folding of the blankets. She acted out strolling as though picking wildflowers, and reenacted a game of tag. She conveyed the emotions of her courtship and honeymoon. With a look of tender affection, Puma pantomimed a full stomach and then rocked a babe in her arms. Her next movement took her to stand in front of Little Doe. Then she invited the child to join in the dance. Mother and daughter used their graceful hands to sign the love they had felt for the departed Patrick.

Next the drama turned violent and angry. The drummers varied the rhythm and intensity of the beat to match Puma's story telling. After falling to her knees, Puma drew an imaginary knife and sawed off her braids and bowed over the hair on the ground. She symbolically rent her clothing, and her fingers traced a path of tears running down her face. As she rose, she signed symbolically stabbing herself in the heart with a knife. Next, she became a puma. She crouched and made some gravity defying leaps. She bared her teeth and pawed the air. Then she went back into her human body and reenacted running and hiding from the rampaging mob. She demonstrated Oscar Jackson's rebuke for schooling the black children. Then Puma-Woman knelt and took Little Doe onto her back and acted out the escape. They demonstrated using reeds to breathe under water. The mother and daughter held hands and ran around the fire one final time and then stopped and opened their arms in gratitude to the men who rescued them, ending the frightening escape.

The drumming abruptly stopped as Puma-Woman and Little Doe bowed in front of Noisy Bird and Moon Woman. An altered drumbeat then signaled the time for all to join in the dance. The entire clan, even the very old and very young joined in, dancing with slow shuffling steps, circling the fire.

After another hour of dancing, Puma-Woman and Little Doe left the dance and walked to the riverbank. The moon was half full and illuminated the path they chose. After a few hundred yards, mother and daughter sat down on the grassy riverbank and listened to the night sounds. The distant drumming from the celebration provided a backdrop for the poignant emotions erupting in the bosoms of mother and daughter. With the innocence of a child, Little Doe asked, "Must I now call you Puma-Woman?" The answer was, "If you wish, but you may continue to call me Mother."

Puma-Woman spoke in a soft and gentle voice, "Little Doe, you must promise to be helpful and obedient to Trotter during my absence. She loves you and will do what is in your best interest. Little Doe, I want you to hold fast the memories of your Father. Keep him in your thoughts, always. You must never forget him. He loved you and was very proud of you. Remember what a good person he was. Allow him to speak to your dreams and give you guidance. Leaving you behind is very hard for me. I will be thinking of you every moment we are apart. I hope to only be gone a few weeks. I plan to come back here to give birth. You can help me care for the babe. Perhaps you and I will return to the Lion's Cave one day and spend time to commune and recover our inter peace. Tears filled Little Doe's eyes, but she did not openly weep. Puma was proud of her strength and control.

As they walked back to the village at a slow pace savoring the moment there was an unmistakable cry from across the river. Puma and Little Doe were startled. Their steps froze mid-stride, and then Little Doe wrapped her arms around her mother. Puma-Woman said, "Listen" as her hands caressed the frightened child's face. Then Puma turned toward the sound and her moonlit face broke into a wide smile. "Little Doe, the stealthy one is here to give me courage and wisdom, the puma is my helper, and is here to consecrate our union."

By the time the Puma-Woman and Little Doe lay down on their bedding it was late, and they fell asleep almost immediately. Pre-dawn stirrings roused Puma-Woman, and she started organizing her plans for the trip before rising from her blanket. Careful not to disturb Little Doe or Trotter's family, Puma dressed in her well-worn doeskin tunic and leggings. She laced the mid-calf moccasins loosely in anticipation of the long trek ahead of her. She knew that her feet were now prone to swell. Her hair had grown but not enough to bind behind her head, so she tied a braided leather band about her forehead. She placed the strap of a leather satchel over her head. The satchel contained, among other items, an extra knife, a whetstone, and a small hatchet. A smaller bag contained extra clothing, sewing sinew and needles. She packed a medicinal herb pouch at the insistence of Noisy Bird and two large water gourds. As she ducked to exit the hut, Little Doe raised her head and smiled. Puma went back and knelt by the child's pallet and embraced her. Then she whispered, "Get dressed, and help me pack the mule. I will be just outside."

Puma had done much of the preparation for the trip over the previous two days. She would be taking two large saddlebags, half a dozen quivers filled with arrows, a roll of skins for bedding. Puma stacked the gear in a pile, ready to load onto the mule. Puma and Little Doe walked to the corral and bridled the mule. Next, they took the animal to the river to drink and allowed it to graze on the abundant green grass. As mules go, the animal appeared to be good natured and gentle. Mother and child listened to the sound of the mule tearing mouthfuls of grass from the moist ground. Hand in hand they led the mule back to the hitching post. Puma strapped a saddle tree behind the riding pad. Once it was cinched in place, she carefully distributed the loaded bags on the beast. Little Doe ducked away and returned with a bowl of leftover food from the night before. As soon as the gear was loaded, they sat on a felled log, and silently ate the food.

The mule stamped and snorted, unhappy with the load on her back. The eastern sky had a twinge of orange. It was a beautiful early summer morning. Fog was rising from the river, and a myriad of birds performed their morning song. As Puma stood, ready to mount the mule, she turned toward the village and saw Trotter, pulling a tunic over her head as she hastily approached. The two women embraced, and then Little Doe turned away and ran toward the river.

Puma started to follow, but Trotter stopped her and said, "It is best that you let her go. I will go to her as soon as you are out of sight. She doesn't want to tell you goodbye. Today we will gather grapes and berries. She will have fun with the other children.

Puma looked into Trotter's kind brown eyes and said, "Thank you dear cousin, for your love and help, you are greatly loved. I hope to return within a few weeks; at least that is my plan." Further words between the two women were unnecessary.

Chapter 14

PUMA-WOMAN PLEDGES RETRIBUTION

The mule shied and jumped sideways, when Puma mounted, but she was able to stay aboard. Puma and the mule would have to get to know each other. Puma estimated that the trip back to the Lion Cave would take at least three days, maybe four. The destination lay in a southwesterly direction from the Otter Clan village. Much of the trip would follow a meandering river. Near the end of the journey, Puma would have to climb over a treacherous rocky ridge and down to the small creek that ran beside the Lion's Cave and farther south also bordered her farm. It was significant that she still considered the farm her property, and rightfully it was. She didn't know what to expect when she returned.

Managing to stow her gear inside the Lion's Cave would be difficult for only one person. She planned to search for an alternate entrance from the surface. Perhaps the opening over the fire pit could be enlarged. The right hiding place for the mule well away from the cave would be important. A small box canyon that could be barricaded was what would work best.

As the sun reached its zenith, Wathena felt unusually warm and noted how pregnancy caused her to perspire more than normal. As if the babe responded to her thoughts, she felt a strong kick, and she saw her tunic move. She smiled and patted her belly. She recognized the movement as a good omen. Puma's face took on an ethereal expression as she sang a traditional lullaby.

The motion of the plodding mule was hypnotic, and Puma's head would droop and jerk upward. She decided to make camp an hour earlier than normal and catch up on sleep. At first, the trail was level, straight, and mostly shaded by giant cottonwood trees. By the second day Puma knew her route would lead through beautiful old oak groves, stately pine forests, and deciduous hardwoods. The warmth from the sun perfumed the air with pine, cedar, and sweet gum essence. Puma allowed her mind to wander. There were so many plans to make. Even with the shade the day was hot. Finally, the time came to choose a campsite. The day of reckoning for the Jackson clan was near. Discomfort brought her back to the present. The Cherokee style blanket saddle was not comfortable compared to the saddles Patrick had provided for her.

Puma opted to alternate between riding astride and leading the animal. Harkening back to her training, she took care not to silhouette herself on a ridge top. Part of her plan for maintaining stealth was to stop every mile or so and walk ahead on foot to listen and look.

The surefootedness of the mule was a plus, but the animal would occasionally and unexpectedly turn loose with a loud, snorting bray. The braying episodes could take a minute or two, and Puma knew she must stop the dumb animal for safety's sake or abandon it to fend for its self. She was trying to recall the method described by a visiting fur trapper that put an end to braying. She wasn't convinced it would work. She decided it was worth experimenting with but knew that placing herself so close to the powerful hooves was risky. Puma decided to spend some time making friends with the cantankerous beast before rigging up the "silencer."

Puma remembered most of the trapper's description, "I braided the frayed end of a rope and the last foot of the mule's tale together and then double tied the joint. Next I passed the rope between the hind legs all the way through to the front legs and used a slip-knot to fasten it to the bridle." The trapper had claimed, "This cinches the mule's tail tight against its underside. Works folks, it sure as shootin' works. No braying!"

Puma went for a walk by the stream where she planned to camp for the night. She returned to the mule with an armload of green grass. Puma offered the grass straight from her arms and spoke soothing words into the mule's ear while she munched on the grass. Next, she used some course cedar branches and groomed the mare. Finally, she led her into the stream and splashed water upon her back. Puma made a point of touching the mule in various places so that she would be desensitized. Then Puma cut more grass and placed it out of sight. Before she began the tail braiding, she placed the grass before the mule. She commenced grooming the hind quarters and brushed tangles from the tail. Then with a soft voice she droned a series of chants as she braided and groomed, alternating between the two. Very slowly, she ran the rope between the hind legs and on to the space between the front legs. The mule stood still basking in the sensation of being brushed. Speaking softly, she threaded the rope through the halter and bridle and secured it. Then she waited for a reaction. She continued the rubbing and patting. Puma backed away and ignored the mule for a few minutes.

Other than looking back at her tail and flicking it a few times, the mule concentrated on grazing. Finally, Friend decided to trumpet her contentment. Puma was resting her back against a tree, waiting for a bray. When the mule extended her head to bray, it cinched up the rope pinning the tail tightly between the hind legs. The surprised mule danced and tried to buck. Then she decided to bray a second time. She looked back while making a choking sound.

The mule gasped for air. Puma was convinced. She tried to bray a few more times before giving up. The tail was securely in place but not to the point of interfering with elimination or causing pain. There was no doubt, it really worked. By afternoon on the third day of travel, fatigue slowed their progress. With steely determination, Puma kept going. She had Patrick in her thoughts almost constantly. How sweet her revenge would be.

As the sun fell lower in the western sky, the trail became more rocky, and difficult. Once she had to double back to choose a better route down an incline. Her body was coated with a reddish dust, and her eyes burned from the sweat droplets trickling from her brow.

Finally, she decided to stop by a spring fed beaver pool, and bathe. She ate some nuts and jerky as she lay on the grass to dry off. After shaking the dust from her buckskins, she dressed and planned to continue along the trail until it was too dark to see. The mule was skittish and did some prancing when Puma re-loaded packs. Friend appeared to accept her tail being held against her body and had quit trying to bray, but Puma would be on alert for any mule shenanigans.

A thicket of plum trees mixed with a few live oaks lay just ahead and would provide cover for camping. She decided that it would be too risky to build a fire and cut some saplings to build a sleeping bench high in the oak tree. This camp was in the same general area where she and Little Doe had encountered the pack of wolves. She took her bag of food and her bow and quiver into the tree with her in the event the pack tried to attack her camp. Sleep did not come quickly, but when she drifted into a dream state, she was back in time going about her everyday routine working around the farmhouse. Her subconscious mind reflected her tragedy with a nightmarish ending. The dream scenario began with the three of them sharing a meal at the kitchen table. A sound alarmed Patrick and he rose from the dinner table, exited the cabin, and walked toward the barn. Puma noticed a look of fear on his face before he disappeared into the darkness. A commotion woke Puma. As she listened, she realized it was the mule reacting to a threat of some kind. By the sounds, she was struggling to break free of the tether.

Puma realized she had been crying. Being with Patrick in her dream world, real or not was something she cherished, but this present intrusion on her dream by the mule? Life had been so good, why did it have to end? She remained still, listening to determine what had the mule so frightened. Suddenly she detected a slight rustling in the tree, near to her bed. She sat up, and in spite of the darkness, was able to make out the outline of a small animal as it baled from the limb that held her food satchel. The lid was partly open, and she realized that the thief was a raccoon. Ah, nothing more than a single raccoon had the mule so jumpy. The rope held, and the mule quickly settled down. Puma could just make out the form of the raccoon scurrying toward a stand of plum thickets. The bandit ran on three feet, holding the stolen food to its chest with an arm. Puma managed to sleep a while longer before first light.

Day four got off to a bad start. Puma would never camp in a plum thicket again. She arose communed with Kanati by singing the Morning Song. It was a clear morning, and she actually felt rested. The skittish mule did not want to be ridden and bucked when she tried to load the gear. Puma tried eye contact and a soft voice, but the wild-eyed brute was not in a friendly mood. Finally, Puma managed to force the mule to accept the load by tying its head close to the tree. Puma decided to forego riding the pack animal and walked. Once away from the campsite, the cantankerous animal tried to bray and tossed its head. Puma jerked the cinch that kept the tail pulled up under her belly. Puma realized that something was frightening the mule. The ripe fruit of the plum thicket had likely drawn a bear. As she surveyed her surroundings, she saw a mother black bear and cub coming up the incline from the stream. Puma fixed an arrow in her bow and then calmly continued her journey. She put her hand on the mule and tried to calm her. When she looked over her shoulder, the sow had stopped and was standing on hind legs, sniffing the air. After walking a dozen steps, Puma looked over her shoulder and could see that the bear and cub had continued to the plum thicket. The day was getting better.

The trail followed a rocky stream that was mostly shaded from the heat. After three hours, she stopped to bathe and give the mule an opportunity to drink from the stream and graze. She continued the journey and just a short distance downstream Puma saw a ford in the river that was heavily traveled. The blackened remains of campfires dotted the creek bank, and trash was scattered here and there. Anger welled up over the scaring of the sacred land.

She decided to withdraw and choose a more remote route and that meant more difficult terrain. As the day grew late, Puma heard a distant gunshot. She was growing more wary and decided to scout ahead on foot. The mule was unpacked and hidden in dense undergrowth beside the creek and a patch of grass. She took her bow and quiver and silently strode in the direction of the gunshot. She needed to know what was out in front. On a ridge she climbed a tall oak and looked out upon the valley below. She heard the crunch of wagons wheels. The winding river was just below and as she watched a group of wagons pulled off the trail and made camp.

Puma checked the direction of the wind and it was favorable. She watched for several minutes to watch for dogs, and there were none. Puma smelled smoke and cooking food. Hunger gripped her insides. The idea of stealing some food drew her closer in the deepening twilight. Night noises came from the surrounding forest. A chorus of bullfrogs blended with the hoo-hooos of an owl.

Curiosity drew her closer to the campsite of the travelers. The moon appeared and was almost full. She was able to make out five hobbled horses, two mules, and six oxen penned inside a rope and post corral. Several toe-headed children were playing in the open area next to the wagons. The three women were preparing the evening meal over a large cooking fire. The men conversed in a relaxed tone while dragging up firewood. The older children carried buckets of water from the stream. When the food was ready, crates for seating were placed by the fire, and one of the men led a prayer. Their hunger was evident, but they still kept up a lively conversation punctuated with laughter. After listening intently, Puma determined that the people were speaking a language other than English. It was a strange dialect, probably European.

Puma carefully approached one of the wagons. She used a dipper and drank from a water barrel mounted on the wagon. Next, she crawled into the bed of the wagon. On the floor was a folded buffalo robe. Ah, what a wonderful winter bed it would make. Upon impulse she stole it. She hid it in the fork of a tree a hundred yards in the direction from which she had come. Then she crept to the next wagon. As she climbed into the bed, she knocked over a long gun. When it fell to the floor, the sound alerted the travelers. The men stopped eating and started walking toward the source of the sound. In a flash, Puma sprang from the wagon bed and hid in some brush. One man spoke to the others in a nervous, high-pitched voice.

Puma silently retreated to the shadow of a large tree. She knew that the tree's foliage was dense enough to hide her if she could climb high in the upper branches. Puma removed the leather strap from her midriff that she sometimes used for tree climbing. The bark of the tree was rough and tore at her legs as she shinnied up the backside of the trunk. A few pieces of bark and some broken twigs fell to the ground, but the men were making so much noise they did not hear. The three men returned to where the wagons were parked. Puma was hardly breathing as she clung to a well-hidden limb. The men had been searching with pistols drawn. Satisfied that it had been a false alarm they holstered their pistols and went back to the fire.

Puma knew that she must stay where she was until the travelers went to bed. Then she could explore the camp for some food. One of the men started playing a musical instrument. He held it to his mouth with one hand and the other hand cupped the outside edge. Puma concluded that he was blowing into the small instrument. The music was odd to her ears, but pleasing. She pictured Little Doe playing the device.

When a sentry was posted for the night Puma prepared for an uncomfortable night. She was already bone tired and hungry. Her stomach was complaining so loudly that she feared the watchman might hear.

Discomfort forced Puma to keep shifting positions. She straddled a limb so that she could rest her head against the trunk. Dosing off while hugging a tree turned out to be dangerous when Puma starting listing to the side. When she woke she was almost sideways on the limb. She was able to reverse her downward momentum by tightening the grip of her legs. This left her briefly hanging upside down from her limb. The close call had her wide awake. In the process of gripping the limb, she sent some chunks of bark to the ground. The night watchmen heard the sound and walked toward Puma's tree. He did a thorough search, looking in every direction but up. Puma was breathless, totally unnerved. Eventually the watchman continued along his surveillance route. His stealthy movements indicated a heightened state of alertness.

Puma tied herself to the tree and prepared to take what rest her discomfort would allow. Puma was continually shifting positions. Every inch of her anatomy that was in contact with the tree hurt. In theory discomfort strengthens one, but on this night the young pregnant Puma-Woman faced reality. Pain and discomfort were not welcome, not tonight. Puma forced her mind to visualize her medicine animal and feel its power and strength in her own body. She offered a silent prayer to the stealthy one.

Finally, dawn broke. It was the fifth day of the journey. One of the men walked directly under Puma's tree, and gathered some firewood. Next the women and girl children walked past Puma's tree on the way to the little stream to bathe. They showed no sense of urgency in completing their tasks quickly. Later the children went to the meadow where they picked wild flowers as a gift for their mother. Breakfast was prepared in a leisurely manner. Puma squirmed and rubbed her numb body parts. She was exhausted and uncomfortable but still engrossed in observing the travelers.

After breakfast they all gathered in a tight group, and one of the men pulled out a black book. He read from the book for several minutes, and then they all bowed. Puma didn't recognize that it was the Lord's prayer that was being read aloud in the strange language.

> *"Unser Vater im Himmel,*
> *dein Name werde geheiligt,*
> *dein Reich komme,*
> *dein Wille geschehe*
> *wie im Himmel, so auf der Erde."*

Puma realized that it must be Sunday. "What if they do not travel on Sunday? What if I have to spend another day and night in this tree!"

Later in the morning one of the older boys began yelling, and everyone ran in his direction. He had found the buffalo robe. Once again, the men drew their pistols and looked around. From their behavior, she could see how frightened they were. They had a short discussion and then began breaking camp with great haste. As the men harnessed the oxen and loaded the wagons, they were anxiously glancing around. What they had suspected was now confirmed. They were not alone. By now Puma didn't care about the buffalo robe, she just needed to come down from the tree. It was an hour before the wagons were out of sight. Puma was weakened from hunger, sore and stiff, and during the descent she fell part of the way down the tree, grasping on to a limb before hitting the ground.

The trek back to the mule and gear was taxing, and she was so hungry she felt weak. Going without food was something she had always tolerated well, but pregnancy changed that. As she walked, she passed another plum thicket. This time she made sure that there were no furry beasts in the area. The plums were ripe, but the birds had been at them. Puma climbed a short tree and shook fruit to the ground. Then she sat on the ground and picked over the fruit for the best plums. Plums had never tasted so good. As Puma slogged her way across a small stream, she saw a catfish hiding in the green moss on the underside of the bank. She took one of her arrows and speared it in the gill. The fish was larger than it appeared from above and put up a mighty fight. Puma fell into the water as she wrestled the creature. It almost escaped a couple of times, but starvation gave Puma the determination to hang on. The arrow would make a nice carrying handle. She drew her knife and opened the belly to clean out the entrails. A sac of yellow eggs was among the intestines, and Puma quickly removed them and washed them in the little stream. Puma had eaten raw fish eggs before. The roe would give Puma some hunger relief. As Puma carried the fish suspended from the arrow, she was glad that it wasn't any larger. She would be building a fire to cook the fish when she got back to the mule. The thought made her salivate.

When Puma arrived at her camp the place where the mule had been tethered, the animal was nowhere to be seen. A section of the rope was still tied to the tree. Alarmed, she dashed to the spot where she had stowed her gear. It was just where she left it, undisturbed. Back where the mule had been, she saw that its hooves had torn up the ground before breaking loose. Something must have frightened the mule.

Immediacy drove Puma to kindle a small cooking fire and cook a portion of the fish. Her body demanded nutritious food. Puma devoured a large portion of the fish as soon as it was hot throughout. The steaming meat burned her tongue and roof of her mouth. She cooled the burns with water and rested beside the shade tree. After dozing for a few minutes, she covered the fire with sand. She secured the food satchel by hanging it in a tree.

The mule's tracks led in a westerly direction. She carried the spare lariat over one shoulder, along with her bow and quiver. She decided to use her tracking stick; it would determine the general direction to follow. Surely the mule would not go far. Some of the ground was rocky, and she would have to circle to find the tracks. The mule was walking, not running. That was good. The sun was getting low in the sky, and Puma needed a good night's sleep.

Over the next hill she came upon the mule grazing in a meadow. Puma knew to hide the rope behind her as she approached offering a handful of grass. She walked up to the lop-eared creature, and rubbed her neck. She spoke in soothing tones as she placed the rope around her neck. She decided that the mule needed a name. Puma stood in front of the mule and rubbed the tender area above her snout, and asked what would you like to be called, my friend? Then Puma thought, friend, yes, "Friend." I will call you Friend. Puma mounted Friend and rode bareback to the camp.

Puma approached the camp cautiously, but there was no sign of what had frightened Friend. She dug into the ashes of her cooking fire and found live coals. The fire soothed her body as she consumed the remaining fish and a handful of ripe plums. Puma began nodding off. She didn't recall ever being so weary. She built up the fire and staged her usual decoy bed a few feet from the flames. Puma attached a rope to the food satchel for hoisting it into the treetop. She would spread her sleeping platform in the tree above the tethered Friend. Puma was sleeping soundly within minutes.

Daylight arrived too soon, and a stiff and bruised Puma was tempted to sleep a while longer. Friend was in a frisky mood, and Puma interrupted her morning routine to calmly speak to the critter while rubbing her coat with an improvised brush of broom weed. She led Friend to drink and let her graze on the succulent grass at the water's edge. Eager to be on the trail Puma decided to eat as she traveled. Now satisfied, Friend stood still for loading. As they rode away, Puma estimated the distance to the cave at a mere ten miles. The vicinity called for extra stealth.

The pain of melancholia manifested itself as Puma relived the desperate escape from the mob of murderers. She was retracing the route she had covered with Little Doe just weeks before. She crossed the stream that had trapped them in a flash flood and recognized the landmarks that marked their race through the hail storm. Puma intercepted a heavily traveled wagon trail headed toward the Cumberland Gap. When the sun was about to set, Puma made camp, certain it would be the last one before she reached the cave. She decided to go without a fire. Her sleeping platform was hastily constructed, and she quickly lapsed into a welcome dream world, a place where her little family was going about their normal daily routine.

Puma awoke eager to be on the road. She used her heels to hurry Friend along. She stopped at the first grassy spot and grazed the mule. Lying on the carpet of grass, Puma was about to doze off when a gunshot and barking dogs startled her. She rolled to all fours and crawled to where she had left her gear.

With bow in hand, she hurried to hide Friend in a dense stand of cottonwoods. An investigation was called for, and she walked in the direction of the noise. Over the next incline, she spotted a new homestead. The land was only recently cleared, and a log cabin was under construction. She didn't recognize the man with the hunting dogs. The wind currents were favorable, and her presence went undetected.

Like her indigenous brethren, Puma resented the waves of thieving settlers usurping sovereign Cherokee territory. Evading detection required a detour of several miles. It was mid-afternoon when Puma reached the Lion's Cave. She tied Friend to a scrub cedar under the shade of a pine. She took her hatchet to the smoke hole in the cave ceiling. Unfortunately, the surface around the smoke vent was part of a huge slab of bed rock that had been pushed to the surface by geological forces millenniums before. No amount of chipping would enlarge that hole.

Puma descended to the cave's entrance, intending to search for a second opening from the inside. The interior reeked with the scent of a lion but was currently unoccupied.

The interior of the cave was just as she and Little Doe had left it. The trickle of water that seeped from a crack in the back wall was still viable. Having an interior water supply enhanced the value of the cave as a hideout. The tangle of vines that covered the cave's entrance made it virtually undetectable. Puma began the arduous chore of transferring her supplies into the cave. As she worked, she devised a plan to construct a rope ladder. She made a mental note to put rope on her shopping list. For the present, she devised a way to lower her food box and satchels on a rope, suspended even with the entrance of the cave.

An exhausted Puma lighted a candle and kindled a small fire. She took time to arrange the satchels and boxes next to the cave wall. She set out a large two-wick beeswax candle with sprigs of dried peppermint grass pressed into its surface. Puma knew from experience the aromatic oil of peppermint is a strong rodent repellant and would protect the wax from being consumed by the pesky field mice that inhabited the crevices of the cave. The firewood on hand would last for the night. She was fairly confident that the peppermint scent from the candle and the smoke from the fire would ward off the former occupant. As an extra layer of caution, Puma urinated at the entrance of the cave. She felt relatively secure. As she thought back over the journey, she became drowsy. She scratched indentions in the sandy floor to accommodate her shoulders and hips. A pile of dried grass padded the surface below her bedroll. She was thinking about finding a hiding place for Friend when her sub-conscious mind took over her brain's activity.

Puma woke after a fitful night. The hard surface of the cave floor was punishing to her pregnant body. She needed a better bed. Lack of restful sleep would impact her ability to concentrate and make her forgetful. As soon as she had a hiding place for Friend, a soft bed was next on her agenda. Pregnancy entitled her to a comfortable bed, so, fortunate for Oscar Jackson, he was granted an extra day or two on earth to enjoy his comfortable lifestyle.

After a quick breakfast of jerky and berries, Puma mounted Friend and struck out to find a hiding place. The terrain east of the cave was a treacherous stretch of geography. Even the sure-footed mule balked and took considerable coaxing to continue. Puma decided it wasn't worth risking injury to Friend and tied her in a shady place with access to grass and water. It was better that she search for the right canyon on foot.

After a couple of hours of hiking, Puma found a promising canyon to explore. Looking down from a promontory, the walls were almost vertical, and she could see a brook in the canyon's crease. The area enclosed was mostly wooded, but there were a few acres of meadow. Puma sat on her behind and scooted down a steep rock wall to the canyon floor. She walked to a pool of water at the head of the stream. What a beautiful little park. Swallows swooped after insects, and butterflies flitted from one wildflower to another.

The pond had a pair of wood ducks. The drake's coloring was a sight to behold. He had a green head, rose colored breast with white spots, a curled over black tail, bright yellow wings, blue and black back, and red ringed eyes. They paddled along together making soft quacking noises. In another part of the pond was a mother mallard with a dozen hatchlings. The surface of the pond was glassy. An island of lily pads was covered with the waxy white blooms with their bright yellow centers. The windless day kept the lovely scent of the blooms near the pond. Puma decided to lie on the grass and feast on nature's exquisiteness.

A fish broke the surface of the water chasing an insect, and Puma watched the waves spread across the pond. From under a rocky overhang a spring poured forth enough water to fill the pond and keep the brook flowing. Moss and ferns blanketed the eastward facing rock wall. Knee deep grass surrounded the pool. The valley appeared to be the perfect place for Friend, assuming the canyon had a way out.

Puma followed the stream to the lower end of the canyon, almost a half mile distance, and found the open end of the canyon had been mostly blocked by a rockslide. The cave-off was likely caused by the series of earthquakes and aftershocks that had shaken the area. The ground's surface was strewn with rocks and boulders and made traversing that it difficult. The only exit to the canyon was about twelve feet wide. That was too wide and blocking the space by building a fence would take too long. Just when she was ready to abandon the canyon an idea occurred to her. What if she created a rockslide to narrow the opening? It would be tricky and even dangerous. She took a long thirsty drink from her gourd and started climbing the unstable rubble.

The looseness of the gravel made the grade almost impossible to scale. A couple of times Puma slid back to the bottom and was forced to start over. When she finally reached the top, she found a limb to use as a lever. What she found was crooked and snarly. She wedged the limb between two boulders, using one as a fulcrum she pulled down with all of her strength. Nothing moved, but she stubbornly tried a second and third time. As an afterthought Puma tied a safety rope around her torso and adjusted it to ride well above her pregnant abdomen. She picked a sturdy shrub well above the slide area as an anchor. She changed her strategy and chose a smaller boulder to dislodge. She went higher and successfully sent a cascade of stones down to the opening below. The effort failed to close the opening, so she continued her destabilization. When she was about to give up on the idea, a large rock moved when she pulled down on her pry bar, and then the entire hill became an avalanche. Puma tumbled down the slide area until her tether stopped her. The shrub that held the rope had pulled out of the ground and slid about 10 feet before hanging up on the jagged tip of a huge buried boulder. The slide happened too fast for Puma to take any protective measures. She fully expected to be buried under tons of falling earth. Her mind flashed to Little Doe and the devastating pain she would suffer. Losing both parents in such a short time would no doubt overwhelm such a young child.

Puma's fall came to a jolting halt, and she was left dangling in space. She grasped the rope to relieve the pressure that was cutting into her upper chest. Puma pumped her feet and began swinging until her arc allowed her to grasp on to a tree limb with her legs. She was forced to ignore the pain the rope was causing. She knew the shrub that held the rope could give away at any moment, so she concentrated on transferring to the limb.

Using some acrobatic moves that far exceeded the capability of most women, especially pregnant women, Puma managed to cross over to a leaning tree and descend. She took a moment to settle her nerves and think about what had just happened. She sat on the debris pile and rode the loose gravel to the canyon floor. Puma was shaking and totally unnerved. She looked about and saw that her landslide had changed the landscape. Her heart sank when she realized that she had shut off the canyon's opening altogether. She prepared to climb over the barrier to return to the mule. Finding a hiding place would have to wait for another day. As she maneuvered over the maze of boulders to exit the canyon, she found a hidden opening between two gigantic boulders that could easily accommodate the width of the mule and would be easy to unclog and then barricade. Elated, she hurried to fetch Friend. The near catastrophe had ended well. Puma returned to her cave covered with cuts, scrapes, and bruises.

By moving a few large rocks that had fractured on impact with the ground, the mule would be able to walk through the opening with a little room to spare. Puma tied her rope to the rocks and used the mule to pull them aside. Puma enticed Friend to follow through the narrow passage with a big bunch of green grass. Friend balked at first, but Puma kept rubbing her nose and speaking to her in warm tones. Friend and Puma had developed a relationship, and by being patient she managed to cajole the lop-eared companion to follow her lead. Puma sprang upon Friend's back and rode bareback to the pond at the head of the canyon. Friend seemed to approve of her new pasture and decided to sample the pond water by wading up to her belly and drinking her fill.

There was a cool, refreshing breeze, and Puma walked over to a grassy area and lay down. Her aching body needed to rest. After a nap, Puma groomed the mule with a handful of dried broom grass. She wished for a soft bristle currycomb. Perhaps Oscar Jackson had one in his store. She left the mule grazing. Puma felt good about leaving Friend at the hiding place. Puma took care to barricade the exit. It was a very sore and weary child of The People who trudged back to the Lion's Cave.

Along the path back to the cave, Puma gathered kindling and firewood. She paused long enough to harvest bark from a willow tree and gathered herbs as she came across them. The sun was getting low, and she felt a chill. She would get a fire going before eating something, anything, it didn't matter. When she climbed down to the cave, she dug in the fire pit and found a few live embers that sped up the process of fire building. She placed a pot water over the flame. The thought of spending another night on the hard pallet in her bone-weary state contributed to a bit of ingenuity. Out of necessity comes creativity, and true to the axiom, Puma visualized and designed the perfect bed, a hammock with a padded mattress.

The fresh smell of cedar branches helped to neutralize the residual scent of the lion. Puma tossed a chunk of jerky into a pot of boiling water and then sprinkled some dried onion flakes, a large amount of sliced cattail shoots, and a handful of ground arrowroot. The meal of porridge made Puma drowsy. As she settled down for the night, her stressed muscles began stiffening. Moving a mountain had very nearly been the end of the Puma-Woman. Her body needed time to regenerate, and that would be difficult on a hard pallet.

The next day Puma went to harvest some cattail shoots along the stream. When she happened to crush a mature cattail pod, the plant exploded into white fuzz that floated on the breeze. The moment would qualify as an epiphany. What if she stuffed the fiber from many cattails into a tube made from a blanket? By day's end she had collected a large quantity of mature cattails and spent the evening fashioning her mattress. To hold the mattress off the floor of the cave, she converted a worn rawhide cloak into a hammock.

Working with the fuzz was aggravating and messy. The escaped fibers floated in the air and brought on fits of sneezing. She tied a wet cloth around her face and focused on finishing the mattress quickly. She was impatient with anything that delayed her mission of revenge.

When Puma went to bed that evening, she was more than pleased with her invention. The hammock and mattress provided her with the first good nights' rest in weeks. The hammock was about two and a half feet off the floor, just right for sitting too. Sleep came quickly. Within an hour or two she was dreaming. It was a recurring dream, the scene, merely a figment of her mind but ever so realistic. In full color, she and Little Doe were walking through a flowering meadow holding hands.

—BONUS EXCERPT—

CHEATIEBO, THE FOLKLORIST SERIES

2

EBONY, BEAUTY IN MOTION

GLENDA SIMPSON

Chapter 1

RETURN TO THE LION'S CAVE

Something awakened Puma. The light radiating from a mostly spent candle gave just enough illumination to see movement at the cave's entrance. The cooking fire had dwindled to a few pulsing coals. Instant fear shattered Puma's fog of sleep as her hand darted to the knife habitually prepositioned at her side. The klandagie's menacing posture signaled that the lioness was stalking prey, and there was no doubt that she herself was the prey. The cat's eyes were narrowed slits, and her ears laid close to her head. Her quivering, spring loaded muscles were ready to launch an attack. Puma knew that the lion had come to reclaim her lair.

Puma leapt from her resting place just as the lion launched its body the entire width of the cave. The impact slammed Puma back onto the mattress. The cat's momentum caused the hammock to swing backward and tilt vertically, spilling them onto the cave's floor. The jarring ferocity of the attack brought Puma to full alertness. The stuffed mattress followed the two of them to the floor. The superior strength of the feline overwhelmed the woman and, but for a fluke, would have been the end of Puma Woman. The swiping claws ruptured the mattress, releasing great puffs of cattail fuzz into the air. The near weightless floating particles disoriented the lion.

Puma was thinking, kill or be killed with the outcome to be decided by the greater of brain or brawn. According to the Cherokee People, pound for pound, the mountain lion is known as one of nature's most ferocious killers. The tawny attacker's slashing claws tore more openings into the mattress, further decreasing visibility. With each breath the combatants drew the floating fuzz into their mouths and nose. The suspended fibers adhered to any moist surface including the surface of the eyeball. The feline was forced to pause and rake the fuzz from her nose and eyes. Puma seized the moment to strike out with her dagger.

Under other circumstances the scene would have been humorous. The strangeness of the battle between the two lionesses, simultaneously struggling with asphyxia created a scenario that was too improbable for fiction. Since the woman's nostrils were smaller and sheltered by her facial architecture, the cattail fibers inhibited her respiration less that the lion's. Due to her superior intellect, she was able to stay focused as the battle raged. Her blade repeatedly found its target. The injured lion didn't run away as expected. Puma prepared herself for a fight to the death.

Oxygen starvation caused the lion to panic! The feline's movements became erratic as she struggled to inhale. Puma capitalized on the situation and managed to stab the beast in an eye as it lunged past her. The lion screamed out in pain and began shaking its head from side to side. Puma moved toward the crazed cat just as it leapt at her. The razor-sharp claws delivered a glancing blow to her upper arm. Puma whirled and sprang upon the lion's back, stabbing repeatedly with all her strength. She knew she had punctured a lung when the cat began spraying blood from its nostrils. A lull in the battle allowed time for the air to partly clear. The klandagie reversed its direction and pinned Puma to the floor of the cave. The lion bit down on Puma's neck and tore at her ear. Puma's reservoir of adrenaline blocked most of her pain and enabled her to continue defending the life of Patrick's unborn child.

The cat paused long enough to sneeze. This opened the nasal passages enough to inhale a breath of oxygen rich air. The lion's stood on hind legs and then sprang toward the adversary viciously biting and clawing. Puma's precise timing helped her stab the lion's remaining eye. Sightless, the screaming lion responded with frantic swiping at the air.

The panther began making the most surreal sound, part growl and part gurgle. Puma reached from behind its back and drove her knife to the hilt into the big cat's heart. Its scream was so loud it was painful to her ears. There was very little fight left by the time Puma slit the animal's jugular vein. She backed off to catch her breath while listening to the lion's weakening gasps and watched its crimson life force puddle and be absorbed by the sandy floor. The odor of warm blood nauseated Puma. She stepped to the cave's entrance for fresh air and expelled the fuzz from her nose and mouth. The lion's raspy breathing stopped. The only sound in the cavern was Puma's own breathing. The layer of cattail down that blanketed the cave's interior transformed it into a snowscape. The sight caused Puma to shiver from the perceived cold.

Puma Woman had narrowly prevailed in an epic clash with a sister lioness. She sank to her knees, weakened by the subsiding adrenaline overload. An eerie sensation caused the hair on Puma's arms to stand up. Some strange force had overshadowed her. The thought came to her that the disembodied spirit of the lioness was fusing with her own spirit. A Klandagi, lord of the forest, had challenged her right to join the elite society, a premier heritage of honor. The former Wathena had validated her right to wear the name Puma-Woman.

Puma felt compelled to honor the lifeless form and dropped to her knees to chant an ancient death song. She ran her hand along the sleek coat and caressed the silken ears. The tears that bathed Puma's face dripped onto the silken fur of the lioness, anointing her for her journey to the unseen world.

Puma's abstraction gave way to the throbbing pain radiating from her injuries. She feared for the welfare of her babe and removed her tunic. Her hands trembled as she ran them over her abdomen. She was relieved when a check found no vaginal bleeding. The most severe pain was coming from her left jaw and ear. After examining the wounds that she could see, she determined that no more than two of her wounds needed to be closed with stitches.

Puma set water to boil for brewing pain medicine. She opened Noisy Bird's satchel and removed a number of herb-filled leather pouches. She spread a blanket on the sandy floor and organized the items she would be using. She bound her wounds with temporary bandages to slow the bleeding. She put a second larger pot of water on the fire to boil. She grimaced as she traced her neck and jaw wounds with her hands. The bites to her neck were superficial, but her ear was dangerous ripped and punctured. It was mostly detached from her head. She hastily bound the ear to her head with a strip of blanket by tying it at the crown of her head.

She was thankful that Noisy Bird had insisted she bring the medicine bag. Puma selected a pouch marked with a charcoal symbol. It contained the crushed dried leaves of the yarrow plant. Puma stepped over the lion's body and built up the fire. She repositioned the lion's carcass to the cave's entrance. She softened a stack of singed and dried prickly pear pads in the hot water. A staple of the medical kit, they were ready for use as bandages.

One of the pouches contained a mixture of kava, chamomile, cannabis, passion-flower leaves, and powdered willow bark. She poured hot water over a bowl filled with the dried leaves and set it aside to steep. In another bowl, she poured just enough hot water to moisten crushed comfrey and sheep sorrel leaves forming the consistency of a poultice. Into the larger pot she dropped a handful of ground sassafras and left it to steep. The tea of sassafras is a time-honored medicine among the Cherokee. Though the medical professionals of the day lacked understanding of bacterial and viral infections, they were armed with the outcome of closely observed trial and error folk medicine. Puma had been told that the Cherokee were better healers than white doctors.

Once the sassafras tea had cooled, Puma irrigated her wounds, ridding them of infectious debris. She followed the sassafras tea by sprinkling yarrow leaf powder directly into the wounds. The stinging brought tears to her eyes. She drew a deep breath and continued by smearing the wounds with the comfrey and sheep sorrel poultice.

There wasn't much she could do to treat her ear. She blotted the blood away and poured sassafras tea over the left side of her head. Working blindly, she inclined her head and covered the wound with the poultice before positioning and bandaging her ear using a softened prickly pear pad held in place with a strip of blanket. She realized that she might lose the ear. It was out of her control. While she worked, she was consuming large gulps of the pain reliever. It was now time to stitch the most serious lacerations. She took out her largest needle, threaded it with animal sinew. With a deep breath she began the painful process. Puma fought off faintness as she forced the dull needle through each side of the torn skin and pulled it together and then used her mouth to help tie each knot. Over and over, she repeated the process until she had to stop and scream. She resumed the stitching. She was forced to stop several times. The task took more than two hours, but it seemed much longer. She was barely able to finish treating the wounds by smearing the cuts with the poultice and properly bandaging them with the prickly pear pads.

Faint and trembling from shock, Puma wrapped a blanket around her shoulders and sat in front of the fire gulping the willow bark tea that merely dulled the pain. Faintness caused her to collapse beside the fire for at least an hour. When she awoke, the cuts were throbbing, and she was experiencing chills while feeling hot. She knew she was running a fever. She consumed two full gourds of willow bark tea. The brew caused Puma to suffer from a strange vertigo, and she didn't dare attempt to stand. What mattered was that it helped relieve the pain.

After a period of sleep Puma changed from her blood-stained blanket to a fresh one. She cut a hole for her head and wore it poncho style. The pain was unrelenting. The slightest movement hurt and caused the forming scabs to crack and resume bleeding.

Puma's mental discipline helped her to function by compartmentalizing her pain. She prepared more willow bark pain reliever. While she waited for the tea to steep, she thought of the lion. It was important to preserve the animal's pelt as a sacred relic. And she wanted to consume a portion of the heart and liver, thereby assimilating its stealth and cunning. It occurred to Puma that she must hasten to prepare the lion's organs for cooking and the hide for tanning before her injuries incapacitated her.

After drinking more of the pain-relieving tea, Puma rose to remove the carcass from the cave to the top of the cliff where she could work on it. She became dizzy and almost fainted. She reconsidered and instead began eviscerating the lion at the cave's entrance? She opened the belly and the first thing she saw were two well developed kittens encapsulated in their uterine sacks. Puma felt heart sick over the sight. Maternal instinct explained the puma's persistence in reclaiming her den.

With tears running down her cheeks, Puma continued the gory task. She was taking an unthinkable short cut because of her injuries. She placed the heart and liver in a large cooking pot after eating a thin slice of each. She knelt to commune with the spirits and sprinkled tobacco on the fire.

Out of an otherwise still daybreak a strong whoosh of wind parted the vines and rushed into the cave. The sudden wind caused Puma to gasp, drawing a great breath of dust and cattail fuzz into her throat. She coughed and spat. How strange, she thought. The wind can only be attributed to a spiritual visitation.

She saved the skull, back, and breast portion of the hide and sent the rest over the edge to the stream below where it would be consumed by fish, otter, and other river creatures.

The pain from Puma's wounds was getting too intense to continue. She gathered the mattress and re-wrapped it tightly before it back in the hammock. Its bulk was half the former size. She was too ill to eat any of the stew and eased her body on to the hammock where she lapsed into a feverish slumber.

When Puma awoke, she was drenched in perspiration. Chills caused her to shutter. She noticed that her scalp contracted, and goosebumps covered her arms. Nausea made it hard to keep down the pain killer. The pain caused her to drink it in great gulps. She relieved herself by the cave's entrance and then splashed cool water on her face. She realized that both she and the baby were in jeopardy. She grasped the medicine bag hanging around her neck and earnestly petitioned the deities known for healing. Such dire times called for burning a pinch of tobacco on the coals of the fire. She added a few sticks to the few remaining coals and fixed her eyes on a puff of rising tobacco smoke. She felt a surge of resolve, tenacity prevailed. Her will to survive was too strong for the demons of darkness. She built up the fire and lighted a new candle before collapsing back on the hammock.

For three days Puma slept, except for brief periods when she applied medicine and took the last of the pain killer.

A week had passed when Puma awoke to a shocking sight. Her wounds were infested with maggots. During her delirium she had threshed about, kicked off her cover and loosened the bandages. Swarms of blow flies laid eggs into her wounds. The sight of the working mass of larvae caused her to swoon. When awareness returned, she recalled Falls-From-Heaven's lesson. He had insisted that maggots promote healing by eating away the dead tissue, and now she knew he had been right. A close inspection revealed that her wounds were much better. The swelling had subsided, and she only felt pain with movement.

After sponge bathing her entire body in sassafras tea to remove the puss and maggots, Puma dressed in a lightweight sleeveless tunic. Ridding her body of the stench of putrid flesh bolstered her mood. The pungent camphor scent of the medicinal herbs masked any remaining odor. The leftover stew was brought to a rolling boil by dropping red-hot stones into the covered cooking pot. After one taste, Puma realized that the stew was spoiled and disposed of it. Her pregnant body was craving fresh food. Recovering her strength for gathering food was an immediate challenge. Puma sang a chant and burned tobacco.

For a second week Puma stayed near the cave, spending most of her recovery resting upon the hammock. As she healed, she became restless and ventured from her sanctuary for a bath in the stream below. She gathered firewood and cut a new supply of cattail pods to replenish the mattress. She could feel her strength returning after a meal of catfish. By the end of the third week, she decided to hike to the canyon and check on Friend. She bathed in the creek and was presented with the opportunity to snatch a plump mallard duck paddling her way. She returned to the cave with the fowl and an armload of cattail pods and a nice mess of cattail shoots. The cattail rhizomes were tough and fibrous and would need to stew for hours. She was too hungry to wait and roasted thin strips of duck over the fire. The fatty duck meat was just what she needed.

Summer had passed midpoint, and the time was right for harvesting the wild food that she craved. The trip to check on Friend would double as a food foraging opportunity.

In preparation for the walk to Friend's box canyon, Puma coiled her braided leather rope and placed it across her upper torso. She slung her bow and quiver over the other shoulder and tied a leather pouch for collecting any fruit or nuts about her waist. She managed to walk the distance by stopping to rest several times.

Little Doe's favorite song came to mind, and Puma sang the words as if her daughter was walking beside her. The blue summer sky was decorated with lovely tuffs of clouds. Puma practiced her birdcalls. Several noisy jays showed curiosity. She spoke to the clamorous birds, "Ahhh, I fooled you!" It occurred to Puma that the pain of losing Patrick was less acute. For some reason this made her feel guilty. She was startled when she realized that she couldn't see his face in her mind or hear his voice. She questioned her sanity.

The barrier she had built at the canyon's entrance was still in place. She moved a small log enough to enter and hiked along the rocky streambed. She removed her moccasins and waded in the creek part of the way. It was second nature for Puma to be alert and aware of her surroundings. A death stench wafted to her nostrils. She hurried to the source of the sickening odor. She walked upon the remains of Friend lying on her side by the pool. Her bloated abdomen was partially torn away, and all the usual scavengers had been to the feast. Dear Friend! It would be lonely traveling without the animal. She recognized the foot prints of a grizzly. Upon approach, a gray fox was forced to end his meal of carrion. High above, three or four buzzards circled on wind currents. There was no way she could have known in advance that the box canyon lay within a grizzly bear's territory. The sobering knowledge demanded extreme caution. Puma hoped that Friend's death had been sudden.

On the walk back to the cave, Puma felt an intense loneliness. She stopped to gather some nuts under a partly dead black walnut tree. It had been struck by lightning in the past. Along a deep ravine Puma found a patch of raspberry vines. The vines had been trampled and crushed, indicating that a bear had napped after eating its fill. Puma took the precaution to locate a tree that she could quickly climb. She had been craving raspberries and ate almost as many as she gathered in the pouch. Puma decided to preserve some of the berries by drying them. There were so many uses for dried berries. If only she had the other ingredients for her favorite pemmican recipe.

Puma closely examined the bear's tracks and marked her tracking stick. From the measurements it was a monster of a bear. She had never hunted a grizzly all alone. Just thinking about such a dangerous task made her heart race. By the time Puma reached the shelter of the cave, she was exhausted and fell upon her bed. She noticed that the baby was unusually active, especially when she lay on her back. Her period of gestation was passing quickly, and without Friend, she would need to get back to the Otter Clan while she could still walk the distance. Ignorance of the future can be a blessing. The Puma-Woman was soon to be tested in ways she would have never imagined.

Puma's mental toughness sped along her recovery from the lion attack. She was regaining stamina and flexibility despite the pain. The thought of Oscar Jackson living a life of plenty consumed her. She was imaging the triumphant finish when justice would be meted out.

First, she would break into Jackson's store and take what she needed. The Jackson family lived in a log cabin a hundred yards from the main compound of buildings. She recalled that they kept hunting hounds. They were known to lounge on the porch of the trading post. They were not characteristically docile but had been trained to dislike people. They would snap at anyone that attempted to pet them. She must silence the dogs before approaching the store.

--End of Excerpt--